William Henry Venable

Dramas and Dramatic Scenes

William Henry Venable

Dramas and Dramatic Scenes

ISBN/EAN: 9783337342326

Printed in Europe, USA, Canada, Australia, Japan

Cover: Foto ©Andreas Hilbeck / pixelio.de

More available books at **www.hansebooks.com**

DRAMAS

AND

DRAMATIC SCENES

EDITED BY

W. H. VENABLE

PREFACE.

THE range and quality of this book are indicated by the table of contents. The editor has endeavored to make a collection of dramatic pieces, various in subject and style, and all within the circle of standard literature. Possibly the volume may have influence in turning attention to some works of genius too much neglected by those who practice elocution as an artistic accomplishment.

Dramatic representation is a fascinating amusement, and it may be made conducive to the best general culture. An art so elegant and intellectual should not be allowed to fall under the contempt of the educator or the censure of the moralist. While it must be admitted that the performance of frivolous, sensational comedies, and coarse farces, exaggerates some of the evils of the common theater, it must be allowed, on the other hand, that the proper acting of choice plays is an exhilarating pastime, at once innocent, pleasant, and profitable. The careful study and appreciative rendering of such a drama, for example, as "The Three Caskets," can not be regarded as otherwise than elevating and refining.

With few exceptions, the plays in these pages are each long

enough to allow the development of a strong interest. The comic selections, in several instances, essentially include, the underplots of the dramas from which they are taken, and are, therefore, quite complete in themselves. Some of the sprightliest pieces, as "Braggadocio" and "Detraction," comprise satisfactory portions of plays that, as a whole, are not adapted to the modern stage. The version of "William Tell" here given is not identical with the common acting edition of that drama.

Though this volume is designed, primarily, to supply scenes for dramatic representation, it may also be used as a rhetorical reader, or as a reference book for students in English literature, since it contains characteristic productions of representative authors, from Shakespeare to Bulwer.

The editor wishes to record his acknowledgment of the great assistance rendered by his wife, in selecting and transcribing material for the entire series of "Eclectic Acting Plays," of which this is the third and last volume. He would also thank Mrs. Robert Rogers, of Cincinnati, for the continued use of her library, rich in dramatic literature.

CONTENTS.

(v)

STAGE TERMS AND DIRECTIONS.

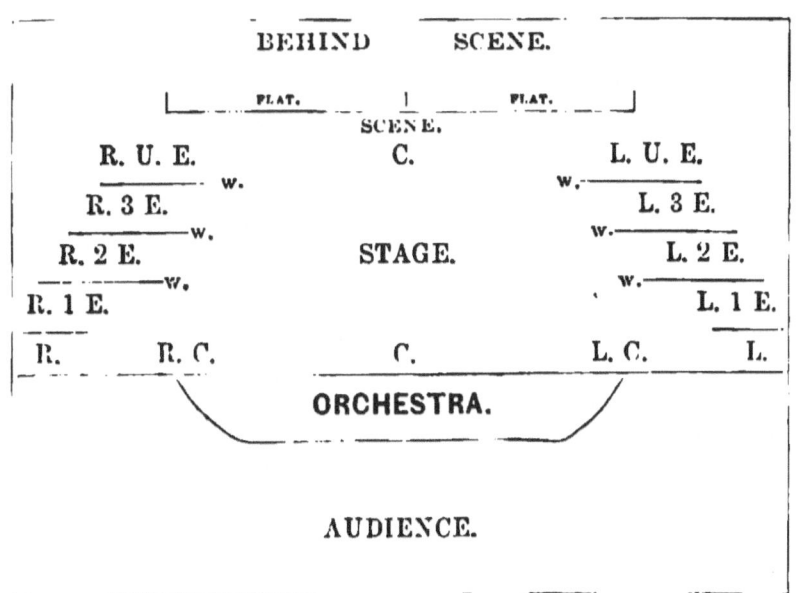

C. means Center; R., Right; L., Left; R. C., Right Center; L. C., Left Center; R. 1 E., Right First Entrance; L. 2 E., Left Second Entrance; R. U. E., Right Upper Entrance; W., Wing; *up* is toward the flat; *down*, toward the footlights. The actor is supposed to face the audience.

Complete directions for constructing a stage and its appurtenances, for providing properties, scenery, and costume, and for selecting, rehearsing, and performing plays, are given in the "AMATEUR ACTOR."

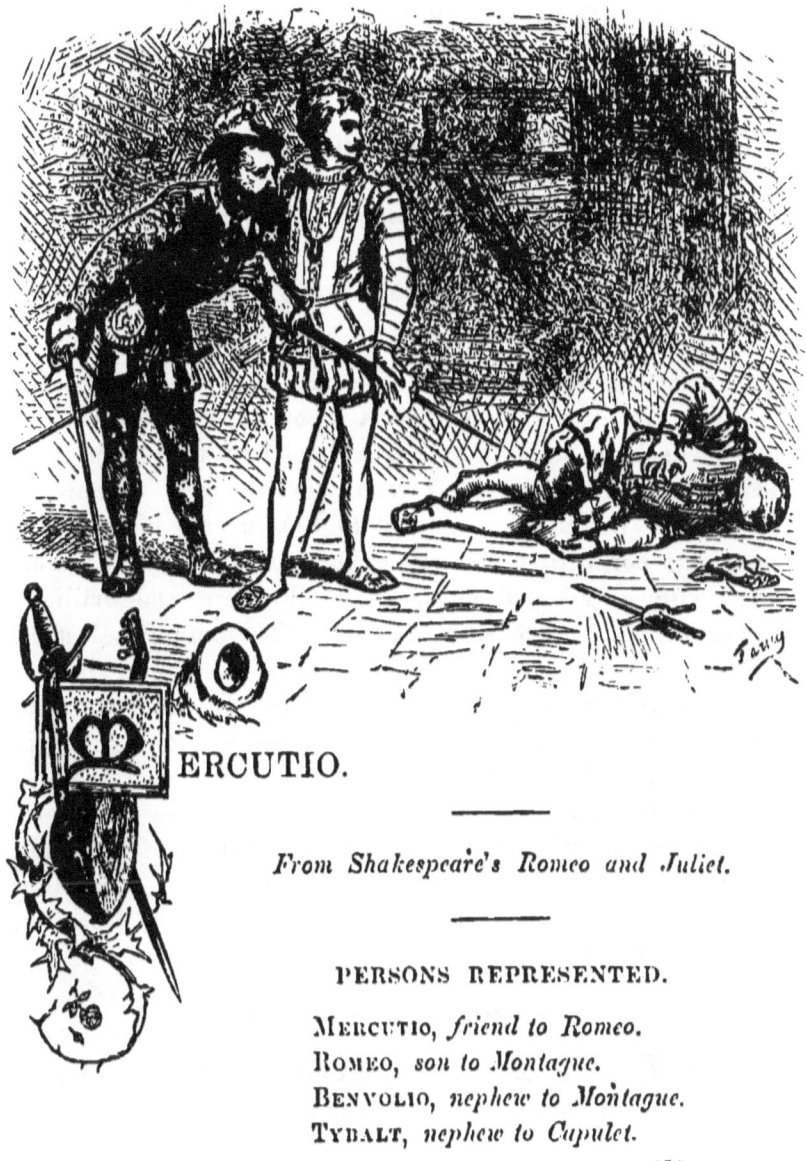

ERCUTIO.

From Shakespeare's Romeo and Juliet.

PERSONS REPRESENTED.

MERCUTIO, *friend to Romeo.*
ROMEO, *son to Montague.*
BENVOLIO, *nephew to Montague.*
TYBALT, *nephew to Capulet.*

(9)

PROLOGUE.

The prologue to Shakespeare's tragedy of Romeo and Juliet begins with these lines:

> *Two households, both alike in dignity,*
> *In fair Verona, where we lay our scene,*
> *From ancient grudge break to new mutiny,*
> *Where civil blood makes civil hands unclean.*

The heads of the houses at variance with each other are Montague and Capulet. Romeo is a son of Montague; Benvolio, a nephew; and Mercutio, a friend of these, and also kinsman to the prince of Verona. Tybalt is a nephew of Capulet, and therefore an enemy to Romeo and his friends. These facts borne in mind will explain our play, which comprises, with a few omissions, the well-known and brilliant *Mercutio Scenes*, from *Romeo and Juliet.* The action is located in Verona's streets. The characters are all young Italian gentlemen, full of passionate life and fire. In the first scene we have the three adherents to the house of Montague preparing for a mad-cap visit, in disguise, to a ball at Capulet's. Scenes second and third derive their interest from the hilarious raillery and wit of the inimitable Mercutio. The fourth and last scene introduces the "fiery Tybalt"; an altercation follows; then a conflict ending in the death, first of Mercutio, and afterward of Tybalt.

SCENE I:—*A Street in Verona. Enter* ROMEO, MERCUTIO, *and* BENVOLIO, L.

Romeo. What, shall this speech be spoke for our excuse,
Or shall we on without apology?

Ben. The date is out of such prolixity:
We'll measure them a measure, and begone.

Rom. Give me a torch; I am not for this ambling;
Being but heavy, I will bear the light.

Mer. Nay, gentle Romeo, we must have you dance.

Rom. Not I, believe me: you have dancing shoes,
With nimble soles; I have a soul of lead,
So stakes me to the ground, I can not move.

Mer. You are a lover; borrow Cupid's wings,
And soar with them above a common bound.

Rom. I am too sore enpierced with his shaft,
To soar with his light feathers; and so bound,
I can not bound a pitch above dull woe:
Under love's heavy burden do I sink.

Mer. And, to sink in it, should you burden love;
Too great oppression for a tender thing.

Rom. Is love a tender thing? it is too rough,
Too rude, too boisterous; and it pricks like thorn.

Mer. If love be rough with you, be rough with
      love:
Give me a case to put my visage in.

                  [Putting on a mask.
A visor for a visor! What care I,
What curious eye doth quote deformities?
Here are the beetle brows, shall blush for me.

Ben. Come, knock, and enter; and no sooner in,
But every man betake him to his legs.

Rom. A torch for me: let wantons, light of heart,
Tickle the senseless rushes with their heels;
I'll be a candle-holder, and look on.

Mer. Tut, 'Romeo,' we'll draw thee from the mire
Of this (save reverence) love, wherein thou stick'st
Up to the ears.—Come, we burn daylight, ho.

Rom.   Nay, that 's not so.

Mer.   I mean, sir, in delay
We waste our lights in vain, like lamps by day.
Take our good meaning; for our judgment sits,
Five times in that, ere once in our five wits.

Rom.   And we mean well in going to this mask;
But 't is no wit to go.

Mer.   Why, may one ask?

Rom.   I dreamed a dream to-night.

Mer.   And so did I.

Rom.   Well, what was yours?

Mer.   That dreamers often lie.

Rom.   In bed, asleep, while they do dream things
    true.

Mer.   O, then, I see, Queen Mab hath been with you.
She is the fairies' midwife; and she comes
In shape no bigger than an agate-stone
On the fore-finger of an alderman,
Drawn with a team of little atomies
Athwart men's noses as they lie asleep:
Her wagon-spokes made of long spinners' legs;
The cover, of the wings of grasshoppers;
The traces, of the smallest spider's web;
The collars, of the moonshine's watery beams:
Her whip, of cricket's bone; the lash, of film:
Her wagoner, a small, grey-coated gnat,
Not half so big as a round little worm
Pricked from the lazy finger of a maid.
Her chariot is an empty hazel-nut,
Made by the joiner squirrel, or old grub,
Time out of mind the fairies' coach-makers:

And in this state she gallops night by night
Through lovers' brains, and then they dream of love:
On courtiers' knees, that dream on court'sies straight:
O'er lawyer's fingers, who straight dream on fees:
O'er ladies' lips, who straight on kisses dream;
Which oft the angry Mab with blisters plagues,
Because their breaths with sweetmeats tainted are.
Sometime she gallops o'er a courtier's nose,
And then dreams he of smelling out a suit:
And sometime comes she with a tithe-pig's tail,
Tickling a parson's nose as 'a lies asleep,
Then dreams he of another benefice:
Sometime she driveth o'er a soldier's neck,
And then dreams he of cutting foreign throats,
Of breaches, ambuscadoes, Spanish blades,
Of healths five fathom deep; and then anon
Drums in his ears, at which he starts and wakes;
And, being thus frighted, swears a prayer or two,
And sleeps again. This is that very Mab —
   Rom. Peace, peace! Mercutio, peace!
Thou talk'st of nothing.
   Mer.   True, I talk of dreams:
Which are the children of an idle brain,
Begot of nothing but vain fantasy;
Which is as thin of substance as the air;
And more inconstant than the wind, who wooes
Even now the frozen bosom of the North;
And, being anger'd, puffs away from thence,
Turning his face to the dew-dropping South.
   Ben. This wind, you talk of, blows us from our-
     selves;

Supper is done, and we shall come too late.

[*Crosses.*

Rom. I fear too early; for my mind misgives,
Some consequence, yet hanging in the stars,
Shall bitterly begin his fearful date
With this night's revels; and expire the term
Of a despised life, closed in my breast,
By some vile forfeit of untimely death:
But He, that hath the steerage of my course,
Direct my sail! — On, lusty gentlemen.   [*Exeunt.*

SCENE II: — *An open Place adjoining Capulet's Garden. Enter* BENVOLIO *and* MERCUTIO, L.

Ben. Romeo! my cousin Romeo!
Mer. He is wise;
And, on my life, hath stolen him home to bed.
Ben. He ran this way, and leaped this orchard
wall.
Call, good Mercutio.
Mer. Nay, I'll conjure, too. —
Romeo! humors! madman! passion! lover!
Appear thou in the likeness of a sigh:
Speak but one rhyme, and I am satisfied;
Cry but — *Ah, me!* — couple but — *love* and *dove;*
Speak to my gossip Venus one fair word,
One nick-name for her purblind son and heir!
Young Adam Cupid, he that shot so trim,
When king Cophetua loved the beggar maid.
He heareth not, he stirreth not, he moveth not;

The ape is dead, and I must conjure him,—
I conjure thee by Rosaline's bright eyes,
By her high forehead, and her scarlet lip,
That in thy likeness thou appear to us.

  Ben. And if he hear thee. thou wilt anger him.

  Mer. This can not anger him ! My invocation
Is fair and honest, and in his mistress' name
I conjure, only but to raise up him.

  Ben. Come, he hath hid himself among these trees,
To be consorted with the humorous night :
Blind is his love, and best befits the dark.

  Mer. Romeo, good night !—I 'll to my truckle-bed,
This field-bed is too cold for me to sleep !
Come, shall we go ?

  Ben. Go, then : for 't is in vain
To seek him here, that means not to be found.

                      [*Exeunt,* L.

SCENE III :— *The Street.* *Enter* BENVOLIO *and*
       MERCUTIO, L.

  Mer. Where the devil should this Romeo be ?
Came he not home to-night?

  Ben. Not to his father's; I spoke with his man.

  Mer. Why, that same pale, hard-hearted wench,
    that Rosaline,
Torments him so, that he will sure run mad.

  Ben. Tybalt, the kinsman to old Capulet,
Hath sent a letter to his father's house.

  Mer. A challenge, on my life !

  Ben. Romeo will answer it.

Mer. Alas, poor Romeo, he is already dead! stabbed with a white wench's black eye; shot through the ear with a love-song; the very pin of his heart cleft with the blind bow-boy's butt-shaft!— And is he a man to encounter Tybalt?

Ben. Why, what is Tybalt?

Mer. Oh, he's the courageous captain of compliments: he fights, as you sing prick-song; keeps time, distance, and proportion; rests me his minim rest — one, two, and the third in your bosom; the very butcher of a silk button, a duellist, a duellist; a gentleman of the very first house — of the first and second cause; ah, the immortal *passado!* the *punto reverso!* the *hai!* —

Ben. The what!

Mer. The plague of such antic, lisping, affected fantasticoes, these new tuners of accents!— *Ma foi,* a very good blade! a very tall man! a very fine wench! — why, is not this a lamentable thing, grandsire, that we should be thus afflicted with these strange flies, these fashion-mongers, these *pardonnez-mois!*

Ben. Here comes Romeo, here comes Romeo!

Mer. Without his roe, like a dried herring. Oh, flesh, flesh, how art thou fishified! Now is he for the numbers that Petrarch flowed in; Laura to his lady was but a kitchen-wench; marry, she had a better love to be-rhyme her: Dido, a dowdy; Cleopatra, a gipsy; Helen and Hero, hildings and harlots; Thisbe, a gray eye or so, but not to the purpose. —

Enter ROMEO, R.

Signior Romeo, *bon jour!* there's a French salutation for you.

Rom. Good morrow to you both.

Mer. You gave us the counterfeit fairly last night.

Rom. What counterfeit did I give you?

Mer. The slip, sir, the slip; can you not conceive? Romeo, will you come to your father's? we'll to dinner there.

Rom. I will follow you. [*Exeunt.*

SCENE IV : — *The Street. Enter* MERCUTIO *and* BENVOLIO, L.

Ben. I pray thee, good Mercutio, let's retire;
The day is hot, the Capulets abroad,
And if we meet, we shall not 'scape a brawl;
For now, these hot days, is the mad blood stirring.

Mer. Thou art like one of those fellows that, when he enters the confines of a tavern, claps me his sword upon the table, and says, *God send me no need of thee;* and by the operation of the second cup, draws it on the drawer, when, indeed, there is no need.

Ben. Am I like such a fellow?

Mer. Come, come, thou art as hot a Jack in thy mood as any in Italy; an there were two such, we should have none shortly, for one would kill the other. Thou! why thou wilt quarrel with a man that hath a hair more or a hair less in his beard

D. S.—2.

than thou hast. Thou wilt quarrel with a man
for cracking nuts, having no other reason but because thou hast hazel eyes: what eye but such an
eye would spy out such a quarrel? Thy head is as
full of quarrels as an egg is full of meat. Thou hast
quarreled with a man for coughing in the street, because he hath wakened thy dog that hath lain asleep
in the sun. Didst thou not fall out with a tailor for
wearing his new doublet before Easter? with another,
for tying his new shoes with old ribbon? and yet
thou wilt tutor me for quarreling!

Ben. An I were so apt to quarrel as thou art,
any man should buy the fee-simple of my life for an
hour and a quarter. — By my head, here come the
Capulets.

Mer. By my heel, I care not.

Enter TYBALT, R.

Tyb. [*Speaking as he enters.*] Follow me close,
  for I will speak to them.
Gentlemen, good den! A word with one of you.

Mer. And but one word with one of us? Couple
it with something: make it a word and a blow.

Tyb. You shall find me apt enough to that, sir,
if you will give me occasion.

Mer. Could you not take some occasion, without
giving?

Tyb. Mercutio, thou consort'st with Romeo.

Mer. Consort! What, dost thou make us minstrels? If thou make minstrels of us, look to hear

nothing but discords: here's my fiddle-stick; here's
that shall make you dance.   Zounds! consort!

[Laying his hand on his sword.

Ben.   We talk here in the public haunt of men:
Either withdraw unto some private place,
Or reason coldly of your grievances,
Or else depart: here all eyes gaze on us.

Mer.   Men's eyes were made to look, and let them
gaze:
I will not budge for no man's pleasure, I.

Tyb.   Well, peace be with you, sir: here comes
my man.

Mer.   But I'll be hanged, sir, if he wear your
livery.

Enter ROMEO, L.

Tyb.   Romeo, the hate I bear thee can afford
No better term than this, — thou art a villain.

Rom.   Tybalt, the reason that I have to love thee,
Doth much excuse the appertaining rage
To such a greeting: — villain I am none;
Therefore, farewell; I see, thou know'st me not.

Tyb.   Boy, this shall not excuse the injuries
That thou hast done me; therefore turn and draw.

Rom.   I do protest, I never injured thee,
But love thee better than thou canst devise,
Till thou shalt know the reason of my love:
And so, good Capulet, (which name I tender
As dearly as my own,) be satisfied.

[Exeunt ROMEO, R., TYBALT, L.

Mer.   Oh, calm, dishonorable, vile submission!
A *la stoccata* carries it away.   [*Draws.*
Tybalt — you rat-catcher! will you walk?

Re-enter TYBALT, L.

Tyb.   What would'st thou have with me?
Mer.   Good king of cats, nothing but one of your
nine lives; that I mean to make bold withal.   Will
you pluck your sword out of his pilcher by the ears?
Make haste, lest mine be about your ears ere it be
out.
Tyb.   I am for you.   [*Drawing.*

Re-enter ROMEO, R.

Rom.   Gentle Mercutio, put thy rapier up.
Mer.   Come, sir, your *passado.*
                    [MERCUTIO *and* TYBALT *fight.*
Rom.   Draw, Benvolio;
Beat down their weapons: — gentlemen, for shame
Forbear this outrage!   Tybalt — Mercutio —
The prince expressly hath forbid this bandying
In Verona streets;
                    Hold, Tybalt; — good Mercutio.
          [*Exit* TYBALT, *having wounded* MERCUTIO, R.
Mer.   I am hurt: —
A plague o' both the houses! — I am sped!
Is he gone, and hath nothing?
Rom.   What, art thou hurt?

Mer. Ay, ay, a scratch, a scratch :—marry, 't is enough.— Go, fetch a surgeon.

Rom. Courage, man : the hurt can not be much.

Mer. No : 't is not so deep as a well, nor so wide as a church door ; but 't is enough — 't will serve : ask for me to-morrow, and you shall find me a grave man. I am peppered, I warrant, for this world. — A plague o' both your houses !— Zounds ! a dog, a rat, a mouse, a cat, to scratch a man to death ! a braggart, a rogue, a villain, that fights by the book of arithmetic !— Why the devil came you between us ? I was hurt under your arm.

Rom. I thought all for the best.

Mer. Help me into some house, Benvolio, Or I shall faint. A plague o' both your houses ! They have made worms'-meat of me : I have it, and soundly, too. — Your houses !

　　　　　Exeunt MERCUTIO *and* BENVOLIO, L.

Rom. This gentleman, the prince's near ally, My very friend, hath got his mortal hurt In my behalf : my reputation stained With Tybalt's slander, Tybalt, that an hour Hath been my kinsman ! Oh, sweet Juliet ! Thy beauty hath made me effeminate, And in my temper softened valor's steel.

　　　　　Enter BENVOLIO, L.

Ben. Oh, Romeo, Romeo, brave Mercutio 's dead : That gallant spirit hath aspired the clouds, Which too untimely here did scorn the earth.

Rom. This day's black fate on more days doth
    depend ;
This but begins the woe, others must end.
    Ben. Here comes the furious Tybalt back again.
    Rom. Alive! in triumph! and Mercutio slain!
Away to heaven, respective lenity,   [*Crosses*, L.
And fire-eyed fury be my conduct now!

Enter TYBALT, L.

Now, Tybalt, take the villain back again, [*Crosses*, R.
That late thou gav'st me ; for Mercutio's soul
Is but a little way above our heads,
Staying for thine to keep him company :
Either thou, or I, or both, must go with him.
    Tyb. Thou, wretched boy, that did'st consort him
    here,
Shalt with him hence.
    Rom. This shall determine that.
          [*They fight.*—TYBALT *falls and dies.*
    Ben. Romeo, away, begone!
The citizens are up, and Tybalt slain —
Stand not amazed ; the prince will doom thee death,
If thou art taken. Hence, begone, away!
    Rom. Oh, I am fortune's fool.

Curtain.

COSTUMES.

ROMEO. — Tight waistcoat, fitting the form down to the middle of the thigh, embroidered, buttoned down front, and girdled about the hips; sleeves close-fitting to elbow, and then hanging in long, wide pendants; hose; long white cloak, with row of buttons down the right shoulder; capuchin, or hood, on head and shoulders; long and pointed shoes; sword.

MERCUTIO. — Same, but scarlet cloak.

BENVOLIO. — Same, but fawn cloak.

TYBALT. — Fawn cloak, lined with buff and yellow.

DETRACTION; OR, THE COQUETTE RENOUNCED.

From Wycherly's Plain Dealer.

DRAMATIS PERSONÆ.

OLIVIA, *a witty, unprincipled coquette.*
ELIZA, *her cousin.*
LETTICE, *Olivia's waiting woman.*
NOVEL, *a pert, railing coxcomb.*
LORD PLAUSIBLE, *a ceremonious, commending hypocrite.*
MANLY, *a plain-dealing sea-captain, betrothed to Olivia.*
BOY.

SCENE:—OLIVIA'S *Lodgings. Enter* OLIVIA, ELIZA, *and* LETTICE.

Olivia. Ah, cousin, what a world 't is we live in; I am so weary of it.

Eliza. Truly, cousin, I can find no fault with it, but that we can not always live in 't; for I can never be weary of it.

Oliv. Oh, hideous! you can not be in earnest, sure, when you say you like the filthy world.

Eliz. You can not be in earnest, sure, when you say you dislike it.

Oliv. You are a very censorious creature, I find.

Eliz. Is it possible that the world, which has such a variety of charms for other women, can have none for you? Let's see — first, what d'ye think of dressing and fine clothes?

Oliv. Dressing! Fie, fie! 't is my aversion. But come hither, you dowdy; methinks you might have arranged this better. [*Arranging* Eliza's *mantle.*] Oh, hideous! d'ye see how it sits?

Eliz. Well enough, cousin, if dressing be your aversion.

Oliv. 'T is so; and for variety of rich clothes, they are more my aversion.

Lettice. Ay, 't is because your ladyship wears 'em too long.

Oliv. Insatiable creature! I have not had this above three days, cousin, and within this month have made some six more.

Eliz. Then your aversion to 'em is not altogether so great.

Oliv. Alas, 't is for Lettice here, only, that I wear 'em, cousin.

Let. If it be for me only, madam, pray do not wear 'em.

Eliz. But what d'ye think of visits — balls? —

Oliv. Oh, I detest 'em.

Eliz. Of plays?

Oliv. I abominate 'em; hideous things!

Eliz. What do you say to masquerading in the winter, and Hyde Park in the summer?

Oliv. Insipid pleasures I taste not.

Eliz. What think you of a rich, young husband?

Oliv. Oh, horrid! Marriage! I nauseate it of all things.

Let. But what does your ladyship think, then, of a handsome, young lover?

Oliv. A handsome young fellow! you impudent! Begone out of my sight! Name a handsome young fellow to me! Fah! a hideous, handsome young fellow I abominate.

Eliz. Indeed! But let's see; will nothing please you?

Oliv. Peace, cousin, or your discourse will be my aversion.

Eliz. Yes; for if any thing be a woman's aversion, 't is plain dealing from another woman; and perhaps that's your quarrel with the world; for that will talk.

Oliv. Talk? not of me, sure; for what men do I converse with? what visits do I admit?

Enter BOY.

Boy. Here's the gentleman to wait upon you, madam.

Oliv. On me! You little, unthinking fop, d'ye know what you say?

Boy. Yes, madam; 't is the gentleman that comes every day to you, who —

Oliv. Hold your peace, you heedless little animal, and get you gone. This country boy, cousin, takes my dancing-master or the milliner for visitors. [*Exit* BOY.

Let. No, madam; 't is Mr. Novel, I 'm sure, by his talking so loud. I know his voice, too, madam.

Oliv. You know nothing, you buffle-headed, stupid creature you; you would make my cousin believe I receive visits. But if it be Mr. — what did you call him?

Let. Mr. Novel, madam; he that —

Oliv. Hold your peace; I 'll hear no more of him; but if it be your Mr. — I can't think of his name again — I suppose he has followed my cousin hither.

Eliz. No, cousin, I will not rob you of the honor of the visit. 'T is you, cousin, for I know him not.

Oliv. Nor did I ever hear of him before, upon my honor, cousin; besides, ha' n't I told you that visits, flattery, and detraction are my aversion? D' ye think, then, I would admit such a coxcomb as he is?

Eliz. I find you do know him, cousin; at least, have heard of him.

Oliv. Yes, now I remember, I have heard of him.

Eliz. Well; but since he is such a coxcomb, for heaven's sake, let him not come up. Tell him, Lettice, that your lady is not in.

Oliv. No, Lettice; tell him my cousin is here, and that he may come up.

Eliz. I know him not, nor desire it. Send him away, Lettice.

Oliv. Upon my word, she sha n't. I must disobey your commands, to comply with your real wishes. Call him up, Lettice.

Eliz. Nay, she shall not stir on this errand.

[*Holds* LETTICE.

Oliv. Well, then, I'll call him myself for you, since you will have it so. Mr. Novel! [*Calls out at door.*] Sir, sir!

Enter NOVEL.

Novel. Madam, I beg your pardon; perhaps you were busy. I did not think you had company with you.

Eliz. [*Aside*] Yet he comes to me, cousin!

Oliv. Chairs there.   [*They sit. Exit* LETTICE.

Nov. Well; but, madam, do you know whence I come now?

Oliv. From some melancholy place, I warrant, sir, since they have lost your good company.

Eliz. So.

Nov. From a place where they treated me, at dinner, with so much kindness and civility, that I could hardly get away to you, dear madam.

Oliv. You have a way with you so new and obliging, sir.

Eliz. [*Aside to* OLIVIA] You hate flattery, cousin!

Nov. Nay, faith, madam, do you think my way new? Then you are obliging, madam. I must confess, I hate imitation — to do any thing like other people. All that know me do me the honor to say I am original. But, as I was saying, madam, I have been treated to-day with all the ceremony and kindness imaginable, at my Lady Autumn's;

but the nauseous old woman at the upper end of the table —

Oliv. I detest her hollow, cherry cheeks; she looks like an old coach new painted; affecting an unseemly smugness, while she is ready to drop in pieces.

Eliz. [*Aside to* OLIVIA] You hate detraction, I see, cousin!

Nov. But the silly old fury, while she affects to look like a woman of this age, talks —

Oliv. Like one of the last.

Nov. Yes, madam; but pray let me give you her character. Then, she never counts her age by the years, but —

Oliv. By the masques she has lived to see.

Nov. Nay, then, madam, I see you think a little harmless railing too great a pleasure for any one but yourself, and therefore I've done.

Oliv. Nay, faith, you shall tell me who you had there to dinner.

Nov. If you would hear me, madam.

Oliv. Most patiently; speak, sir.

Nov. Then we had her daughter —

Oliv. Ay, her daughter, the very disgrace to good clothes, which she always wears but to heighten her deformity, not mend it; for she is still more splendidly, gallantly ugly, and looks like an ill piece of daubing in a rich frame.

Nov. So! But have you done with her, madam, and can you spare her to me a little now?

Oliv. Ay, ay, sir.

Nov. Then she is like —

Oliv. She is, you 'd say, like a city bride, the greater fortune, but not the greater beauty for her dress.

Nov. Well; have you done, madam? Then, she —

Oliv. Then she bestows as unfortunately on her face all the graces in fashion, as the languishing eye, or the pouting lip.

Eliz. Cousin, I find one may have a collection of all one's acquaintances' pictures at your house as at an artist's.

Oliv. I draw after the life; I do nobody wrong, cousin.

Eliz. No; you hate flattery and detraction.

Oliv. But, Mr. Novel, who had you besides at dinner?

Nov. Nay, I 'll not tell you, unless you will allow me the privilege of railing in my turn; but, now I think on 't, the women ought to be your province, as the men are mine; and you must know we had him whom —

Oliv. Him whom —

Nov. What! invading me already, and giving the character before you know the man?

Eliz. No, that is not fair, though it be usual.

Oliv. I beg your pardon, Mr. Novel; pray go on.

Nov. Then, I say, we had that familiar coxcomb who is at home wheresoe'er he comes.

Oliv. Ay, that fool —

Nov. Nay then, madam, your servant; I 'm gone.

Taking a fool out of one's mouth is worse than taking the bread out of one's teeth.

Oliv. I 've done ; your pardon, Mr. Novel ; pray proceed.

Nov. I say, the rogue, that he may be the only wit in the company, will let nobody else talk, and —

Oliv. Ay, those fops who love to talk all themselves are my aversion.

Nov. Then you 'll let me speak, madam, sure.

Oliv. Pr'ythee, tell us who else was with you there.

Nov. We had nobody else.

Oliv. Nay faith, you had. Come, my Lord Plausible was there, too, who is, cousin, a —

Eliz. You need not tell me what he is, cousin ; for I know him to be a civil, good-natured, harmless gentleman, that speaks well of all the world, and is always in good humor, and —

Oliv. Hold, cousin, hold ; I hate detraction, but I must tell you, cousin, his civility is cowardice ; his good nature, want of wit ; and he has neither courage nor sense to rail ; and for his being always in humor, 't is because he is never dissatisfied with himself. In fine, he is my aversion ; and I never admit his visits beyond my hall.

Nov. No ; he visit you ! cringing, grinning rogue ! If I should see him coming up to you, I would make bold to kick him down again. Ha ! —

Enter LORD PLAUSIBLE.

My dear Lord Plausible, your most humble servant.
        [*Rises and salutes* PLAUS., *and kisses him.*

Eliz. [*Aside*] So I find kissing and railing follow each other with angry men, as well as with angry women.

L. P. Your most faithful, humble servant, generous Mr. Novel; and, madam, I am your eternal slave, and kiss your fair hands, which I had done sooner, according to your commands, but —

Oliv. No excuses, my lord.

Eliz. [*Aside*] What! you sent for him, then, cousin.

Nov. [*Aside*] Ha! invited!

Oliv. I know you must divide yourself; for your good company is too general a good to be engrossed by any particular friend.

L. P. Oh Lord, madam, my company! Your most obliged, faithful, humble servant. But I could have brought you good company, indeed, for I parted at the door with two of the worthiest, bravest men —

Oliv. Who were they, my lord?

Nov. Who do you call the worthiest, bravest men, pray?

L. P. O, the wisest, bravest gentlemen! men of such honor and virtue! of such good qualities! Ah —

Eliz. [*Aside*] This is a coxcomb that speaks ill of all people in a different way, and libels every body with dull praise, and commonly in the wrong place, so as to make his panegyrics abusive lampoons.

L. P. Ah! such patterns of heroic virtue! such—

Oliv. But pray let me know who they were.

L. P. The honor of our nation, the glory of our age. Ah! I could dwell a twelvemonth on their praise, which, indeed, I might spare by telling their names — Sir John Current and Sir Richard Court-title.

Nov. Court-title! Ha, ha!

Oliv. And Sir John Current! Why will you keep such a wretch company, my lord?

L. P. Oh, madam, seriously, you are a little too severe, for he is a man of unquestioned reputation in every thing.

Oliv. Yes, because he endeavors only with the women to pass for a man of courage, and with the bullies for a wit; with the wits for a man of business, and with the men of business for a favorite at court; and at court for good city security.

Nov. And for Sir Richard, he —

L. P. He loves your choice, picked company; persons that —

Oliv. He loves a lord, indeed; but —

Nov. Pray, dear madam, let me have but a bold stroke or two at his picture. He loves a lord, as you say, though —

Oliv. Though he borrowed his money, and ne'er paid him again.

Nov. And would bespeak a place three days before, at the back end of a lord's coach, to Hyde Park.

L. P. Nay, i' faith, i' faith, you are both too severe.

Oliv. Then, to show yet more his passion for quality, he makes love to that fulsome coach-load of honor, my Lady Goodly; for he is always at her lodging.

L. P. Because it is the conventicle-gallant, the meeting-house of all the fair ladies, and glorious, superfine beauties of the town.

Nov. Very fine ladies! There is, first —

Oliv. Her honor, as fat as an hostess.

L. P. She is something plump, indeed; a good, comely, graceful person.

Nov. Then, there 's my Lady Frances — what d' ye call her? Ugly —

L. P. She has wit in abundance, and the very handsomest heel, elbow, and tip of an ear you ever saw.

Nov. Heel and elbow! ha, ha! And there 's my lady Betty, you know —

Oliv. As slatternly as an Irish woman bred in France.

L. P. Ah! all she has hangs with a loose air, indeed, and becoming negligence.

Eliz. You see all faults with lover's eyes, I find, my lord.

L. P. Ah, madam, your most obliged, faithful, humble servant to command! But you can say nothing, sure, against the superfine Mrs. —

Oliv. I know who you mean. She is as censorious and detracting a jade as a superannuated spinster.

L. P. She has a smart way of raillery, it must be confessed.

Nov. And then, for Mrs. Grideline —

L. P. She, I 'm sure, is —

Oliv. One that never spoke ill of any body, 't is confessed; for she is as silent in conversation as a country lover, and no better company than a clock or a weather-glass; for, if she sounds, 't is but once an hour, to put you in mind of the time of day, or to tell you 't will be cold or hot, rain or snow.

L. P. Ah, poor creature! she's extremely good and modest.

Nov. And for Mrs. Bridlechin, she —

Oliv. As proud as a churchman's wife.

L. P. She's a woman of great spirit and honor, and will not make herself cheap, 't is true.

Nov. Then Mrs. Hoyden, that calls all people by their sirnames, and is —

Oliv. As familiar as a duck.

L. P. Mrs. Hoyden! a poor, affable, good-natured soul. But the divine Mrs. Trifle comes thither, too; sure, her beauty, virtue, and conduct you can say nothing to?

Oliv. No!

Nov. No! — Pray let me speak, madam.

Oliv. First, can any one be called beautiful that squints?

L. P. Her eyes languish a little, I own.

Nov. Languish! ha, ha!

Oliv. Languish! Then for her conduct —

Eliz. [*Rising*] Cousin, pardon me; I must be going.

Oliv. You will not, sure; nay, you shall not, venture your reputation by going, and mine by leaving me alone with two men here; nay, you 'll disoblige me forever, if —

Eliz. If — I stay. Your servant. [*Exit.*

Nov. I saw your old lover this morning, Captain — [*Whispers.*

Enter CAPTAIN MANLY *behind.*

Oliv. Whom? You need not whisper.

Man. [*Aside*] I am luckily got here unobserved.
How! In close conversation with these supple
rascals?

Oliv. Manly returned, do you say? And is he
safe?　　　　　　　　　　[*Whispers to* PLAUSIBLE.

Man. [*Aside*] She yet seems concerned for my
safety; and perhaps they are admitted here now
but for their news of me.

Oliv. I heard of his fighting only, without particulars; and confess I always loved his brutal
courage, because it made me hope it might rid me
of his more brutal love.

Man. [*Aside*] What's that?

Nov. He has no use of his arms but to set 'em on
kimbo; for he never pulls off his hat, at least not
to me, I'm sure; for you must know, madam, he has
a fantastical hatred to good company; he can't abide
me.

L. P. Oh, be not so severe on him as to say he
hates good company; for I assure you he has a great
respect, esteem, and kindness for me.

Oliv. Well, if he be returned, Mr. Novel, then
shall I be pestered again with his boisterous sea love;
have my alcove smell like a cabin, my chamber per-
fumed with his tarpaulin Brandenburg, and hear
volleys of brandy sighs enough to make a fog in
one's room. Fah! I hate a lover that smells like
Thames Street!

Man. [*Aside*] I can bear no longer, and need hear
no more. [*Comes forward.*] But since you have
these two pulvillio-boxes, these essence-bottles, this
pair of musk-cats here, I hope I may venture to
come yet nearer you.

Oliv. Overheard us, then!

Nov. [*Aside*] I hope he heard not me.

L. P. Most noble and heroic captain, your most
obliged, faithful, humble servant.

Nov. Dear tar, thy humble servant.

Man. Away. — Madam —

Oliv. Nay, I think I have fitted you for listening.

Man. [*Thrusts* NOVEL *and* PLAUSIBLE *on each side,
and confronts* OLIVIA.] You have fitted me for be-
lieving you could not be fickle, though you were
young; nor be vain, though you were handsome;
nor break your promise, though to a parting lover;
nor abuse your best friend, though you had wit : but
I take your contempt of me not worse than your
esteem of these things here, though you know 'em.

Nov. Things!

L. P. Let the captain rally a little.

Man. Yes, things. Canst thou be angry, thou
thing? [*Coming up to* NOVEL.] Madam, tell me,
pray, what was it about this spark could take you?
Was it the merit of his fashionable impudence, the
briskness of his noise, the wit of his laugh, his judgment or fancy in his garniture? or was it a well-
trimmed glove, or the scent of it that charmed you?
Then, madam, [*turning to* LORD PLAUS.] for *this*
gentle piece of courtesy, this man of tame honor,

what could you find in him? Was it his languishing, affected tone, his mannerly look, his second-hand flattery, his slavish obsequiousness, or his jaunty way of playing with your fan that won your heart?

Nov. Ha, ha! I can not hold; I must laugh.

L. P. And, i' faith, dear captain, I beg your pardon and leave to laugh at you, too, though I protest I mean you no hurt. Ha, ha!

Man. Why, you impudent, pitiful wretches; you presume, sure, upon your effeminacy to urge me; for you are in all things so like women, that you may think it in me a kind of cowardice to beat you.

Nov. No hectoring, good captain.

Man. Or perhaps you think this lady's presence secures you. But have a care; she has talked herself out of all the respect I had for her, and by using me ill before you, has given me a privilege of using you so before her; but if you would preserve your respect to her, and not be beaten before her, go, begone immediately.

Nov. Begone! What?

L. P. Nay, worthy, noble, generous captain!

Man. Begone, I say.

Nov. Begone again! to us, begone!*

Man. No chattering, baboons! instantly begone! or — [MANLY *puts them out of the room;* NOVEL *struts,* PLAUSIBLE *cringes.*]

Oliv. Turn hither your rage.

Man. Olivia, you heard that chance has used me scurvily, therefore you do, too. Well, persevere in your ingratitude, falsehood, and disdain.; have constancy in something, and I promise you to be as just to your real scorn as I was to your feigned love, and henceforth will despise, contemn, hate, loathe, and detest you most faithfully.

Curtain.

COSTUMES.

OLIVIA. — Elegant dress of silk or satin, with voluminous train; simple trimmings; arms bare to the elbow; pearl necklace; hair in long ringlets, confined by a band of pearls.

ELIZA. — Rich train dress; lace mantle; hair adorned with a rose; hat and feathers.

LETTICE. — Short dress; brown Holland apron; profusion of jewelry.

LORD PLAUSIBLE. — Short doublet, open in front, displaying a rich, ruffled shirt-bosom; loose breeches, fastened around the waist by an embroidered band; large, full sleeves, ornamented with ribbons; beneath the knee, long, drooping lace ruffles; lace collar; high-crowned hat, with plume of feathers; periwig, consisting of a profusion of curls hanging down the back and shoulders; dress sword.

NOVEL. — Similar to Plausible, but more negligent.

MANLY. — Blue pants and jacket; belt; low-crowned hat with long band; sword.

BONIFACE.

From Farquhar's Beaux Stratagem.

DRAMATIS PERSONÆ.

BONIFACE.   AIMWELL.   ARCHER.   TAPSTER.

SCENE:—*An Inn.   Enter* BONIFACE, *conducting* AIM-
WELL, *in a riding habit; and* ARCHER, *as footman,
carrying a portmanteau.*

Bon.   This way, this way, gentlemen.

Aim.   Set down the things; go to the stable and
see my horse well rubbed.

Arch.   I shall, sir.   [*Exit.*

Aim.   You 're my landlord, I suppose?

Bon.   Yes, sir; I 'm old Will Boniface; pretty
well known on this road, as the saying is.

Aim.   Oh, Mr. Boniface, your servant.

Bon.   Oh, sir. — What will your honor please to
drink, as the saying is.

Aim.   I have heard your town of Litchfield much
famed for ale; I think I 'll taste that.

Bon.   Sir, I have now in my cellar ten tun of the
best ale in Staffordshire; 't is smooth as oil, sweet
as milk, clear as amber, and strong as brandy, and

will be just fourteen years old the fifth day of March next, old style.

Aim. You're very exact, I find, in the age of your ale.

Bon. As punctual, sir, as I am in the age of my children. I'll show you such ale. Here, tapster, broach number 1706, as the saying is. Sir, you shall taste my anno Domini. I have lived in Litchfield, man and boy, above eight-and-fifty years, and, I believe, have not consumed eight-and-fifty ounces of meat.

Aim. At a meal, you mean, if one may guess your sense by your bulk.

Bon. Not in my life, sir; I have fed purely upon ale; I have eat my ale, drank my ale, and I always sleep upon ale.

Enter TAPSTER *with a tankard.*

Now, sir, you shall see. [*Filling it out.*] Your worship's health. Ha! delicious, delicious! — fancy it Burgundy, only fancy it, and 't is worth ten shillings a quart.

Aim. [*Drinks.*] 'T is confounded strong.

Bon. Strong! It must be so, or how would we be strong that drink it?

Aim. And have you lived so long upon this ale, landlord?

Bon. Eight-and-fifty years, upon my credit, sir; but it killed my wife, poor woman! as the saying is.

Aim. How came that to pass?

Bon. I do n't know how, sir; she would not let the ale take its natural course, sir; she was for qualifying it every now and then with a dram, as the saying is; and an honest gentleman that came this way from Ireland made her a present of a dozen bottles of usquebaugh — but the poor woman was never well after; — but, however, I was obliged to the gentleman, you know.

Aim. Why, was it the usquebaugh that killed her?

Bon. My lady Bountiful said so. She, good lady, did what could be done; she cured her of three disorders, but the fourth carried her off; but she's happy, and I'm contented, as the saying is.

Enter ARCHER.

Arch. Landlord, there are some French gentlemen below that ask for you.

Bon. I'll wait on 'em. — Does your master stay long in town, as the saying is? [*Aside to* ARCHER.

Arch. I can't tell, as the saying is.

Bon. Come from London?

Arch. No.

Bon. Going to London, mayhap?

Arch. No.

Bon. An odd fellow, this! [*Bar bell rings.*] I beg your worship's pardon; I'll wait on you in half a minute. [*Exit.*

Aim. The course is clear, I see. Now, my dear Archer, welcome to Litchfield.

Arch. I thank thee, my dear brother in iniquity.

Aim. Iniquity! pr'ythee, leave canting. You need not change your style with your dress.

Arch. Do n't mistake me, Aimwell; for 't is still my maxim that there 's no scandal like rags, nor any crime so shameful as poverty. Men must not be poor: idleness is the root of all evil: the world 's wide enough, let 'em bustle: fortune has taken the weak under her protection, but men of sense are left to their industry.

Aim. Upon which topic we proceed, and, I think, luckily, hitherto. Would not any man swear, now, that I am a man of quality, and you my servant, when, if our intrinsic value were known —

Arch. Come, come; we are the men of intrinsic value who can strike our fortunes out of ourselves; whose worth is independent of accidents in life, or revolutions in government: we have heads to get money, and hearts to spend it.

Enter BONIFACE.

Bon. What will your worship please to have for supper?

Aim. What have you got?

Bon. Sir, we have a delicate piece of beef in the pot, and a pig at the fire.

Aim. Good supper-meat, I must confess; but I can't eat beef, landlord.

Arch. And I hate pig.

Aim. Hold your prating, sirrah! Do you know who you are?   [*Aside.*

Bon. Please to bespeak something else; I have every thing in the house.

Aim. Have you any veal?

Bon. Veal! sir, we had a delicate loin of veal on Wednesday last.

Aim. Have you got any fish or wild-fowl?

Bon. As for fish, truly, sir, we are an inland town, and indifferently provided with fish, that's the truth on 't; but, then, for wild-fowl — we have a delicate couple of rabbits.

Aim. Get me the rabbits fricasseed.

Bon. Fricasseed! La, sir, they'll eat much better smothered with onions.

Arch. Pshaw! Rot your onions.

Aim. Again, sirrah! — Well, landlord, what you please; — but hold, I have a small charge of money, and your house is so full of strangers, that I believe it may be safer in your custody than mine; for when this fellow of mine gets drunk, he minds nothing. — Here, sirrah, reach me the strong box.

Arch. Yes, sir. — This will give us reputation.

[*Aside. Brings the box.*

Aim. Here, landlord; the locks are sealed down, both for your security and mine; it holds somewhat above two hundred pounds; if you doubt it, I'll count them to you after supper; but be sure you lay it where I may have it at a minute's warning; for my affairs are a little dubious at present; perhaps I may be gone in half an hour; perhaps I may be your guest till the best part of that be spent;—and, pray, order your ostler to keep my horses ready saddled; — but one thing above the rest, I must beg, that you will let this fellow have none of your anno Domini, as you call it; for he's the most insufferable sot. — Here, sirrah, light me to my chamber.

[*Exit, lighted by* ARCHER.

Arch. Yes, sir.

Bon. [*Following with box.*] I shall do your worship's commands, as the saying is.

BRAGGADOCIO.

From The Old Bachelor, by Congreve.

DRAMATIS PERSONÆ.

CAPTAIN BLUFFE, *a boasting coward.*
BELLMOUR, *a gay young fellow.*
SIR JOSEPH WITTOL, *a credulous, silly knight.*
SHARPER, *friend to Bellmour.*

SCENE I : — *The Street.   Enter* BELLMOUR *and*
SHARPER. R.. *the latter speaking as he enters.*

Sharp. Well, but, George, I have one question to ask you —

Bell. Pshaw, I have prattled away my time — I hope you are in no haste for an answer; for I shan't stay now. [*Looks at his watch.*

Sharp. Nay, pr'ythee, George —

Bell. No; besides my business, I see a fool coming this way.

Sharp. Whom do you mean? Oh, here he comes! Stand close, let 'em pass. [*They go up.* BLUFFE *and* WITTOL *cross the stage.*] What in the name of wonder is he? [*Comes down.*

Bell. (R. C.) Why, a fool.

Sharp. (L. C.) 'T is a tawdry outside.

Bell. And a very beggarly lining; yet he may be worth your acquaintance. A little of thy chemistry, Tom, may extract gold from that dirt.

Sharp. Say you so? Faith, I am as poor as a chemist, and would be as industrious. But what was he that followed him? Is not he a dragon that watches those golden pippins?

Bell. Hang him, no — he a dragon! If he be, 't is a very peaceful one; I can insure his anger dormant; or, should he seem to rouse, 't is but well lashing him, and he will sleep like a top.

Sharp. Ay, is he of that kidney?

Bell. Yet is adored by that bigot, Sir Joseph Wittol, as the image of valor: he calls him his Back, and, indeed, they are never asunder. Yet, last night, I know not by what mischance, the knight was alone, and had fallen into the hands of some night-walkers,

who, I suppose, would have pillaged him; but I
chanced to come by, and rescued him; though, I
believe, he was heartily frightened; for, as soon as
ever he was loose, he ran away, without staying to
see who helped him.

Sharp. Is that bully of his in the army?

Bell. No, but is a pretender, and wears the habit
of a soldier, which, now-a-days, as often cloaks cowardice as a black gown does atheism. You must
know, he has been abroad — went purely to run
away from a campaign — enriched himself with the
plunder of a few oaths, and here vents 'em against
the general, who, slighting men of merit, and pre-
ferring only those of interest, has made him quit the
service.

Sharp. Wherein, no doubt, he magnifies his own
performance.

Bell. Speaks miracles; is the drum to his own
praise — the only implement of a soldier he resem-
bles: like that, being full of blustering noise and
emptiness.

Sharp. And, like that, too, of no use but to be
beaten.

Bell. Right: but there the comparison breaks;
for he will take a drubbing with as little noise as a
pulpit cushion.

Sharp. His name, and I have done.

Bell. Why, that, to pass it current, too, he has
gilded with a title: he is called Captain Bluffe.

Sharp. Well, I'll endeavor his acquaintance.

[*Exeunt* L.

SCENE II :— *Enter* SIR JOSEPH WITTOL, SHARPER
following.

Sharp. (L.) [*Aside*] Sure, that's he, and alone.

Sir Jo. (R.) Um!—Ay, this,—this is the very
place the inhuman cannibals, the bloody-minded
villains, would have butchered me last night; no
doubt they would have flayed me alive, have sold
my skin, and devoured my members.

Sharp. [*Aside*] How's this?

Sir Jo. An it had n't been for a civil gentleman
as came by, and frightened 'em away.—But, egad,
I durst not stay to give him thanks.

Sharp. [*Aside*] This must be Bellmour he means.
Ha! I have a thought.

Sir Jo. Zooks! would the captain would come.
The very remembrance makes me quake. Egad, I
shall never be reconciled to this place heartily.

Sharp. [*Aside*] 'T is but trying, and being where
I am at worst. Now, luck! [*Looking about as in
search.*] Cursed fortune! this must be the place,
this unlucky place —

Sir Jo. [*Aside*] Egad, and so 't is. [*Sees* SHARPER.]
Why, here has been more mischief done, I perceive.

Sharp. [*Still looking about*] No, 't is gone, 't is lost.
Ten thousand evils on that chance which drew me
hither! Ay, here, just here — nothing to be found
but the despair of what I 've lost.

Sir Jo. [*Aside*] Poor gentleman! By the Lord
Harry, I 'll stay no longer; for I 've found, too —

D. S.—5.

Sharp. Ha! who is 't that has found? What have you found? Restore it quickly, or —

[*Goes up to* Sir Joseph.

Sir Jo. Not I, sir, not I, as I 've a soul to be saved; I have found nothing but what has been to my loss, as I may say, and as you were saying, sir.

Sharp. Oh, your servant, sir; you are safe, then, it seems; 't is an ill wind that blows nobody good. Well you may rejoice over my ill fortune, since it paid the price of your ransom.

Sir Jo. I rejoice! egad, not I, sir; I 'm very sorry for your loss, with all my heart blood, sir; and if you did but know me, you 'd ne'er say I was so ill-natured.

Sharp. Know you! Why, can you be so ungrateful to forget me?

Sir Jo. O La, forget him! No, no, sir, I do n't forget you — because I never saw your face before, egad! Ha, ha, ha!

Sharp. [*Angrily*] How!

Sir Jo. Stay, stay, sir; let me recollect. [*Aside*] He 's a terribly angry fellow. I believe I had better remember him till I can get out of his sight; but out o' sight out o' mind, egad.

Sharp. Methought the service I did you last night, sir, in preserving you from those ruffians, might have taken better root in your shallow memory.

Sir Jo. [*Aside*] Gads — daggers, belts, blades, and scabbards! this is the very gentleman! How shall I make him a return suitable to the greatness of his merit? I had a pretty thing to that purpose, if he

ha' n't frightened it out of my memory. Hem, hem.
[*To* SHARP.] Sir, I must submissively implore your
pardon for my transgression of ingratitude and
omission; having my entire dependence, sir, upon
the superfluity of your goodness, which, like an
inundation, will, I hope, totally immerge the recol-
lection of my error, and leave me floating, in your
sight, upon the full-blown bladders of repentance,
by the help of which I shall hope to once more
swim into your favor.   [*Bows.*

Sharp. So-h. — Oh, sir, I am easily pacified; the
acknowledgment of a gentleman --

Sir Jo. Acknowledgment, sir! I am all over acknowledgment, and will not stick to show it in the
greatest extremity, by night or by day, in sickness
or in health, winter or summer; all seasons and occasions shall testify the reality and gratitude of your
superabundant humble servant, Sir Joseph Wittol,
knight. — Hem, hem.

Sharp. Sir Joseph Wittol?

Sir Jo. The same, sir; of Wittol Hall, in *comitatu*
Bucks.

Sharp. Is it possible? Then I am happy to have
obliged the mirror of knighthood and pink of courtesy in the age. Let me embrace you.

Sir Jo. O La, sir!

Sharp. My loss I esteem as a trifle paid with interest, since it has purchased me the friendship and
acquaintance of the person in the world whose character I admire.

Sir Jo. You are only pleased to say so, sir. But

pray, if I may be so bold, what is the loss you mention?

Sharp. Oh, term it so no longer, sir. In the scuffle last night I only dropped a bill of a hundred pound, which, I confess, I came half despairing to recover; but, thanks to my better fortune —

Sir Jo. You have found it, sir, then, it seems. I profess I 'm heartily glad —

Sharp. Sir, your humble servant. I do n't question but you are, that you have so cheap an opportunity of expressing your generosity and gratitude; since the refunding of so trivial a sum will wholly acquit you and doubly engage me.

Sir Jo. [*Aside*] What a dickins does he mean by a trivial sum! But have you found it, sir?

Sharp. No otherwise, I vow, but in my hopes in you, sir.

Sir Jo. Hum!

Sharp. But that 's sufficient. 'T were injustice to doubt the honor of Sir Joseph Wittol.

Sir Jo. O La, sir!

Sharp. You are above, I 'm sure, a thought so low, to suffer me to lose what was ventured in your service; nay, 't was in a manner paid down for your deliverance; 't was so much lent you; and you scorn, I 'll say that for you —

Sir Jo. Nay, I 'll say that for myself, with your leave, sir; I do scorn a dirty thing; — but, egad, I 'm a little out of pocket at present.

Sharp. Pshaw! you can't want a hundred pound. Your word is sufficient anywhere. "T is but bor-

rowing so much dirt. You have large acres, and
can soon repay it. Money is but dirt, Sir Joseph —
mere dirt.

Sir Jo. But I profess, 't is a dirt I have washed
my hands of at present; I have laid it all out upon
my back.

Sharp. Are you so extravagant in clothes, Sir
Joseph?

Sir Jo. Ha, ha, ha! a very good jest, I profess.
Ha, ha, ha! a very good jest. And I did n't know
that I had said it, and that's a better jest than
t'other. 'Tis a sign you and I ha'n't been long
acquainted. You have lost a good jest for want of
knowing me. I only mean a friend of mine whom
I call my Back; he sticks as close to me, and follows
me through all dangers; he is, indeed, back, breast,
and head-piece, as it were, to me. Egad, he's a
brave fellow. Paugh! I am quite another thing
when I am with him; I do n't fear the devil, (God
bless us,) almost, if he be by. Ah, had he been with
me last night —

Sharp. [*Angrily*] If he had, sir, what then? He
could have done no more, nor, perhaps, have suffered
so much. Had he a hundred pound to lose?

Sir Jo. O La, sir, by no means. [*Aside*] But
I might have saved a hundred pound. I meant
innocently, as I hope to be saved, sir. [*Aside*] What
a hot fellow. Only, as I was saying, I let him have
all my ready money to redeem his great sword from
limbo. But, sir, I have a letter of credit to Alderman Fondlewife, as far as two hundred pound; and,

this afternoon, you shall see I am a person such a
one as you would wish to have met with.

Sharp. [*Aside*] That you are, I'll be sworn. Why,
that's great, and like yourself.

Enter BLUFFE, L.

Sir Jo. (c.) Oh, here he comes — my Hector of
Troy! Welcome, my bully, my Back! Egad, my
heart has gone a-pit-pat for thee.

Bluffe. How now, my young knight, not for
fear, I hope? He that knows me must be a stranger
to fear.

Sir Jo. Nay, egad, I hate fear ever since I had
like to have died of a fright. But —

Bluffe. But look you here, boy, here's your antidote, here's your powder for a shaking fit. [*Puts
his hand upon his sword.*] But who hast thou got
with thee? Is he of mettle?

Sir Jo. Ay, bully, a very smart fellow, and will
fight like a cock.

Bluffe. Say you so? then I honor him. But has
he been abroad? for every cock will fight upon his
own dunghill.

Sir Jo. I don't know; but I'll present you —

Bluffe. I'll recommend myself. [*Crosses to* c.
Sir, I honor you; I understand you love fighting;
I reverence a man that loves fighting; sir, I kiss
your hilts.

Sharp. (R.) Sir, your servant; but you are mis-
informed; for, unless it be to serve my particular

friend, as Sir Joseph here, my country, or my religion, or in some very justifiable cause, I'm not
for it.

Bluffe. O La, I beg your pardon, sir; I find you
are not of my palate; you can't relish a dish of
fighting without sweet sauce. Now, I think

Fighting for fighting's sake's sufficient cause;
Fighting to me's religion and the laws.

Sir Jo. (L.) Ah, well said, my hero. Was not
that great, sir? By the Lord Harry, he says true:
fighting is meat, and drink, and cloth to him. But,
Back, this gentleman is one of the best friends I
have in the world, and saved my life last night.—
You know, I told you.

Bluffe. Ay! then I honor him again. Sir, may I
crave your name?

Sharp. Ay, sir, my name's Sharper.

Sir Jo. Pray, Mr. Sharper, embrace my Back.
[SHARPER *and* BLUFFE *embrace*, c.] Very well.—
By the Lord Harry, Mr. Sharper, he's as brave a
fellow as Cannibal — are you not, bully Back?

Sharp. Hannibal, I believe you mean, Sir Joseph.

Bluffe. Undoubtedly he did, sir: faith Hannibal
was a very pretty fellow, but, Sir Joseph, compari-
sons are odious. — Hannibal was a very pretty fellow in those days, it must be granted; but, alas!
sir, were he alive now, he would be nothing, nothing in the earth.

Sharp. How, sir! — I make a doubt if there be at
this day a greater general breathing.

Bluffe. Oh, excuse me, sir—Have you served abroad?

Sharp. Not I, really, sir.

Bluffe. Oh, I thought so. Why, then, you can know nothing, sir: I 'm afraid you scarce know the history of the late war in Flanders, with all its particulars.

Sharp. Not I, sir; no more than public letters, or the gazette tells us.

Bluffe. Gazette! Why there again now.—Why, sir, there are not three words of truth, the year round, put into the gazette. I 'll tell you a strange thing now as to that:—You must know, sir, I was resident in Flanders the last campaign—had a small post there: but no matter for that. Perhaps there was scarce any thing of moment done, but an humble servant of yours, that must be nameless, was an eye-witness of,—I wo n't say had the greatest share in 't; though I might say that, too, since I name nobody, you know. Well, Mr. Sharper, as I hope for a truncheon, this gazette-writer never so much as once mentioned me—not once, by the wars—took no more notice than as if Nol. Bluffe had not been in the land of the living!

Sharp. Strange!

Sir Jo. Yet, by the Lord Harry, it 's true, Mr. Sharper; for I went every day to coffee-houses to read the gazette myself.

Bluffe. Ay, ay! no matter. You see, Mr. Sharper, after all, I am content to retire—live a private person—Scipio and others have done it.

Sharp. [*Aside*] Impudent rogue!

Sir Jo. Ay, this confounded modesty of yours. — Egad, if he would put in for 't, he might be made general himself yet.

Bluffe. Oh, fie! no, Sir Joseph; you know I hate this. [*Crosses to* R.

Sir Jo. Let me but tell Mr. Sharper a little how you ate fire out of the mouth of a cannon. — Egad, he did; those impenetrable whiskers of his have confronted flames —

Bluffe. Death! what do you mean, Sir Joseph?

Sir Jo. Look you now, I tell you he 's so modest he 'll own nothing.

Bluffe. Pish! you have put me out; I have forgot what I was about. [*Angrily*] Pray hold your tongue, and give me leave.

Sir Jo. I am dumb.

Bluff. This sword, I think I was telling you of, Mr. Sharper, — this sword I 'll maintain to be the best divine, anatomist, lawyer, or casuist in Europe; it shall decide a controversy or split a cause.

Sir Jo. Nay, now I must speak — it will split a hair; by the Lord Harry, I have seen it.

Bluffe. Zounds! sir, it 's a lie, you have not seen it, nor sha'n't see it; sir, I say you can't see it: what d 'ye say to that now? [*In* SIR JOSEPH'S *face*.

Sir Jo. I am blind.

Bluffe. Death! had any other man interrupted me — [*Returns angrily to* R.

Sir Jo. Good Mr. Sharper, speak to him; I dare not look that way.

Sharp. (c.) Captain, Sir Joseph is penitent.

Bluffe. (R.) Oh, I am calm, sir, calm as a dis-
charged culverin. But 't was indiscreet, when you
know what will provoke me. Nay, come, Sir Joseph, you know my heat 's soon over.

Sir Jo. Well, I 'm a fool sometimes; but I 'm
sorry —

Bluffe. Enough.

Sir Jo. Come, we 'll go take a glass to drown an-
imosities. Mr. Sharper, will you partake?

Sharp. I wait on you, sir; nay, pray, Captain,
you are Sir Joseph's back.   [*Exeunt,* L.

SCENE III : — *Enter* SIR JOSEPH *and* BLUFFE, L.

Bluffe. And so, out of your unwonted generosity—

Sir Jo. And good nature, Back; I am good-natured, and can't help it.

Bluffe. You have given him a note upon Fondlewife for a hundred pound.

Sir Jo. Ay, ay, poor fellow, he ventured fair
for it.

Bluffe. You have disobliged me in it — for I have
occasion for the money; and, if you would look me
in the face and live, go, and force him to redeliver
you the note — go — and bring it me hither. I 'll
stay here for you.

Sir Jo. You may stay till the day of judgment,
then, by the Lord Harry. I know better things
than to be run through the body for a hundred
pounds. Why, I gave that hundred pound for be-

ing saved, and d 'ye think I 'd be so ungrateful to
take it from the gentleman again?

Bluffe. Well, go to him from me — tell him I say
he must refund, or bilbo 's the word, and slaughter
will ensue. If he refuse, tell him — but whisper
that — tell him I 'll pink his soul — but whisper
that softly to him.

Sir Jo. So softly that he shall never hear on 't.
Why, what 's the matter, bully, are you mad? Or
do you think I 'm mad? Egad! for my part I
do n't love to be the messenger of ill news; 't is an
ungrateful office — so tell him yourself.

Bluffe. By these hilts I believe he frightened you
into this composition: I believe you gave it him out
of fear, pure, paltry fear — confess.

Sir Jo. No, no; hang 't I was not afraid neither — though I confess he did in a manner snap
me up; — yet I can't say it was altogether out of
fear, but partly to prevent mischief, — for he was a
very choleric fellow: and [*blustering*] if my choler
had been up, too, egad, there would have been mischief done, that 's flat. And yet, I believe if you
had been by I would as soon have let him have
had a hundred of my teeth. Odds heart, if he
should come just now, when I am angry — I 'd tell
him — Mum!

Enter SHARPER *and* BELLMOUR, L.

Bell. (L.) Thou 'rt a lucky rogue! There 's your
benefactor; you ought to return him thanks now
you have received the favor.

Sharp. [*Advancing*] Sir Joseph, your note was accepted, and the money paid at sight. I'm come to return my thanks.

Sir Jo. [*Sulkily*] They wont be accepted so readily as the bill, sir.

Bell. (L.) I doubt the knight repents, Tom; he looks like the knight of the sorrowful face.

Sharp. (C.) This is a double generosity — do me a kindness and refuse my thanks. But I hope you are not offended that I offered them.

Sir Jo. May be I am, sir; may be I am not, sir; may be I'm both, sir: what then? I hope I may be offended, without any offense to you, sir.

Sharp. (C.) Heyday! Captain, what's the matter? you can tell.

Bluffe. (R.) Mr. Sharper, the matter is plain — Sir Joseph has found out your trick, and does not care to be put upon, being a man of honor!

Sharp. Trick, sir?

Sir Jo. Ay, trick, sir; and won't be put upon, sir, being a man of honor, sir! and so, sir —

Sharp. Hark ye, Sir Joseph, a word with ye. In consideration of some favors lately received, I would not have you draw yourself into a *præmunire*, by trusting to that sign of a man there — that pop-gun charged with wind.

Sir Jo. O La! O La! Captain, come, justify yourself. I'll give him the lie, if you'll stand to it.

Sharp. Nay, then, I'll be beforehand with you; take that—oaf! [*Cuffs him.*

Sir Jo. Captain, will you see this? Wo n't you pink his soul?

Bluffe. (R.) Hush! 't is not so convenient now — I shall find a time.

Sharp. What do you mutter about a time, rascal? You were the incendiary. There 's to put you in mind of your time — a memorandum.

[*Kicks him.*

Bluffe. Oh! this is your time, sir, you had best make use on 't.

Sharp. Egad, and so I will: there 's again for you. [*Kicks him.*

Bluffe. You are obliging, sir; but this is too public a place to thank you in; but, in your ear, you are to be seen again.

Sharp. Ay, you inimitable coward, and to be felt — as for example — [*Kicks him.*

Bell. Ha, ha, ha! Pr'ythee come away; 't is scandalous to kick this puppy, without a man were cold, and had no other way to get himself aheat.

[*Exeunt* BELLMOUR *and* SHARP., L.

Bluffe. Very well — very fine — but 't is no matter. Is not this fine, Sir Joseph?

Sir Jo. Indifferent; egad, in my opinion, very indifferent. I 'd rather go plain all my life than wear such finery.

Bluffe. Death! To be affronted thus! I 'll die before I suffer it. [*Draws.*

Sir Jo. O La! His anger was not raised before. Nay, dear Captain, do n't be in a passion, now he 's gone. Put up, put up, dear Back! 't is your Sir

Joseph who begs. Come, let me kiss thee. — So, so, put up, put up!

Bluffe. By my valor! 't is not to be put up!

Sir Jo. What, bully?

Bluffe. The affront!

Sir Jo. No, egad! no more 't is, for that 's put up already: thy sword, I mean.

Bluffe. Well, Sir Joseph, at thy entreaty. But were not you, my friend, abused, and cuffed, and kicked?   [*Putting up his sword.*

Sir Jo. Ay, ay! so were you, too. No matter, 't is past.

Bluffe. By the immortal thunder of great guns! 't is false. He sucks not vital air who dares affirm it to this face!   [*Looks big.*

Sir Jo. To that face I grant you, Captain. — No, no, I grant you — not to that face, by the Lord Harry! If you had put on your fighting face before you had done his business, he durst as soon have kissed you as kicked you to your face. But a man can no more help what 's done behind his back than what 's said. Come, we 'll think no more of what 's past.

Bluffe. I 'll call a council of war within, to consider of my revenge to come.   [*Exeunt.*

COSTUMES.

BLUFFE. — Tight jacket with sleeves; short trowsers; high boots; metallic back, breast, and head-piece, the last a pot-helmet; immense beard; sword; two large pistols.

WITTOL.—Swallow-tailed buff coat, embroidered with tarnished gilt, with large, loose sleeves, and the collar covered by a falling band of dirty lace;. breeches tied below the knee with ribbon; hose; shoes fastened with yellow ribbon; felt hat with a soiled plume; sword; peaked beard.

BELLMOUR.—Silk doublet with loose sleeves slashed up the front; collar of rich pointed lace; short cloak, worn carelessly on one shoulder; long breeches; wide boots, ruffled at top with lace or lawn; broad-leafed Flemish beaver hat, with rich hat-band and plume of feathers; a Spanish rapier, hung from a rich sash worn over the right shoulder; small mustaches turned up.

SHARPER.—Same as Bellmour, except as to colors and style of ornamentation.

RIENZI, THE TRIBUNE OF THE PEOPLE.

From Mitford's Rienzi.

DRAMATIS PERSONÆ.

COLA DI RIENZI, *afterward Tribune of the People.*
ALBERTI, *Captain of the Guard.*
PAOLO, *a Roman Citizen.*
ANGELO COLONNA, *Son of a Roman Nobleman.*
Soldiers and Citizens.

Prologue.

No declamation is more familiar to the lips of school-boys than Rienzi's Address to the Romans. In our Play, which is a Scene from the Second Act of Miss Mitford's Tragedy, this famous speech appears in its proper setting. The harangue of Rienzi is, indeed, the prelude to an exciting scene, which culminates in the temporary success of a popular conspiracy. You will please to imagine the events represented on our stage as occurring at night, before the gates of the Roman Capitol, and in the fourteenth century.

Scene:— *Before the Gates of the Capitol. — The Stage darkened.*

Alberti, Paolo, Citizens, etc., *crowd in background.*

1st Cit. (R.) This is the chosen spot. A brave
assemblage!

2d Cit. (R. C.) Why, yes. No marvel that Rienzi
struck
So bold a blow. I had heard shrewd reports
Of heats, and discontents, and gathering bands,
But never dreamed of Cola.

Pao. (R.) 'T is the spot!
Where loiters he? The night wears on apace.

Alb. (C.) It is not yet the hour.

1st Cit. Who speaks?

Another Cit. Alberti,
The captain of the guard; he and his soldiers
Have joined our faction.

Alb. Comrades, we shall gain
An easy victory. The Ursini,
Drunk with false hope and brute debauch, feast high
Within their palace. Never wore emprise
A fairer face.

Pao. And yet the summer heaven,
Sky, moon, and stars, are overcast. The saints
Send that this darkness—

Enter Rienzi, *from 2 E. L., down C.*

Rienzi. [*Advancing to the front*] Darkness! Did ye
never
Watch the dark glooming of the thunder-cloud
D. S.—6.

Ere the storm burst? We'll light this darkness, sir,
With the brave flash of spear and sword.
 Citizens. Rienzi!
Live, brave Rienzi — honest Cola!
 Rie. Friends!
 Citizens. Long live Rienzi!
 Alb. Listen to him.
 Rie. Friends,
I come not here to talk. Ye know too well
The story of our thralldom. We are slaves!
The bright sun rises to his course, and lights
A race of slaves! — He sets, and his last beam
Falls on a slave, —
.   Slaves to a horde
Of petty tyrants, feudal despots, lords,
Rich in some dozen paltry villages, —
Strong in some hundred spearmen, — only great
In that strange spell — a name! Each hour, dark fraud,
Or open rapine, or protected murder,
Cries out against them. But this very day,
An honest man, my neighbor — [*Pointing to* PAOLO,
  R. *corner.*] — there he stands, —
Was struck, — struck like a dog, by one who wore
The badge of Ursini; because, forsooth,
He tossed not high his ready cap in air,
Nor lifted up his voice in servile shouts,
At sight of that great ruffian! Be we men,
And suffer such dishonor? Men, and wash not
The stain away in blood? Such shames are common:
I have known deeper wrongs. I that speak to ye,

I had a brother once, — a gracious boy,
Full of all gentleness, of calmest hope,
Of sweet and quiet joy; there was a look
Of heaven upon his face, which limners give
To the beloved disciple. How I loved
That gracious boy! Younger by fifteen years;
Brother at once and son! He left my side,
A summer bloom on his fair cheeks,— a smile
Parting his innocent lips. In one short hour
The pretty harmless boy was slain! I saw
The corse, the mangled corse, and then I cried
For vengeance! — Rouse, ye Romans! rouse, ye
    slaves!
Have ye brave sons? — Look in the next fierce brawl
To see them die! Have ye fair daughters? — Look
To see them live, torn from your arms, disdained,
Dishonored; and if ye dare call for justice,
Be answered by the lash! Yet this is Rome,
That sat on her seven hills, and from her throne
Of beauty ruled the world! And we are Romans!
Why, in that elder day, to be a Roman
Was greater than a king! — And once again,
Hear me, ye walls, that echoed to the tread
Of either Brutus! — once again, I swear
The eternal city shall be free! her sons
Shall walk with princes! Ere to-morrow's dawn,
The tyrants —   [*tire back.*
   1st Cit. Hush! Who passes there? [CITIZENS *re-*
   Alb. A foe,
By his proud bearing. Seize him!
   Rie. As I deem,

'T is Angelo Colonna. Touch him not;
I would hold parley with him. Good Alberti,
The hour is nigh. Away! [*Exit* ALBERTI, R. U. E.

Enter ANGELO COLONNA, L.

Now, sir! [*To* ANGELO.

    Ang. (L.) What be ye,
That thus in stern and watchful mystery
Cluster beneath the veil of night, and start
To hear a stranger's foot?
    Rie. Romans.
    Ang. And wherefore
Meet ye, my countrymen?
    Rie. For freedom.
    Ang. Surely
Thou art Cola di Rienzi!
    Rie. Ay, that voice,—
The traitor voice.
    Ang. I knew thee by the words.
Who, save thyself, in this bad age, when man
Lies prostrate like yon temple, dared conjoin
The sounds of Rome and freedom?
    Rie. I shall teach
The world to blend those words, as in the days
Before the Cæsars. Thou shalt be the first
To hail the union. I have seen thee hang
On tales of the world's mistress; thy young hand
Hath clenched thy maiden sword. Unsheath it now,
Now, at thy country's call! What! dost thou pause?
Is the flame quenched? Dost falter? Hence with
    thee.

Pass on! pass whilst thou may!   [*Crosses to* L.

Ang. Hear me, Rienzi!
Even now my spirit leaps up at the thought
Of those brave storied days — a treasury
Of matchless visions, bright and glorified,
Paling the dim lights of this darkling world
With the golden blaze of heaven; but past and gone,
As clouds of yesterday, as last night's dream.

Rie. A dream! Dost see yon phalanx, still and
  stern?
An hundred leaders, each with such a band,
Wait with suppressed impatience till they hear
The great bell of the Capitol, to spring
At once on their proud foes. Join them.

Ang. My father!

Rie. Already he hath quitted Rome.

Ang. My kinsmen!

Rie. We are too strong for contest. Thou shalt
  see
No other change within our peaceful streets
Than that of slaves to freemen. Such a change
As is the silent step from night to day,
From darkness into light. We talk too long.

Ang. Yet reason with them; — warn them.

Rie. And their answer —
Will be the gaol, the gibbet, or the ax,
The keen retort of power. Why, I have reasoned;
And, but that I am held, amongst your great ones,
Half madman and half fool, these bones of mine
Had whitened on yon wall. Warn them! They met
At every step dark warnings.

              Friend met friend, nor smiled,
Till the last footfall of the tyrant's steed
Had died upon the ear.
              Sir, the boys, —
The unfledged boys, march at their mother's hest,
Beside their grandsires; even the girls of Rome, —
The gentle and the delicate, array
Their lovers in this cause. I have one yonder,
Claudia Rienzi, — thou hast seen the maid —
A silly trembler, a slight fragile toy,
As ever nursed a dove, or reared a flower, —
Yet she, even she, is pledged —

   Ang. To whom? to whom?

   Rie. To liberty!
A king's son
Might kneel in vain for Claudia. None shall wed her,
Save a true champion of the cause.

   Ang. I 'll join ye: [*Gives his hand to* RIENZI.
How shall I swear?

   Rie. [*To the people*] Friends, comrades, country-
      men!
I bring unhoped-for aid. Young Angelo craves
To join your band.

   Citizens. He 's welcome! [*Coming forward,* R. *and* L.

   Ang. Hear me swear
By Rome — by freedom — by Rienzi! Comrades,
How have ye titled your deliverer? Consul —
Dictator, emperor?

   Rie. No:
Those names have been so often steeped in blood,
So shamed by folly, so profaned by sin,

The sound seems ominous, — I 'll none of them.
Call me the Tribune of the people; there
My honoring duty lies.

> [*The* CITIZENS *shout*, Hail to our Tribune! — *The
> bell sounds thrice; shouts again; and a military
> band is heard playing a march without,* R. U. E.

Hark! the bell, the bell!
That, to the city and the plain,
Proclaims the glorious tale
Of Rome re-born, and Freedom.   See, the clouds
Are swept away, and the moon's boat of light
Sails in the clear blue sky, and million stars
Look out on us, and smile.

> [*The gate of the Capitol opens,* C. F., *and* ALBERTI
> *and* SOLDIERS *join the* PEOPLE, *and lay the keys
> at* RIENZI's *feet.*

Hark! that great voice
Hath broke our bondage.   Look, without a stroke
The Capitol is won — the gates unfold —
The keys are at our feet.   Alberti, friend,
How shall I pay the service?   Citizens!
First to possess the palace citadel —
The famous strength of Rome; then to sweep on,
Triumphant, through her streets.

> [*As* RIENZI *and the* PEOPLE *are entering the Capitol,
> he pauses.*

Oh, glorious wreck
Of gods and Cæsars! thou shalt reign again.

Queen of the world; and I — come on, come on,
My people!

Citizens. Live Rienzi — live our Tribune!

[*Exeunt through the gates, in the center of the flat,
into the Capitol.*

COSTUMES.

Rienzi. — White toga; buff hose; black sandals.

Paolo and Colonna. — Togas, and sandals.

Alberti. — Scarlet and gold Roman uniform; sword.

Citizens. — Brown stuff dresses; flesh legs; russet sandals.

Soldiers. — Roman shirts of mail; helmets; spears or battle-
axes; shields.

ILL-GOTTEN GOLD.

From Milman's Fazio.

DRAMATIS PERSONÆ.

GIRALDI FAZIO.   BARTOLO.

SCENE I : — *A room with crucibles and apparatus of Alchymy.* FAZIO *discovered seated.* (R. C.)

Faz. Yet he, Bartolo, he is of our rich ones :
There 's not a galiot on the sea, but bears
A venture of Bartolo's ; not an acre,
Nay, not a villa of our proudest princes,
But he hath cramped it with a mortgage ; he,
He only stocks our prisons with his debtors.
I saw him creeping home last night : he shuddered
As he unlocked his door, and looked around
As if he thought that every breath of wind
Were some keen thief : and when he locked him in,
I heard the grating key turn twenty times,
To try if all were safe.   I looked again
From our high window by mere chance, and saw
The motion of his scanty moping lantern ;
And, where his wind-rent lattice was ill stuffed
With tattered remnants of a money-bag,

D. S.—7.

Through cobwebs and thick dust I spied his face,
Like some dry wither-boned anatomy,
Through a huge chest-lid, jealously and scantily
Uplifted, peering upon coin and jewels,
Ingots and wedges, and broad bars of gold,
Upon whose luster the wan light shone muddily,
As though the New World had outrun the Spaniard,
And emptied all its mines in that coarse hovel.
His ferret eyes gloated as wanton o'er them,
As a gross Satyr on a sleeping Nymph!
And then, as he heard something like a sound,
He clapped the lid to, and blew out the lantern.

    [*He pauses a moment, then, rising, speaks on with
        enthusiastic energy.*

Oh, what a star of the first magnitude
Were poor young Fazio, if his skill should work
The wond'rous secret your deep-closeted sages
Grow gray in dreaming of! Why, all our Florence
Would be too narrow for his branching glories;
It would o'erleap the Alps, and all the north
Troop here to see the great philosopher.
He would be wealthy, too — wealthy in fame;
And that's more golden than the richest gold.
                        [*A groan without.*
Holy St. Francis! what a groan was there!
   Bar. (*Without*) Within there! — Oh, within there,
       neighbor! Death!
Murder, and merciless robbery!

       F*azio opens the door* — *Enter* BARTOLO.

Faz. What! Bartolo!

Bar. Thank ye, my friend! Ha! ha! ha! my old limbs!

I did not think them half so tough and sinewy.

St. Dominic! but their pins pricked close and keen.

Six of 'em, strong and sturdy, with their daggers,

Tickling the old man to let loose his ducats!

Faz. Who, neighbor, who?

Bar. Robbers — black crape-faced robbers,

Your only blood-suckers, that drain your veins,

And yet their meager bodies aye grow sparer.

They knew that I had moneys from the Duke,

But I o'erreached them, neighbor; not a ducat,

Nay, not a doit, to cross themselves withal,

Got they from old Bartolo.——Oh, I bleed!

And my old heart beats minutes like a clock.

Faz. A surgeon, friend!

Bar. Ay, one of your kind butchers,

Who cut and slash your flesh for their own pastime,

And then, God bless the mark! they must have money!

Gold, gold, or nothing! Silver is grown coarse,

And rings unhandsomely. Have I 'scaped robbing,

Only to give?——Oh, there! there! there! Cold, cold,

Cold as December.

Faz. Nay, then, a confessor!

Bar. A confessor! one of your black smooth talkers,

That drone the name of God incessantly,

Like the drear burden of a doleful ballad!

That sing to one of bounteous codicils
To the Franciscans or some hospital!
Oh! there 's a shooting! — Oozing here! — Ah, me,
My ducats and my ingots scarcely cold
From the hot Indies! Oh! and I forgot
To seal those jewels from the Milan Duke!
Oh! misery, misery! — Just this very day,
And that mad spendthrift Angelo hath not signed
The mortgage on those meadows by the Arno.
Oh! misery, misery! — Yet I 'scaped them bravely,
And brought my ducats off!—   [*Dies.*

   Faz. Why, e'en lie there, as foul a mass of earth
As ever loaded it. 'T were sin to charity
To wring one drop of brine upon thy corpse.
In sooth, death 's not nice-stomached, to be crammed
With such unsavory offal. What a god
'Mong men might this dead, withered thing have
      been,
That now must rot beneath the earth, as once
He rotted on it! Why, his wealth had won
In better hands an atmosphere around him,
Musical ever with the voice of blessing,—
Nations around his tomb, like marble mourners,
Vied for their pedestals. — In better hands?
Methinks these fingers are nor coarse nor clumsy.
Philosophy! Philosophy! thou 'rt lame
And tortoised-paced to my fleet desires!
I scent a shorter path to fame and riches.
The Hesperian trees nod their rich clusters at me,
Tickling my timorous and withdrawing grasp;—
I would, yet dare not;—that 's a coward's reckoning.

Half of the sin lies in "I would." To-morrow,
If that it find me poor, will write me fool,
And myself be a mock unto myself.
Ay, and the body murdered in my house!
Your carrion breeds most strange and loathsome in-
       sects —
Suspicion 's of the quickest and the keenest —
So, neighbor, by your leave, your keys! In sooth
Thou hadst no desperate love for holy church ;
Long-knolled bell were no sweet music to thee.
A " God be with thee " shall be all thy mass ;
Thou never loved'st those dry and droning priests.
Thou 'lt rot most cool and quiet in my garden ;
Your gay and gilded vault would be too costly.

                [*Exit, with body of Bartolo.*

SCENE II : — *A Street.*

Enter FAZIO *with a dark lantern,* R.

Faz. I, wont to rove like a tame household dog,
Caressed by every hand, and fearing none,
Now prowl e'en like a gray and treasonous wolf.
'T is a bad deed to rob, and I 'll have none on 't :
'T is a bad deed to rob — and whom ? the dead ?
Ay, of their winding-sheets and coffin nails.
'T is but a quit-rent for the land I sold him,
Almost two yards to house him and his worms ;
Somewhat usurious in the main, but that
Is honest thrift to your keen usurer.   .
Had he a kinsman, nay, a friend, 't were devilish.
But now whom rob I ? why, the state. — In sooth,

Marvelous little owe I this same state,
That I should be so dainty of its welfare.
Methinks our Duke hath pomp enough; our Senate
Sit in their scarlet robes and ermine tippets,
And live in proud and pillared palaces,
Where their Greek wines flow plentiful. — Besides,
To scatter it abroad amid so many,
It were to cut the sun out into spangles,
And mar its brilliance by dispersing it.
Away! away! his burying is my Rubicon!
Cæsar or nothing! Now, ye close-locked treasures,
Put on your gaudiest hues, outshine yourselves!
With a deliverer's, not a tyrant's hand,
Invade I thus your dull and peaceful slumbers,
And give you light and liberty. Ye shall not
Molder and rust in pale and pitiful darkness,
But front the sun with light bright as his own.

[*Exit*, L.

SCENE III : — FAZIO'S *House.*

Enter FAZIO, *with a sack*, R.: *he rests it.*

Faz. My steps were ever to this door, as though
They trod on beds of perfume and of down.
The wingéd birds were not by half so light,
When through the lazy twilight air they wheel
Home to their brooding mates. But now, methinks,
The heavy earth doth cling around my feet.
I move as every separate limb were gyved
With its particular weight of manacle.
The moonlight that was wont to seem so soft,

So balmy to the slow respired breath,
Icily, shiveringly cold falls on me.
The marble pillars, that soared stately up,
As though to prop the azure vault of heaven,
Hang o'er me with a dull and dizzy weight.
The stones whereon I tread do grimly speak,
Forbidding echoes, ay, with human voices :
Unbodied arms pluck at me as I pass,
And socketless pale eyes look glaring on me.
But I have passed them : and methinks this weight
Might strain more sturdy sinews than mine own.
Howbeit, thank God, 't is safe! — Thank God! — for
    what?
That a poor honest man 's grown a rich villain.

[*Bows his head upon his hands with remorse, while the
curtain descends to music expressive of his emotion.*

COSTUMES.

FAZIO. — Brown doublet and trunks, trimmed and puffed, with
    black hat and stockings to match; brown Spanish cloak.
BARTOLO. — Dark-colored doublet and trunks; dark breeches,
    and hat.

REMARKS.

This play, though of a somber cast, will be found quite effective
in representation. The action is extremely simple, and the long
soliloquies afford excellent practice in sustained dramatic reading. The piece also gives opportunity for simulating the passions
of avarice, terror, ambition, scorn, and remorse.

THE THREE CASKETS; OR, BASSANIO'S CHOICE.

From Shakespeare's Merchant of Venice.

DRAMATIS PERSONÆ.

BASSANIO, *a Venetian gentleman.*
GRATIANO, *his friend.*
PRINCE OF MOROCCO, } *suitors to Portia.*
PRINCE OF ARRAGON,
PORTIA, *a rich heiress of Belmont.*
NERISSA, *her waiting-maid.*
ATTENDANTS OF PORTIA.

SCENE I: — *Belmont. A room in* PORTIA's *house. At back of stage and hidden by a curtain, a table, upon which are three caskets. one of gold. one of silver, one of lead. Enter* PORTIA *and* NERISSA.

Por. (c.) By my troth, Nerissa, my little body is aweary of this great world.

Ner. (R. c.) You would be, sweet madam, if your miseries were in the same abundance as your good fortunes are. And yet, for aught I see, they are as sick that surfeit with too much, as they that starve with nothing. It is no small happiness, therefore, to be seated in the mean: superfluity comes sooner by white hairs, but competency lives longer.

Por. Good sentences, and well pronounced.

Ner. They would be better, if well followed.

Por. If to do were as easy as to know what were good to do, chapels had been churches, and poor men's cottages princes' palaces. It is a good divine that follows his own instructions. I can easier teach twenty what were good to be done, than be one of the twenty to follow mine own teaching. The brain may devise laws for the blood; but a hot temper leaps o'er a cold decree. Such a hare is madness, the youth, to skip o'er the meshes of good counsel, the cripple. But this reasoning is not in the fashion to choose me a husband.— O me! the word *choose!* I may neither choose whom I would, nor refuse whom I dislike: so is the will of a living daughter curbed by the will of a dead father. Is it not hard, Nerissa, that I can not choose one nor refuse none?

[*Crosses,* R.

Ner. Your father was ever virtuous; and holy men, at their death, have good inspirations: therefore the lottery that he hath devised in these three chests of gold, silver, and lead, (whereof who chooses his meaning, chooses you,) will, no doubt, never be chosen by any rightly but one who you shall rightly love. But what warmth is there in your affection toward any of these princely suitors that are already come?

Por. I pray thee, overname them; and as thou namest them, I will describe them; and according to my description, level at my affection.

Ner. First, is there the Neapolitan prince.

Por. Ay, that's a colt indeed, for he doth nothing but talk of his horse; and he makes it a great appropriation to his own good parts, that he can shoe him himself.

Ner. (c.) Then is there the County Palatine.

Por. (R.) He doth nothing but frown, as who should say, 'An you will not have me, choose.' He hears merry tales and smiles not. I fear he will prove the weeping philosopher when he grows old, being so full of unmannerly sadness in his youth. I had rather be married to a death's-head with a bone in his mouth, than to either of these. Heaven defend me from these two.

Ner. How say you by the French lord, Monsieur Le Bon?

Por. God made him, and therefore let him pass for a man. In truth, I know it is a sin to be a mocker; but he!—why, he hath a horse better than the Neapolitan's; a better bad habit of frowning than the Count Palatine; he is every man in no man. If a throstle sing, he falls straight a-capering; he will fence with his own shadow. If I should marry him, I should marry twenty husbands. If he would despise me, I would forgive him; for if he love me to madness, I shall never requite him.

Ner. What say you, then, to Falconbridge, the young baron of England?

Por. You know I say nothing to him, for he understands not me, nor I him. He hath neither Latin, French, nor Italian; and you will come into the court and swear that I have a poor penny-worth in the English. He is a proper man's picture; but, alas! who can converse with a dumb-show? How oddly he is suited! I think he bought his doublet in Italy, his round hose in France, his bonnet in Germany, and his behavior every-where.

Ner. What think you of the Scottish lord, his neighbor?

Por. That he hath a neighborly charity in him; for he borrowed a box of the ear of the Englishman, and swore he would pay him again when he was able. I think the Frenchman became his surety and sealed under for another.

Ner. How like you the young German, the Duke of Saxony's nephew?

Por. Very vilely in the morning, when he is sober, and most vilely in the afternoon, when he is drunk. When he is best, he is a little worse than a man; and when he is worst, he is little better than a beast. An the worst fall that ever fell, I hope I shall make shift to go without him.

[*Crosses*, R.

Ner. If he should offer to choose, and choose the

right casket, you should refuse to perform your father's will, if you should refuse to accept him.

Por. Therefore, for fear of the worst, I pray thee, set a deep glass of Rhenish wine on the contrary casket; for if the devil be within, and that temptation without, I know he will choose it. I will do any thing, Nerissa, ere I will be married to a sponge.

Ner. You need not fear, lady, the having any of these lords; they have acquainted me with their determinations, which is, indeed, to return to their home, and to trouble you with no more suit, unless you may be won by some other sort than your father's imposition depending on the caskets.

Por. If I live to be as old as Sibylla, I will die as chaste as Diana, unless I be obtained by the manner of my father's will. I am glad this parcel of wooers are so reasonable, for there is not one among them but I dote on his very absence; and I wish them a fair departure.

Ner. Do you not remember, lady, in your father's time, a Venetian, a scholar and a soldier, that came hither in company of the Marquis of Montferrat?

Por. Yes, yes; it was Bassanio; as I think, so was he called.

Ner. True, madam: he, of all the men that ever my foolish eyes looked upon, was the best deserving a fair lady.

Por. I remember him well, and I remember him worthy of thy praise.

Enter a SERVING-MAN.

How now? what news?   [*Crosses to* L.

Serv. The four strangers seek you, madam, to
take their leave; and there is a forerunner come
from a fifth, the Prince of Morocco, who brings
word the Prince, his master, will be here to-night.

Por. If I could bid the fifth welcome with so good
heart as I can bid the other four farewell, I should
be glad of his approach. Come, Nerissa — sirrah, go
before. Whilst we shut the gate upon one wooer,
another knocks at the door.   [*Exeunt.*

SCENE II : — *The same. Flourish of cornets. Enter
the* PRINCE OF MOROCCO *and his train;* PORTIA,
NERISSA, *and others attending.*

Morocco. Mislike me not for my complexion,
The shadowed livery of the burnished sun,
To whom I am a neighbor and near bred.

Por. In terms of choice I am not solely led
By nice direction of a maiden's eye;
Besides, the lottery of my destiny
Bars me the right of voluntary choosing:
But if my father had not scanted me,
And hedged me by his wit, to yield myself
His wife who wins me by that means I told you,
Yourself, renowned prince, then stood as fair
As any comer I have looked on yet,
For my affection.

Mor.   Even for that I thank you:

Therefore, I pray you, lead me to the caskets,
To try my fortune.   By this scimetar,
That slew the Sophy and a Persian prince,
That won three fields of Sultan Solyman,
I would o'er-stare the sternest eyes that look,
Outbrave the heart most daring on the earth,
Pluck the young sucking cubs from the she-bear,
Yea, mock the lion when he roars for prey,
To win thee, lady.

Por.   You must take your chance;
And either not attempt to choose at all,
Or swear, before you choose, if you choose wrong,
Never to speak to lady afterward
In way of marriage ; therefore be advised.

Mor.   Nor will not.   Come, bring me unto my
        chance.

Por.   Go draw aside the curtains, and discover
The several caskets to this noble Prince.
Now make your choice.   [*An* ATTENDANT *obeys.*

Mor.   The first, of gold, who this inscription bears :
Who chooseth me, shall gain what many men desire.
The second, silver, which this promise carries : —
Who chooseth me, shall get as much as he deserves.
This third, dull lead, with warning all as blunt : —
Who chooseth me, must give and hazard all he hath.
How shall I know if I do choose the right?

Por.   The one of them contains my picture, Prince :
If you choose that, then I am yours withal.

Mor.   Some god direct my judgment!   Let me see ;
I will survey the inscriptions back again :
What says this leaden casket?

Who chooseth me, must give and hazard all he hath.
Must give — for what? For lead? hazard for lead?
A golden mind stoops not to shows of dross;
I'll then nor give nor hazard aught for lead.
What says the silver, with her virgin hue?
Who chooseth me, shall get as much as he deserves.
As much as he deserves? — Pause there, Morocco,
And weigh thy value with an even hand.
As much as I deserve? Why, that's the lady:
Let's see once more this saying graved in gold:
Who chooseth me, shall gain what many men desire.
Why, that's the lady; all the world desires her:
From the four corners of the earth they come,
To kiss this shrine, this mortal breathing saint.
            Deliver me the key:
Here do I choose, and thrive I as I may!
   Por. There, take it, Prince; and if my form lie
     there,
Then I am yours.   [*He unlocks the golden casket.*
   Mor.   What have we here!
A carrion death, within whose empty eye
There is a written scroll. I'll read the writing:
    All that glitters is not gold;
    Often have you heard that told:
    Many a man his life hath sold,
    But my outside to behold:
    Gilded tombs do worms infold.
    Had you been as wise as bold,
    Young in limbs, in judgment old,
    Your answer had not been inscrolled:
    Fare you well; your suit is cold.

Cold, indeed; and labor lost:
Then, farewell, heat, and welcome, frost!
Portia, adieu! I have too grieved a heart
To take a tedious leave. Thus losers part.
[*Exit with his train.*
Por. A gentle riddance. — Draw the curtains; go.
Let all of his complexion choose me so. [*Exeunt.*

SCENE III: — *The same. Enter* NERISSA *with a* SERVITOR.

Ner. Quick, quick, I pray thee; draw the curtain
straight:
The Prince of Arragon hath ta'en his oath,
And comes to his election presently.
[*Flourish of cornets. Enter the* PRINCE OF ARRAGON,
PORTIA, *and their trains.*
Por. Behold, there stand the caskets, noble Prince:
If you choose that wherein I am contained,
Straight shall our nuptial rites be solemnized:
But if you fail, without more speech, my lord,
You must be gone from hence immediately.
Arragon. I am enjoined by oath to observe three
things:
First, never to unfold to any one
Which casket 't was I chose; next, if I fail
Of the right casket, never in my life
To woo a maid in way of marriage;
Lastly, if I do fail in fortune of my choice,
Immediately to leave you and be gone.

Por. To these injunctions every one doth swear
That comes to hazard for my worthless self.

Arr. And so have I addressed me. Fortune, now,
To my heart's hope! Gold, silver, and base lead.
Who chooseth me, must give and hazard all he hath:
You shall look fairer, e'er I give or hazard.
What says the golden chest? Ha! let me see:
Who chooseth me, shall gain what many men desire.
I will not choose what many men desire;
Because I will not jump with common spirits,
And rank me with the barbarous multitudes.
Why, then to thee, thou silver treasure-house;
Tell me, once more, what title thou dost bear:
Who chooseth me, shall get as much as he deserves:
I will assume desert. — Give me a key for this,
And instantly unlock my fortunes here.

[*He opens the silver casket.*

Por. Too long a pause for that which you find
there.

Arr. What's here? the portrait of a blinking idiot,
Presenting me a schedule. I will read it.
How much unlike art thou to Portia!
How much unlike my hopes and my deservings!
Who chooseth me, shall have as much as he deserves.
Did I deserve no more than a fool's head?
Is that my prize? Are my deserts no better?

Por. To offend and judge are distinct offices,
And of opposed natures.

Arr. What is here?

      The fire seven times tried this:
      Seven times tried that judgment is,

D. S.—8.

> *That did never choose amiss.*
> *Some there be that shadows kiss;*
> *Such have but a shadow's bliss.*
> *There be fools alive, I wis,*
> *Silvered o'er; and so was this.*
> *Take what wife you will to bed,*
> *I will ever be your head:*
> *So be gone: you are sped.*

Still more fool I shall appear,
By the time I linger here:
With one fool's head I came to woo,
But I go away with two.
Sweet, adieu! I'll keep my oath,
Patiently to bear my wroth.

                             [*Exeunt* ARRAGON *and train.*

    Por. Thus hath the candle singed the moth.
O these deliberate fools! when they do choose,
They have the wisdom by their wit to lose.
    Ner. The ancient saying is no heresy, —
Hanging and wiving goes by destiny.
    Por. Come, draw the curtain, Nerissa.

Enter a SERVANT.

    Serv. Where is my lady?
    Por.   Here: what would my lord?
    Serv. Madam, there is alighted at your gate
A young Venetian, one that comes before
To signify the approaching of his lord,
From whom he bringeth sensible regreets;
To wit, (besides commends and courteous breath,)

Gifts of rich value. Yet I have not seen
So likely an ambassador of love :
A day in April never came so sweet,
To show how costly Summer was at hand,
As this forespurrer comes before his lord.

Por. No more, I pray thee : I am half afeard
Thou wilt say anon he is some kin to thee,
Thou spend'st such high-day wit in praising him.
Come, come, Nerissa ; for I long to see
Quick Cupid's post, that comes so mannerly.

Ner. Bassanio, lord Love, if thy will be.

[*Exeunt.*

Scene IV : — *The same. Enter* BASSANIO, PORTIA,
GRATIANO, NERISSA, *and* ATTENDANTS.

Por. I pray you, tarry ; pause a day or two
Before you hazard : for, in choosing wrong,
I lose your company : therefore forbear awhile.
There's something tells me, but it is not love,
I would not lose you : and you know yourself,
Hate counsels not in such a quality.
But lest you should not understand me well, —
And yet a maiden hath no tongue but thought, —
I would detain you here some month or two,
Before you venture for me : I could teach you
How to choose right, but then I am forsworn ;
So will I never be : so may you miss me ;
But if you do, you 'll make me wish a sin, —
That I had been forsworn.

Bassanio. Let me choose ;
For as I am. I live upon the rack.

Por. Upon the rack, Bassanio! then confess
What treason there is mingled with your love.

Bass. None but that ugly treason of mistrust,
Which makes me fear the enjoying of my love
There may as well be amity and life
'Tween snow and fire, as treason and my love.

Por. Ay, but I fear you speak upon the rack;
And men, enforced, do speak any thing.

Bass. Promise me life, and I'll confess the truth.

Por. Well, then, confess and live.

Bass. Confess and love
Had been the very sum of my confession.
O happy torment, when my torturer
Doth teach me answers for deliverance!
But let me to my fortune and the caskets.

Por. Away, then! I am locked in one of them :
If you do love me, you will find me out.
Nerissa, and the rest, stand all aloof.
Let music sound while he doth make his choice;
Then, if he lose, he makes a swan-like end,
Fading in music : that the comparison
May stand more proper, my eye shall be the stream
And watery death-bed for him. He may win,
And what is music then? Then music is
Even as the flourish when true subjects bow
To a new-crowned monarch : such it is
As are those dulcet sounds in break of day;
That creep into the dreaming bridegroom's ear,
And summon him to marriage. *[Soft music.*

Bass. So may the outward shows be least themselves :

The world is still deceived with ornament.
In law, what plea so tainted and corrupt
But, being seasoned with a gracious voice,
Obscures the show of evil? In religion,
What deadly error, but some sober brow
Will bless it, and approve it with a text,
Hiding the grossness with fair ornament?
There is no vice so simple but assumes
Some mark of virtue on his outward parts:
How many cowards, whose hearts are all as false
As stairs of sand, wear yet upon their chins
The beards of Hercules and frowning Mars;
Who, inward searched, have livers white as milk;
And these assume but valor's excrement,
To render them redoubted! Look on beauty,
And you shall see 't is purchased by the weight,
Which therein works a miracle in nature,
Making them lightest that wear most of it:
So are those crisped, snaky, golden locks,
Which make such wanton gambols in the wind,
Upon supposed fairness, often known
To be the dowry of a second head;
The skull that bred them, in the sepulcher.
Thus ornament is but the guiled shore
To a most dangerous sea; the beauteous scarf
Veiling an Indian beauty; -- in a word,
The seeming truth which cunning times put on
To entrap the wisest. Therefore, thou gaudy gold,
Hard food for Midas, I will none of thee;
Nor none of thee, thou pale and common drudge
'Tween man and man: but thou, thou meager lead,

Which rather threat'nest than dost promise aught,
Thy plainness moves me more than eloquence;
And here choose I.   Joy be the consequence!
    Por. [*Aside*] How all the other passions fleet to air,
As doubtful thoughts, and rash-embraced despair,
And shuddering fear, and green-eyed jealousy.
O love! be moderate; allay thy ecstasy;
In measure rain thy joy: scant this excess:
I feel too much thy blessing; make it less,
For fear I surfeit.
    Bass.   What find I here?
                        [*Opening the leaden casket.*
Fair Portia's counterfeit!   What demi-god
Hath come so near creation?   Move, these eyes?
Or whether, riding on the balls of mine,
Seem they in motion?   Here are severed lips,
Parted with sugar breath: so sweet a bar
Should sunder such sweet friends.   Here'in her hairs
The painter plays the spider, and hath woven
A golden mesh to entrap the hearts of men,
Faster than gnats in cobwebs: but her eyes!
How could he see to do them? having made one,
Methinks it should have power to steal both his,
And leave itself unfurnished.   Yet look, how far
The substance of my praise doth wrong this shadow
In underprizing it, so far this shadow
Doth limp behind the substance.—Here's the scroll,
The continent and summary of my fortune.
        You that choose not by the view,
        Chance as fair, and choose as true:
        Since this fortune falls to you.

Be content, and seek no new :
If you be well pleased with this,
And hold your fortune for your bliss,
Turn you where your lady is,
And claim her with a loving kiss.

A gentle scroll. — Fair lady, by your leave ;
I come by note to give and to receive. [*Kissing her.*
Like one of two contending in a prize,
That thinks he hath done well in people's eyes,
Hearing applause and universal shout,
Giddy in spirit, still gazing in a doubt
Whether those peals of praise be his or no ;
So, thrice fair lady, stand I even so,
As doubtful whether what I see be true,
Until confirmed, signed, ratified by you.

Por. You see me, Lord Bassanio, where I stand,
Such as I am : though for myself alone
I would not be ambitious in my wish,
To wish myself much better; yet, for you
I would be trebled twenty times myself,
A thousand times more fair, ten thousand times more
     rich ;
That only to stand high in your account,
I might in virtues, beauties, livings, friends,
Exceed account : but the full sum of me
Is sum of nothing : which, to term in gross,
Is an unlessoned girl, unschooled, unpracticed :
Happy in this, she is not yet so old
But she may learn ; happier than this,
She is not bred so dull but she can learn ;
Happiest of all is that her gentle spirit

Commits itself to yours to be directed,
As from her lord, her governor, her king.
Myself and what is mine to you and yours
Is now converted : but now I was the lord
Of this fair mansion, master of my servants,
Queen o'er myself; and even now, but now,
This house, these servants, and this same myself
Are yours, my lord. I give them with this ring,
Which, when you part from, lose, or give away,
Let it presage the ruin of your love,
And be my vantage to exclaim on you.

Bass. Madam, you have bereft me of all words;
Only my blood speaks to you in my veins:
And there is such confusion in my powers
As, after some oration fairly spoke
By a beloved prince, there doth appear
Among the buzzing, pleased multitude;
Where every something, being blent together,
Turns to a wild of nothing, save of joy,
Expressed and not expressed. But when this ring
Parts from this finger, then parts life from hence:
O then be bold to say, Bassanio's dead !

Ner. My lord and lady, it is now our time,
That have stood by and seen our wishes prosper,
To cry, good joy. Good joy, my lord and lady !

Gratiano. My Lord Bassanio, and my gentle lady,
I wish you all the joy that you can wish;
For I am sure you can wish none from me:
And when your honors mean to solemnize
The bargain of your faith, I do beseech you,
Even at that time I may be married too.

Bass. With all my heart, so thou canst get a wife.

Grat. I thank your lordship, you have got me one.
My eyes, my lord, can look as swift as yours :
You saw the mistress, I beheld the maid ;
You loved, I loved ; for intermission
No more pertains to me, my lord, than you.
Your fortune stood upon the caskets there,
And so did mine, too, as the matter falls ;
For wooing here until I sweat again,
And swearing till my very roof was dry,
With oaths of love, at last, if promise last,
I got a promise of this fair one here
To have her love, provided that your fortune
Achieved her mistress.

Por.   Is this true, Nerissa?

Ner. Madam, it is, so you stand pleased withal.

Bass. And do you, Gratiano, mean good faith?

Grat. Yes, faith, my lord.

Bass. Our feast shall be much honored in your
marriage.

Tableau.   Curtain.

COSTUMES.

BASSANIO. — White tunic, trimmed with silver; blue satin waistcoat, embroidered, and blue sash-belt; white silk stocking
pantaloons; white shoes, with rosettes.

GRATIANO. — Green velvet coat; white waistcoat; worsted pantaloons, and russet boots.

PORTIA. — Salmon-colored gown, trimmed with silver.

NERISSA. — White dress spangled, with colored body.

D. S.—9.

PRINCE OF MOROCCO. — Long crimson tunic, girt around the waist by a rich sash; over the tunic, a long flowing robe, or gabardine, of a dark green color, reaching almost or quite to the feet; wide flowing sleeves; high turban of crimson and gold, ornamented with gems; scimetar, worn suspended from a narrow scarf or band hung over the right shoulder.

PRINCE OF ARRAGON. — Slashed doublet; hose; hat with feather; sword. The costume should be of very rich material.

THE POSITIVE MAN.

From The Positive Man, by John O'Keefe.

DRAMATIS PERSONÆ.

SIR TOBY TACIT.   LADY TACIT.
RUPEE.   CORNELIA.
SERVANT.

SCENE: — SIR TOBY TACIT'S *House.* *Enter* SIR TOBY *and* LADY TACIT.

Sir Toby. You know, my Lady Tacit, I am not to be controlled; I will have my way.

Lady T. Will! And have, my sweet Sir Toby. Do I ever presume to have a will of my own? But indeed, my dear love, you are a little too positive.

Sir T. I am, I am a positive man, I own it; and I will insist, and persist, too, that this new house I've taken in Portland Place is charmingly situated. I challenge England to afford such a delightful prospect.

Lady T. Sir Toby, pardon me; do you really think the view of Highgate and Hampstead so very beautiful?

Sir T. Me! not I. Visto, the landscape painter, commends it, indeed; but he knows no more of a prospect than a hedgehog. The house, though, has a lofty hall; it strikes you with an air of grandeur.

Lady T. The hall lofty, Sir Toby! Pardon me, my dear, but I protest it did n't seem so to me.

Sir T. Nor to me, my Lady. I thought, indeed, it seemed tolerably high, till t' other day, trying to cut one of Vestris' capers, I hit my head against the lantern. — But the great parlor, my Lady; I 'll lay any man an hundred guineas that parlor dines forty.

Lady T. Nay, Sir Toby, when once you form an opinion, you will persist in it; you are exceedingly obstinate.

Sir T. True, Lady Tacit; when once I 'm determined, I 'm not to be moved by the rhetoric of Oxford, Cambridge, Sorbonne, or Salamanca.

Enter SERVANT.

Serv. Mr. Rupee, sir.   [*Exit.*

Sir T. My new East India son-in-law. Here, my Lady Tacit, pull up my cravat and pull down my ruffles.

Lady T. Sir Toby! ask me such a thing!

Sir T. Then, my Lady, I will pull down my ruffles and pull up my cravat; I am determined.

Enter RUPEE.

Rupee. My Lady Tacit, your ladyship's slave. I have — *Apropos,* Sir Toby, your most obedient.

Lady T. Sir, we are exceedingly proud of this honor.

Sir T. Sir, we are exceedingly proud.

Lady T. Sir Toby!

Sir T. Proud! I mean, sir, we are your humble—

Rupee. I hope, madam, my lovely Cornelia is well?

Sir T. She is exceedingly well, indeed, sir.

Lady T. What are you at, my sweet?

Sir T. Only at present she has got a most dangerous cold.

Lady T. Cornelia! a cold!

Sir T. But now she's perfectly recovered; and my daughter will be so happy when she hears —

Lady T. Your daughter! Sir Toby!

Sir T. Mine? I'm an obstinate man, but in this particular I will not be positive.

Lady T. Mr. Rupee, dear sir, I shall beg but for a few moments, though, to deprive myself of the egregious felicity of your very agreeable company.

[*Exit.*

Sir T. Egregious felicity! Mr. Rupee, what a fine spoken woman!

Rupee. Very, Sir Toby; but that phrase of egregious felicity is —

Sir T. Nonsense.

Rupee. Nonsense! *Apropos*, did you ever hear me speak in Leadenhall street upon Indian affairs?

Sir T. Poor Lady Tacit! all obedience — humble as a forsaken sultana. But, sir, in this house I am Turk and tyrant. Sir, I am a very Bajazet. Not

my fault, though, Mr. Rupee; I was formed with a
hard heart. As Othello says, "I strike it, and it hurts
my hand." Now, sir, as to my wife — she's a lady,
thanks to my knighthood, but the most silly, ignorant, ridiculous —

[*Re-enter* LADY TACIT *and* CORNELIA.

Hem! — sensible, elegant, and finest spoken woman
in England. Ah, my Lady Tacit, we were just talking of you.

Lady T. Cornelia, child, receive Mr. Rupee as a
gentleman who is shortly to be your husband.

Rupee. Oh, my charming Cornelia! [*Aside*] Now
if I can but recollect my oriental compliment; it has
pleased both black, brown, and yellow: now I'll try
it on the fair. Cornelia, speak, my love; the melody
of your voice is sweeter than the sound of a Nankin
bell; your breath is cinnamon of Ceylon, diffusing
fragrance through teeth of the sagacious elephant,
and coral of the Ormus. Permit me, madam, to
touch this fair hand, soft as weft of the Indostan
worm. Your eyes, arched with camels' hair, brilliant
as the diamond of Golconda; and the porcelain tower
of Pekin is but a faint emblem of the excellent sym-
metry of your beautiful *tout ensemble*.

Sir T. Oh, charming! elegant! Cornelia, speak
and make a handsome curtsey.

Cor. I confess, sir, I am incapable of answering
so lavish and polite a compliment.

Sir T. What a delightful curtsey she makes! eh,
Mr. Rupee?

Lady T. O fie, Sir Toby!

Sir T. True, my Lady;—so, so, Corney; you are a good girl, but confound your dancing-master. Well, Mr. Rupee, what say you to a bottle?

Lady T. What! do you mean to bottle a gentleman at this time of day? Richard! [*Enter* SERVANT] Get tea.

Sir T. Look ye, my Lady Tacit, I am the lord and master in this house; I will be positive; therefore I say, Richard, get tea! [*Exit* SERVANT.

Rupee. Tea!—*Apropos,* ma'am, do you take snuff?

Cor. No, sir. [*Aside*] Insignificant coxcomb!

Rupee. True, madam; it was formerly in style, quite the rage with people of *ton;* but now it's a vile bore. I took snuff once in such profusion, that in most polite circles I was distinguished by the title of Count Macabah.

Sir T. When I was encamped, I took so much snuff that they called me Captain Strasborough.

Rupee. Strasborough!—*Apropos,* I presume from to-morrow I date my felicity?

Sir T. Yes; you and my daughter Cornelia here shall be married to-morrow morning; that is, my Lady, if you have no objection.

Lady T. Ah, Mr. Rupee, they talk of female prerogative; you see how weak my influence with such a positive man.

Sir T. Yes, Mr. Rupee, when the gust of passion blows, my Lady Tacit is the gentle osier of compliance, and I am the sturdy oak of opposition.

[*Exeunt.*

COSTUMES. — Modern English dresses.

PANGLOSS.

From The Heir-at-Law, by Geo. Colman the Younger.

DRAMATIS PERSONÆ.

LORD DUBERLY, *alias* DANIEL DOWLAS.
DICK DOWLAS.
DR. PANGLOSS, LL.D. *and* A. S. S.
LADY DUBERLY, *alias* DEBORAH DOWLAS.
JOHN, *a Servant.*

SCENE I :— *An Apartment in* LORD DUBERLY's *House.*
LORD *and* LADY DUBERLY *discovered at breakfast.*

Lord D. But what does it matter, my Lady,
whether I drink my tea out of a cup or a saucer?

Lady D. A great deal in the polite circles, my
Lord. We have been raised, by a strange freak of
fortune, from nothing, as a body may say ; and —

Lord D. Nothing! as reputable a trade as any in
all Gosport. You hold a merchant as cheap as if he
trotted about with all his property in a pack, like a
peddler.

Lady D. A merchant, indeed! curious merchan-
dise you dealt in, truly!

Lord D. A large assortment of articles: coal, cloth, herrings, linen, candles, eggs, sugar, treacle, tea, bacon, and brick-dust; with many more, too tedious to mention in this here advertisement.

Lady D. Well, praise the bridge that carried you over; but you must now drop the tradesman and learn life. Consider, by the strangest accident, you have been raised to neither more nor less than a peer of the realm.

Lord D. Oh! 't was the strangest accident, my Lady, that ever happened on the face of the universal yearth.

Lady D. True; 't was, indeed, a windfall; and you must now walk, talk, eat and drink as becomes your station. 'T is befit a nobleman should behave as sich, and know summut of breeding.

Lord D. Well, but I ha n't been a nobleman more nor a week; and my throat is n't noble enough yet to be proof against scalding. Hand over the milk, my Lady.

Lady D. Hand over! Ah! what 's bred in the bone will never come out of the flesh, my Lord.

Lord D. Pshaw! here 's a fuss, indeed! When I was plain Daniel Dowlas, of Gosport, I was reckoned as cute a dab at discourse as any in town. Nobody found fault with me then.

Lady D. But why so loud? I declare, the servants will hear.

Lord D. Hear! and what will they hear but what they know? Our story a secret! Tell 'em Queen Anne 's dead, my Lady. Do n't every body know

old Duberly was supposed to die without any *hair*
to his estate — as the doctors say, of an implication
of disorders? and that his son, Henry Morland, was
lost, some time ago, in the salt sea?

Lady D.   Well, there's no occasion to —

Lord D.   Don't every body know that lawyer
Ferret, of Furnival's Inn, owed the legatees a
grudge, and popped a bit of an advertisement into
the *News:* — "Whereas, the heir-at-law, if there be
any reviving, of the late Baron Duberly, will apply—
so and so — he'll hear of summut greatly to his
advantage."

Lady D.   But why bawl it to the —

Lord D.   Didn't he hunt me out to prove my
title, and lug me from the counter to clap me into a
coach, a house here in Hanover Square, and an estate
in the country worth fifteen thousand per annum?
Why, bless you, my Lady, every little black sweep
with a soot-bag cries it about the streets as often as
he says "Sweep!"

Lady D.   'T is a pity but my Lord had left you
some manners with his money.

Lord D.   He! what, my cousin twenty thousand
times removed? He must have left them by word
of mouth. Never spoke to him but once in all my
born life — upon an electioneering matter. That's
a time when most of your proud folks make no
bones of tippling with a tallow-chandler, in his back
room, on a melting day. But he! — except calling
me cousin, and buying a lot of damaged huckaback
to cut into kitchen towels, he was as cold and as

stiff as he is now, though he has been dead and
buried these nine months, rot him!

Lady D. There again, now! rot him!

Lord D. Why, what is a man to say when he
wants to consecrate his old, stiff-rumped relations?

[*Rings the bell.*

Lady D. Why, an oath now and then may slip
in, to garnish genteel conversation; but then it
should be done with an air to one's equals, and with
a kind of careless condescension to menials.

Lord D. Should it? Well, then; here, John.

Enter JOHN, R.

My good man, take away the tea.

John. Yes, my Lord. [*Exit,* R.

Lady D. And now, my Lord, I must leave you
for the concerns of the day. We elegant people are
as full of business as an egg 's full of meat.

Lord D. Yes, we elegant people find the trade of
the *tone*, as they call it, plaguy fatiguing. What!
you are for the *wis a wis* this morning? Much good
may it do you, my Lady. It makes me sit stuck up
and squeezed like a bear in a bathing-tub.

Lady D. I have a hundred places to call at.
Folks are so civil since we came to take possession.
There's dear Lady Littlefigure, Lord Sponge, Mrs.
Holdbank, Lady Betty Pillory, the Hon. Mrs. Cheat-
well, and —

Lord D. Ay, ay; you may always find plenty
in this here town to be civil to fifteen thousand a
year, my Lady.

Lady D. Well, there's no learning you life. I'm sure they are as kind and friendly. The supper Lady Betty gave to us, and a hundred friends, must have cost her fifty good pounds, if it cost a brass farden; and she does the same thing, I'm told, three times a week. If she isn't monstrous rich, I wonder, for my part, how she can afford it.

Lord D. Why, my Lady, that would have puzzled me, too, if they hadn't hooked me into a game of cocking and punting, I think they call it, where I lost as much in half a hour as would keep her and her company in fricasees and whip sullibubs for a fortnight. But I may be even with her some o' these a'ternoons. Only let me catch her at Put, that's all!

Enter JOHN, L.

John. Doctor Pangloss is below, my Lord.

Lord D. Oddsbobs, my Lady! That's the man as learns me to talk English.

Lady D. Hush! consider —   [*Pointing to* JOHN.

Lord D. Hum! I forgot. My honest fellow, show him up stairs, d'ye hear? [*Exit* JOHN, L.] There, was that easy?

Lady D. Tolerable.

Lord D. Well, now, get along, my Lady; the Doctor and I must be snug.

Lady D. Then I bid you good morning, my Lord. As Lady Betty says, I wish you a *bon repos.*

[*Exit,* R.

Lord D. A *bon repos!* I do n't know how it is, but the women are more cuter at these here matters nor the men. My wife, as every body may see, is as genteel already as if she had been born a duchess. This Doctor Pangloss will do me a deal of good in the way of fashioning my discourse. So here he is.

Enter PANGLOSS, L.

Doctor, good morning. I wish you a *bon repos!* Take a chair, Doctor.

Pang. Pardon me, my Lord; I am not inclined to be sedentary. I wish, with permission, "*erectus ad sidera tollere vultus.*"—Ovid. Hem!

Lord D. *Tollory vultures!* I suppose that *that* means you had rather stand?

Pang. Fye, this is a locomotive morning with me. Just hurried, my Lord, from the Society of Arts, whence, I may say, "I have borne my blushing honors thick upon me."—Shakespeare. Hem!

Lord D. And what has put your honors to the blush, this morning, Doctor?

Pang. To the blush! a ludicrous perversion of the author's meaning — he, he, he! Hem! You shall hear, my Lord. "Lend me your ears."— Shakespeare again. Hem! 'T is not unknown to your lordship, and the no less literary world, that the Caledonian University of Aberdeen long since conferred upon me the dignity of LL.D.; and, as I never beheld that erudite body, I may safely say

they dubbed me with a degree from sheer con-
siderations of my celebrity.

Lord D. True.

Pang. For nothing, my Lord, but my own innate
modesty, could suppose that Scotch college to be
swayed by one pound fifteen shillings and three
pence three farthings, paid on receiving my diploma,
as a handsome compliment to the numerous and
learned head of that seminary.

Lord D. Oh, no; it was n't for the matter of
money.

Pang. I do not think it was altogether the *"auri*
sacra fames."—Virgil. Hem! But this very day,
my Lord, at eleven o'clock A. M., the Society of
Arts, in consequence, as they were pleased to say,
of my merits — he, he, he! my *merits*, my Lord —
have admitted me as an unworthy member; and I
have henceforward the privilege of adding to my
name the honorable title of *A double S*.

Lord D. And I make no doubt, Doctor, but you
have richly deserved it. I warrant a man does n't
get A double S tacked to his name for nothing.

Pang. Decidedly not, my Lord. Yes, I am now
artium societatis socius. My two last publications did
that business. *"Exegi monumentum ære perennius."*—
Horace. Hem!

Lord D. And what might them there two books
be about, Doctor?

Pang. The first, my Lord, was a plan to lull the
restless to sleep by an infusion of opium into their
ears. The efficacy of this method originally struck

me in St. Stephen's chapel, while listening to the oratory of a worthy country gentleman.

Lord D. I wonder it wa'n't hit upon before by the doctors.

Pang. Physicians, my Lord, put their patients to sleep in another manner — he, he, he! " To die — to sleep; no more."— Shakespeare. Hem! My second treatise was a proposal for erecting dove-houses, on a principle tending to increase the propagation of pigeons. This, I may affirm, has received considerable countenance from many who move in the circles of fashion. " *Nec gemere cessabit turtur.*" — Virgil. Hem! I am about to publish a third edition by subscription. May I have the honor to pop your lordship down among the pigeons?

Lord D. Ay, ay; down with me, Doctor.

Pang. My Lord, I am grateful. I ever insert names and titles at full length : what may be your lordship's sponsorial and patronymic appellations?

[*Taking out his pocket-book.*

Lord D. My what?

Pang. I mean, my Lord, the designations given to you by your lordship's godfathers and parents.

Lord D. Oh! what my Christian and surname? I was baptized Daniel.

Pang. " *Abolens baptismate labem.*" — I forget where; no matter. Hem! The Right Honorable Daniel — [*Writing.*

Lord D. Dowlas.

Pang. [*Writing*] Dowlas — " Filthy Dow!" — Hem! Shakespeare.—The Right Honorable Daniel

Dowlas, Baron Duberly.—And now, my Lord, to your lesson for the day.   [*They sit.*

Lord D.   Now for it, Doctor.

Pang.   The process which we are now upon is, to eradicate that blemish in your lordship's language which the learned denominate *cacology*, and which the vulgar call *slip-slop.*

Lord D.   I am afraid, Doctor, my *cakelology* will give you a tolerable tight job on 't.

Pang.   " *Nil desperandum.*" — Horace.   Hem ! We 'll begin in the old way, my Lord.   Talk on : when you stumble, I check.   Where was your lordship yesterday evening ?

Lord D.   At a consort.

Pang.   Umph ! *tête à tête* with Lady Duberly, I presume.

Lord D.   *Tête à tête* with five hundred people, hearing of music.

Pang.   Oh ! I conceive : your lordship would say a concert.   Mark the distinction : a *concert*, my Lord, is an entertainment visited by fashionable lovers of harmony.   Now, a *consort* is a wife — little conducive to harmony in the present day, and seldom visited by a man of fashion, unless she happens to be his friend's or his neighbor's.

Lord D.   A difference, indeed !   Between you and I, Doctor, (now my Lady 's out of hearing,) a wife is the plague.

Pang.   He, he, he ! there are plenty of Jobs in the world, my Lord.

Lord D.   And a sight of Jezebels, too, Doctor.

But patience, as you say; for I never gives my Lady no bad language. Whenever she gets in her tantrums, and talks high, I always sits mumchance.

Pang. "So spake our mother Eve, and Adam heard."—Milton. Hem! [*They rise*] Silence is most secure, my Lord, in these cases; for if once your lordship opened your mouth, 't is twenty to one but bad language would follow.

Lord D. Oh, that's a sure thing; and I never liked to disperse the women.

Pang. Asperse.

Lord D. Humph! there's another stumble! After all, Doctor, I shall make but a poor progress in my vermicular tongue.

Pang. Your knowledge of our native or *vernacular* language, my Lord, time and industry may meliorate. *Vermicular* is an epithet seldom applied to tongues, but in the case of puppies who want to be wormed.

Lord D. Oh, then, I a'n't so much out, Doctor. I've met plenty of puppies, since I came to town, whose tongues are so troublesome, that worming might chance to be of service. But, Doctor, I've a bit of a proposal to make to you concerning my own family.

Pang. Disclose, my Lord.

Lord D. Why, you must know, I expect my son Dicky in town this here very morning. Now, Doctor, if you would but mend his cakelology, mayhap it might be better worth while than the mending of mine.

D. S.—10.

Pang [*Aside*] I smell a pupil. Whence, my Lord, does the young gentleman come?

Lord D. You shall hear all about it. You know, Doctor, though I 'm of good family distraction —

Pang. *Ex.*

Lord D. Though I 'm of a good family extraction, 't was but t' other day I kept a shop at Gosport.

Pang. The rumor has reached me. "*Fama volat viresque.*" —

Lord D. Do n't put me out.

Pang. Virgil. Hem! Proceed.

Lord D. A tradesman, you know, must mind the main chance; so, when Dick began to grow as big as a porpus, I got an old friend of mine, who lives in Derbyshire — humph! close to the peak — to take Dick 'prentice at half-price. He 's just now out of his time; and I warrant him as wild and as rough as a rock. Now, if you, Doctor, if you would but take him in hand, and soften him a bit —

Pang. Pray, my Lord — "to soften rocks." — Congreve. Hem! Pray, my Lord, what profession may the Honorable Mr. Dowlas have followed?

Lord D. Who? Dick? He has served his clerkship to an attorney at Castleton.

Pang. An attorney! Gentlemen of his profession, my Lord, are very difficult to soften.

Lord D. Yes, but the pay may make it worth while. I 'm told that Lord Spindle gives his eldest son, Master Drumstick's tutorer, three hundred a year; and, besides learning his pupil, he has to read my lord to sleep of an afternoon, and walk out with the lap-dogs and children. Now, if three hundred a year, Doctor, will do the business for Dick, I sha'n't begrudge it you.

Pang. Three hundred a year! say no more, my Lord. LL.D., A. double S., and three hundred a year! I accept the office. " *Verbum sat.*"—Horace. Hem! I 'll run to my lodgings, settle with Mrs. Suds, put my wardrobe into a — no, I 've got it all on, and — [*Going —*]

Lord D. Hold, hold! not so hasty, Doctor. I must first send you for Dick to the Blue Boar.

Pang. The Honorable Mr. Dowlas, my pupil, at the Blue Boar!

Lord D. Ay, in Holborn. As I a'n't fond of telling people good news beforehand, for fear they may be baulked, Dick knows nothing of my being made a lord.

Pang. *Three* hundred a year!

> " *I 've often wished that I had clear,*
> *For life, six* " — *no, three —*
> ——— " *Three hundred* " —

Lord D. I wrote him just before I left Gosport, to tell him to meet me in London with —

Pang. " *Three* hundred pounds a year." — Swift. Hem!

Lord D. With all speed, upon business; d' ye mind me?

Pang. Dr. Pangloss, with an income of — no lap-dogs, my Lord?

Lord D. Nay, but listen, Doctor; — and as I

did n't know where old Ferret was to make me live
in London, I told Dick to be at the Blue Boar this
morning by the stage-coach. Why, you do n't hear
what I 'm talking about, Doctor.

Pang. Oh, perfectly, my Lord — three hundred —
Blue Boars — in a stage-coach !

Lord D. Well, step into my room, Doctor, and
I 'll give you a letter which you shall carry to the
inn, and bring Dick away with you. I warrant the
boy will be ready to jump out of his skin.

Pang. Skin! jump! I 'm ready to jump out of
mine! I follow your lordship. — Oh, Dr. Pangloss,
where is your philosophy now! — I attend you, my
Lord. "*Equam memento.*" — Horace. *Servare mentem.*
Hem! bless me, I 'm all in a fluster — LL.D., A.
double S., and three hundred a — I attend your
lordship.

SCENE II : — *A Room in the Blue Boar Inn. Enter*
DR. PANGLOSS *and* WAITER, L.

Pang. Let the chariot turn about. Dr. Pangloss
in a lord's chariot ! " *Curra portabur eodem.*" — Juve-
nal. Hem ! — Waiter !

Wait. Sir.

Pang. Have you any gentleman here who arrived
this morning ?

Wait. There 's one in the house now, sir.

Pang. Is he juvenile ?

Wait. No, sir; he 's Derbyshire.

Pang. He, he, he! — Of what appearance is the gentleman?

Wait. Why, plaguy poor, sir.

Pang. "I hold him rich, al had he not a sherte."— Chaucer. Hem! — Denominated the Honorable Mr. Dowlas?

Wait. Honorable! He left his name plain Dowlas at the bar, sir.

Pang. Plain Dowlas, did he? That will do; "for all the rest is leather — "

Wait. Leather, sir!

Pang. "And prunello."—Pope. Hem! Tell Mr. Dowlas a gentleman requests the honor of an interview.

Wait. This is his room, sir. He is but just stepped into our parcel warehouse; he'll be with you directly.

[*Exit*, R.

Pang. Never before did honor and affluence let fall such a shower on the head of Dr. Pangloss! Fortune, I thank thee! propitious goddess, I am grateful! I, thy favored child, who commenced his career in the loftiest apartment of a muffin-maker, in Milk Alley. Little did I think, "good, easy man" — Shakespeare — hem! — of the riches and literary dignities which now —

Enter DICK DOWLAS, R.

My pupil!

Dick. [*Speaking while entering*] Well, where is the man that wants — oh! you are he, I suppose —

Pang. I *am* the man, young gentleman. "*Homo sum.*"—Terence. Hem! Sir, the person who now presumes to address you is Peter Pangloss, to whose name, in the College of Aberdeen, is subjoined LL.D., signifying Doctor of Laws; to which has been recently added the distinction of A. double S., the Roman initials for a Fellow of the Society of Arts.

Dick. Sir, I am your most obedient, Richard Dowlas; to whose name, in his tailor's bill, is subjoined DR., signifying debtor; to which are added L. S. D., the Roman initials for pounds, shillings, and pence.

Pang. Ha! this youth was doubtless designed by destiny to move in the circles of fashion; for he is dipped in debt, and makes a merit of telling it.

Dick. But what are your commands with me, Doctor?

Pang. I have the honor, young gentleman, of being deputed an ambassador to you from your father.

Dick. Then you have the honor to be an ambassador of as good-natured an old fellow as ever sold a ha'porth of cheese in a chandler's shop.

Pang. Pardon me, if on the subject of your father's cheese, I advise you to be as mute as a mouse in one, for the future. 'T were better to keep that "*alta menta repositum.*"—Virgil. Hem!

Dick. Why, what's the matter? any misfortune? Broke, I fear!

Pang. No, not broke; but his name, as 't is customary in these cases, has appeared in the *Gazette.*

Dick. Not broke, but Gazetted!

Pang. Check your passions; learn philosophy. When the wife of the great Socrates threw a — hum! threw a tea-pot at his erudite head, he was as cool as a cucumber. When Plato —

Dick. Hang Plato! what of my father?

Pang. Don't hang Plato! The bees swarmed round his mellifluous mouth as soon as he was swaddled. " *Cum in cunis apes in labellis consedissent.*" — Cicero. Hem!

Dick. I wish you had a swarm round yours, with all my heart. Come, to the point.

Pang. In due time. But calm your choler. " *Ira furor brevis est.*" — Horace. Hem! Read this.

[*Gives a letter.*

Dick. [*Snatches the letter, breaks it open, and reads*] "Dear Dick. This comes to inform you I am in a perfect state of health, hoping you are the same." Ay, that's the old beginning. " It was my lot, last week, to be made "— ay, a bankrupt, I suppose — "to be made a "— what? — "to be made a p-e-a-r " — a pear! to be made a pear! What does he mean by that?

Pang. A peer — a peer of the realm. His lordship's orthography is a little loose; but several of his equals countenance the custom. Lord Loggerhead always spells *physician* with an *f.*

Dick. A peer! what, my father! I'm electrified. Old Daniel Dowlas made a peer! But let me see — [*reads on*] — "pear of the realm. Lawyer Ferret got me my titt "— oh, title — "and an estate of fifteen thousand per ann., by making me out next of kin to old Lord Duberly, because he died without — without *hair.*" 'T is an odd reason, by the by, to be next of kin to a nobleman because he died bald.

Pang. His lordship means *heir* — heir to his estate. We shall meliorate his style speedily — " reform it altogether." — Shakespeare. Hem!

Dick. [*Reads on*] " I sent my carrot " — carrot!

Pang. He, he, he! *Chariot,* his lordship means.

Dick. [*Reading*] " With Dr. Pangloss in it."

Pang. That 's me.

Dick. [*Reading*] " Respect him ; for he 's an LL.D., and, moreover, an A. double S." [*They bow.*

Pang. His lordship kindly condescended to insert that at my request.

Dick. [*Reading*] " And I have made him your tutorer, to mend your cakelology."

Pang. Cacology : from Κακος, *malus,* and Λογος, *verbum.* — Vide Lexicon. Hem!'

Dick. [*Reading*] " Come with the Doctor to my house in Hanover Square." — Hanover Square ! — " I remain your affectionate father, to command, Duberly."

Pang. That 's his lordship's title.

Dick. Is it?

Pang. It is.

Dick. Say *sir* to a lord's son. You have no more manners than a bear !

Pang. Bear! Under favor, young gentleman, I am the bear leader, being appointed your tutor.

Dick. And what can you teach me?

Pang. Prudence. Do n't forget yourself in sudden success. "*Tecum habita.*" — Persius. Hem!

Dick. Prudence to a nobleman's son with fifteen thousand a year!

Pang. Do n't give way to your passions.

Dick. Give way! I 'm wild — mad! You teach me, pooh! I have been in London before, and know it requires no teaching to be made a modern fine gentleman. Why, it all lies in a nut-shell: — sport a curricle — walk Bond street — play at faro — get drunk — dance reels — go to the opera — cut off your tail — pull on your pantaloons — and there 's a buck of the first fashion in town for you. D' ye think I do n't know what 's going?

Pang. Mercy on me! I shall have a very refractory pupil.

Dick. Not at all; we 'll be hand-and-glove together, my little Doctor. I 'll drive you down to all the races, with my terrier between your legs, in a tandem.

Pang. Doctor Pangloss, the philosopher, with a terrier between his legs, in a tandem!

Dick. I 'll tell you what, Doctor, I 'll make you my long-stop at cricket — you shall draw corks when I'm president — laugh at my jokes before company — squeeze lemons for punch — cast up the reckoning — and woe betide you if you do n't keep sober enough to see me safe home after a jollification!

Pang. Make me a long-stop and a squeezer of lemons! This is more fatiguing than walking out
D. S.—11.

with the lap-dogs.   And are these the qualifications for a tutor, young gentleman ?

Dick.   To be sure they are.   'T is the way that half the prig parsons, who educate us honorables, jump into fat livings.

Pang.   'T is well they jump into something fat at last, for they must wear all the flesh off their bones in the process.

Dick.   Come now, tutor, go and call the waiter.

Pang.   Go and call! sir, sir! I 'd have you to understand, Mr. Dowlas —

Dick.   Ay, let us understand one another, Doctor. My father, I take it, comes down handsomely to you for your management of me.

Pang.   My lord has been liberal.

Dick.   But 't is I must manage you, Doctor.   Acknowledge this, and, between ourselves, I 'll find means to double your pay.

Pang.   Double my —

Dick.   Do you hesitate?   Why, man, you have set up for a modern tutor without knowing your trade.

Pang.   Double my pay! say no more — done — " *actum est.*"—Terence.   Hem !—Waiter!   [*Bawling.*

Dick.   That 's right.   Tell him to pop my clothes into the carriage.   They are in that bundle.

Enter WAITER, R.

Pang.   Waiter, here! put up the Honorable Mr. Dowlas's clothes and linen into his father's, Lord Duberly's chariot.

Wait. Where are they all, sir?

Pang. All wrapped up in the Honorable Mr. Dowlas's pocket-handkerchief.

[Exit WAITER *with bundle,* L.

Dick. See 'em safe in, Doctor.

Pang. I go, most worthy pupil. — Six hundred pounds a year! However deficient in the classics, his knowledge of arithmetic is admirable.

" *I've often wished that I had clear,*
For life, six hundred pounds a year." —

Dick. Nay, nay; don't be so slow.

Pang. Swift. Hem! — I'm gone. *[Exeunt,* L.

COSTUMES.

DANIEL DOWLAS. — Green coat, richly embroidered; flowered waistcoat, silver button-holes; salmon-colored breeches; white silk stockings; shoes; paste buckles; lace ruffles; cornered hat, etc.

DICK DOWLAS. — Green coat; white waistcoat; light breeches; white silk stockings; dress shoes.

DOCTOR PANGLOSS. — Black velvet coat, with glass buttons; black cloth breeches; silk stockings; shoes and buckles; small cane; ruffles; three-cornered hat.

WAITER. — Plain blue coat; yellow waistcoat and breeches; white stockings and shoes.

LADY DUBERLY. — White satin petticoat; lace apron; loose pink satin gown, ornamented; short sleeves; old-fashioned head-dress; high-heeled shoes.

INKLE AND YARICO.

By Geo. Colman the Elder.

DRAMATIS PERSONÆ.

INKLE, *an avaricious speculator.*
SIR CHRISTOPHER CURRY, *Governor of Barbadoes.*
CAPTAIN CAMPLEY, *a brave young officer.*
MEDIUM, *father to Inkle; a trader.*
TRUDGE, *Inkle's attendant.*
MATE.
YARICO, *an Indian maiden.*
NARCISSA, *Inkle's intended, but married to Campley.*
WOWSKI, *an Indian girl attending Yarico.*
PATTY, *a servant girl.*

TIME — The Seventeenth Century.

SCENE: — *The Quay at Barbadoes. Enter* SIR
CHRISTOPHER CURRY, R.

Sir C. Od's my life! I can scarce contain my
happiness. I have left them safe in church, in the
middle of the ceremony. I ought to have given
Narcissa away, they told me; but I capered about
so much for joy, that old Spintext advised me to go

and cool my heels on the quay, till it was all over.
Oh, I'm so happy! and they shall see, now, what an
old fellow can do at a wedding.

Enter INKLE, L. 1. E.

Inkle. (L.) Now for dispatch! Hark'ee, old gentleman! [*To the Governor.*
Sir C. (R.) Well, young gentleman!
Inkle. If I mistake not, I know your business
here.
Sir C. Egad, I believe half the island knows it by
this time.
Inkle. Then to the point: I have a female whom
I wish to part with.
Sir C. Very likely; it's a common case, now-a-
days, with many a man.
Inkle. If you could satisfy me you would use her
mildly, and treat her with more kindness than is
usual — for I can tell you she's of no common
stamp — perhaps we might agree.
Sir C. Oho! a slave! Faith, now I think on't,
my daughter may want an attendant or two extra-
ordinary; and as you say she's a delicate girl, above
the common run, and none of your thick-lipped, flat-
nosed, squabby, dumpling dowdies, I don't much
care if —
Inkle. And for her treatment —
Sir C. Look ye, young man; I love to be plain:
I shall treat her a good deal better than you would,
I fancy; for, though I witness this custom every day,

I can't help thinking the only excuse for buying our
fellow-creatures, is to rescue 'em from the hands of
those who are unfeeling enough to bring them to
market.

Inkle. Fair words, old gentleman; an Englishman
won't put up with an affront.

Sir C. An Englishman! more shame for you! Men
who so fully feel the blessings of liberty, are doubly
cruel in depriving the helpless of their freedom.

Inkle. Let me assure you, sir, 'tis not my occu-
pation; but for a private reason — an instant pressing
necessity —

Sir C. Well, well, I have a pressing necessity, too;
I can't stand to talk now; I expect company here
presently; but if you'll ask for me to-morrow, at the
Castle —

Inkle. The Castle!

Sir C. Ay, sir, the Castle — the Governor's Castle;
known all over Barbadoes.

Inkle. [*Aside*] 'Sdeath! this man must be on the
Governor's establishment — his steward, perhaps —
and sent after me, while Sir Christopher is impatiently waiting for me. I've gone too far; my secret
may be known. As 'tis, I'll win this fellow to my
interest. [*To Sir C.*] One word more, sir: my business must be done immediately; and, as you seem
acquainted at the Castle, if you should see me there—
and there I mean to sleep to-night —

Sir C. Oh, you do?

Inkle. Your finger on your lips; and never breathe
a syllable of this transaction.

Sir C. No! Why not?

Inkle. Because, for reasons which, perhaps, you 'll know to-morrow, I might be injured with the Governor, whose most particular friend I am.

Sir C. [*Aside*] So! here 's a particular friend of mine, coming to sleep at my house, that I never saw in my life. I 'll sound this fellow. — I fancy, young gentleman, as you are such a bosom friend of the Governor's, you can hardly do any thing to alter your situation with him?

Inkle. Oh! pardon me; but you 'll find that hereafter. Besides, you doubtless know his character?

Sir C. Oh, as well as I do my own. But let 's understand one another. You may trust me, now you 've gone so far. You are acquainted with his character, no doubt, to a hair?

Inkle. I am — I see we shall understand each other. You know him, too, I see, as well as I — a very touchy, testy, hot old fellow.

Sir C. [*Aside*] Here 's a scoundrel! I hot and touchy! I can hardly contain my passion! — But I won't discover myself. I 'll see the bottom of this. [*To Inkle.*] Well, now, as we seem to have come to a tolerable explanation, let 's proceed to business; bring me the woman.

Inkle. No; there you must excuse me. I rather would avoid seeing her more; and wish it to be settled without my seeming interference. My presence might distress her — you conceive me?

Sir C. [*Aside*] What an unfeeling rascal! The poor girl 's in love with him, I suppose. — No, no;

fair and open. My dealing's with you, and you
only. I see her now, or I declare off.

Inkle. Well, then, you must be satisfied. Yonder's
my servant. — Ha! a thought has struck me. Come
here, sir.

Enter TRUDGE, L.

I'll write my purpose, and send it her by him. It's
lucky that I taught her to decipher characters; my
labor now is paid. [*Takes out his pocket-book and
writes, still talking to himself.*] This is somewhat less
abrupt; 'twill soften matters. [*To* TRUDGE] Give this
to Yarico; then bring her hither with you.

Trudge. I shall, sir.   [*Going,* L.

Inkle. Stay; come back. [*Aside*] This soft fool,
if uninstructed, may add to her distress: his drivel-
ling sympathy may feed her grief, instead of soothing
it. — When she has read this paper, seem to make
light of it; tell her it is a thing of course, done purely
for her good. I here inform her that I must part
with her. D'ye understand your lesson?

Trudge. Pa—part with Ma—Madam Ya—ric—o!

Inkle. Why does the blockhead stammer? — I
have my reasons. No muttering — and let me tell
you, sir, if your rare bargain were gone, too, 'twould
be the better: she may babble our story of the forest,
and spoil my fortune.

Trudge. I'm sorry for it, sir. I have lived with
you a long while; I've half a year's wages, too, due
the 25th *ult.*, for dressing your hair and scribbling

your parchments; but take my scribbling, take my frizzing, take my wages, and I and Wows will take ourselves off together: she saved my life, and nothing but death shall part us.

Inkle. Impertinent! go and deliver your message.

Trudge. I'm gone, sir. I never carried a letter with such ill-will in all my born days. [*Exit,* L.

Sir C. Well, shall I see the girl?

Inkle. She'll be here presently. One thing I had forgot: when she is yours, I need not caution you, after the hints I've given, to keep her from the Castle. If Sir Christopher should see her, 't would lead, you know, to a discovery of what I wish concealed.

Sir C. Depend upon *me;* Sir Christopher will know no more of our meeting than he does at this moment.

Inkle. Your secrecy shall not be unrewarded; I'll recommend you particularly to his good graces.

Sir C. Thank ye, thank ye; but I'm pretty much in his good graces as it is: I do n't know any body he has a greater respect for.

Re-enter TRUDGE, L.

Inkle. Now, sir, have you performed your message?

Trudge. Yes, I gave her the letter.

Inkle. And where is Yarico? Did she say she'd come? Did n't you do as you were ordered? Did n't you speak to her?

Trudge. I could n't, sir, I could n't. I intended
to say what you bid me; but I felt such a pain in my
throat, I could n't speak a word for the soul of me;
and so, sir, I fell a-crying.

Inkle. (c.) Blockhead!

Sir C. (R.) 'Sblood! but he's a very honest blockhead. Tell me, my good fellow, what said the girl?

Trudge. (L.) Nothing at all, sir. She sat down,
with her two hands clasped on her knees, and looked
so pitifully in my face I could not stand it. Oh, here
she comes. I'll go and find Wows. If I must be
melancholy, she shall keep me company.   [*Exit*, L.

Sir C. Od's my life! as comely a girl as ever I
saw!

Enter YARICO, L., *who looks for some time in* INKLE'S
face, bursts into tears, and falls on his neck.

Inkle. (c.) In tears! Nay, Yarico, why this?

Yar. (L.) Oh, do not — do not leave me!

Inkle. Why, simple girl! I'm laboring for your
good. My interest here is nothing; I can do nothing
from myself. You are ignorant of our country's
customs. I must give way to men more powerful,
who will not have me with you. But see, my Yarico,
ever anxious for your welfare, I've found a kind,
good person who will protect you.

Yar. Ah! why not you protect me?

Inkle. I have no means. — How can I?

Yar. Just as I sheltered you. Take me to yonder

mountain, where I see no smoke from tall, high houses, filled with your cruel countrymen. None of your princes there will come to take me from you. And should they stray that way, we'll find a lurking-place just like my own poor cave, where many a day I sat beside you, and blessed the chance that brought you to it, that I might save your life.

Sir C. (R.) His life! Zounds! my blood boils at the scoundrel's ingratitude!

Yar. Come, come, let us go. I always feared these cities. Let's fly and seek the woods; and there we'll wander hand in hand together. No cares shall vex us then: we'll let the day glide by in idleness; and you shall sit in the shade, and watch the sunbeam playing on the brook, while I sing the song that pleases you. No cares, love, but for food; and we'll live cheerily, I warrant. In the fresh, early morning, you shall hunt down our game, and I will pick you berries. And then, at night, I'll trim our bed of leaves, and lie down in peace.—Oh! we shall be so happy!

Inkle. Hear me, Yarico. My countrymen and yours differ as much in minds as in complexions. We were not born to live in woods and caves—to seek subsistence by pursuing beasts. We Christians, girl, hunt money—a thing unknown to you. But, here, 't is money which brings us ease, plenty, command, power—every thing; and, of course, happiness. You are the bar to my attaining this; therefore, 't is necessary for my good—and which I think you value—

Yar. You know I do; so much, that it would break my heart to leave you.

Inkle. But we must part. If you are seen with me, I shall lose all.

Yar. I gave up all for you — my friends, my country — all that was dear to me; and still grown dearer, since you sheltered there — all, all was left for you; and were it now to do again, again I'd cross the seas, and follow you all the world over.

Inkle. We idle time, sir: she is yours. See you obey this gentleman; 't will be the better for you.

        [*Going. Puts* YARICO *across to* C.

Yar. Oh, barbarous! Do not, do not abandon me!

Inkle. (L.) No more.

Yar. Stay but a little: I sha'n't live long to be a burden to you: your cruelty has cut me to the heart. Protect me but a little. Or I'll obey this man, and undergo all hardships for your good: stay but to witness them: I soon shall sink with grief: tarry till then, and hear me bless your name when I am dying; and beg you, now and then, when I am gone, to heave a sigh for your poor Yarico.

Inkle. I dare not listen. You, sir, I hope, will take good care of her.   [*Going.*

Sir C. Care of her! that I will. I'll cherish her like my own daughter, and pour balm into the heart of a poor, innocent girl that has been wounded by the artifices of a scoundrel.

Inkle. Ha! 'Sdeath, sir, how dare you!

Sir C. 'Sdeath, sir, how dare you look an honest man in the face!   [*Crosses,* C.

Inkle. (L.) Sir, you shall feel —

Sir C. (c.) Feel! — It's more than ever you did, I believe. Mean, sordid wretch! dead to all sense of honor, gratitude, or humanity! I never heard of such barbarity! I have a son-in-law who has been left in the same situation; but if I thought him capable of such cruelty, I would return him to sea, with a peck loaf, in a cockle-shell! — Come, come; cheer up, my girl! You sha'n't want a friend to protect you, I warrant you. [*Taking* YARICO *by the hand.*

Inkle. Insolence! The Governor shall hear of this insult.

Sir C. The Governor! — Liar! cheat! rogue! impostor! — breaking all ties you ought to keep, and pretending to those you have no right to. The Governor never had such a fellow in the whole catalogue of his acquaintance. The Governor disowns you — the Governor disclaims you — the Governor abhors you! and, to your utter confusion, here stands the Governor to tell you so! here stands old Curry, who never talked to a rogue without telling him what he thought of him.

Inkle. Sir Christopher! — Lost and undone!

Medium. [*Without,* L.] Hollo! young Multiplication! Zounds! I have been peeping in every cranny of the house. Why, young Rule-of-three! [*Enters from the inn,* L. S. E.] Oh! here you are, at last. — Ah, Sir Christopher! what, are you there! Too impatient to wait at home. But here's one that will make you easy, I fancy.

[*Clapping* INKLE *on the shoulder.*

Sir C. (c.) How came you to know him?

Med. Ha, ha! Well, that's curious enough, too. So you have been talking here without finding out each other?

Sir C. No, no; I have found him out, with a vengeance.

Med. Not you. Why, this is the dear boy. It's my nephew, that is; your son-in-law, that is to be. It's Inkle.

Sir C. It's a lie! and you're a purblind old booby! and this dear boy is a scoundrel!

Med. Heyday, what's the meaning of this? One was mad before, and he has bit the other, I suppose.

Sir C. But here comes the dear boy — the true boy — the jolly boy, piping hot from church, with my daughter.

Enter CAMPLEY, NARCISSA, *and* PATTY, R.

Med. Campley!

Sir C. Who? Campley? It's no such thing.

Camp. That's my name, indeed, Sir Christopher.

Sir C. And how came you, sir, to impose upon me, and assume the name of Inkle? — a name which every man of honesty ought to be ashamed of.

Camp. [*Crosses to* SIR C.] I never did, sir. Since I sailed from England with your daughter, my affection has daily increased; and when I came to explain myself to you, by a number of concurring circum-

stances, which I am now partly acquainted with,
you mistook me for that gentleman. Yet, had I
even then been aware of your mistake, 1 must
confess, the regard for my own happiness would
have tempted me to let you remain undeceived.

Sir C. And did you, Narcissa, join in —

Nar. How could I, my dear sir, disobey you?

Patty. But, your Honor, what young lady could
refuse a captain?

Camp. I am a soldier, Sir Christopher. Love
and war is the soldier's motto. Though my income
is trifling to your *intended* son-in-law's, still the
chance of war has enabled me to support the object
of my love above indigence. Her fortune, Sir Christopher, I do not consider myself by any means entitled to.

Sir C. 'Sblood! but you must, though. Give me
your hand, my young Mars, and bless you both together. Thank you, thank you, for cheating an old
fellow into giving his daughter to a lad of spirit,
when he was going to throw her away upon one in
whose breast the mean passion of avarice smothers
the smallest spark of affection or humanity.

Nar. I have this moment heard a story of a transaction in the forest, which, I own, would have rendered compliance with your former demands very
disagreeable.

Patty. Yes, sir; I told my mistress he had brought
over a Hotty-pot gentlewoman.

Sir C. [*To* Narcissa] Yes, but he would have left
her for you, and you for his interest; and sold you,

perhaps, as he has this poor girl to me, as a requital
for preserving his life.

Nar.   How!

Enter TRUDGE *and* WOWSKI, L.

Trudge.   Come along, Wows! take a long last
leave of your poor mistress: throw your pretty
ebony arms about her neck.

Wows.   No, no; she not go.   You not leave poor
Wowski?   [*Throwing her arms about* YARICO.

Sir C.   Poor girl!   A companion, I take it.

Trudge.   A thing of my own, sir.   I could n't help
following my master's example in the woods.   "Like
master, like man," sir.

Sir C.   But you would not sell her, you dog, would
you?

Trudge.   Hang me, like a dog, if I would, sir!

Sir C.   So say I to every fellow that breaks an
obligation due to the feelings of a man.   But, old
Medium, what have you to say for your hopeful
nephew?

Med.   I never speak ill of my friends, Sir Christopher.

Sir C.   Pshaw!

Inkle. [*Comes down,* L.] Then let me speak: hear
me defend a conduct —

Sir C.   Defend!   Zounds!   plead guilty at once:
it 's the only hope left of obtaining mercy.

Inkle.   Suppose, old gentleman, you had a son.

Sir C.   'Sblood!   Then I 'd make him an honest

fellow; and teach him that the feeling heart never knows greater pride than when it's employed in giving succor to the unfortunate. I'd teach him to be his father's own son to a hair.

Inkle. Even so my father tutored me from infancy, bending my tender mind, like a young sapling, to his will. Interest was the grand prop round which he twined my pliant, green affections. Taught me in childhood to repeat old sayings, all tending to his own fixed principles: and the first sentence that I ever lisped was, " Charity begins at home."

Sir C. I shall never like a proverb again, as long as I live.

Inkle. As I grew up, he'd prove — and by example — were I in want, I might e'en starve for what the world cared for their neighbors; why, then, should I care for the world? Men now lived for themselves. These were his doctrines. Then, sir, what would you say, should I, in spite of habit, precept, education, fly in my father's face and spurn his counsels?

Sir C. Say? Why, that you were an honest, undutiful fellow. Oh, away with such principles! — principles which destroy all confidence between man and man; principles which none but a rogue could instil, and none but a rogue could imbibe. Principles —

Inkle. Which I renounce!

Sir C. Eh!

Inkle. Renounce entirely. Ill-founded precept too long has steeled my breast; but still 't is

vulnerable. This trial was too much. Nature,
'gainst habit, combating within me, has penetrated
to my heart — a heart, I own, long callous to the
feelings of sensibility : but now it bleeds, and bleeds
for my poor Yarico. Oh, let me clasp her to it while
't is glowing, and mingle tears of love and penitence!

Trudge. [*Capering about*] Wows, listen to that!

[Wowski *goes to* Trudge.

Yar. And shall we, shall we be happy?

Inkle. Ay — ever, ever, Yarico.

Yar. I knew we should — and yet I feared. But
shall I still watch over you? Oh, love, you surely
gave your Yarico such pain only to make her feel
this happiness the greater.

Wows. [*Going to* Yarico] Oh, Wowski so happy!
and yet I think I not glad, neither.

Trudge. Eh, Wows! How? — why not?

Wows. 'Cause I can't help cry.

Sir C. Then, if that's the case, bless me if I
think I 'm very glad, either. What is the matter
with my eyes? — Young man, your hand ; I am now
proud and happy to shake it.

Med. Well, Sir Christopher, what do you say to
my hopeful nephew now?

Sir C. Say! why, confound the fellow, I say that
it is ungenerous enough to remember the bad action
of a man who has virtue left in his heart to repent
it. [*To* Trudge] As for you, my good fellow, I must,
with your master's permission, employ you myself.

Trudge. Oh, rare! Bless your honor! Wows,
you 'll be lady to a Governor's factotum.

Wows. Iss — I Lady Jactotum.

Sir C. And now, my young folks, we'll drive home and celebrate the wedding. Od's my life! I long to be shaking a foot at the fiddles; and I shall dance ten times the lighter for reforming an Inkle, while I have it in my power to reward the innocence of a Yarico.

Tableau. Curtain.

COSTUMES.

INKLE. — Nankeen trowsers and jacket; white waistcoat; light hat; white stockings; black belt and hanger.

SIR CHRISTOPHER. — Blue coat, embroidered button-holes; white waistcoat and breeches; white hat, gold button and loop; knee and shoe buckles; and white silk stockings.

CAMPLEY. — Regimental coat; white trowsers; sash, sword, hat etc.

MEDIUM. — Plain brown coat and waistcoat; blue striped trowsers; white stockings; shoes; black leather belt and hanger.

TRUDGE. — Nankeen trowsers and jacket; white waistcoat and stockings; shoes; hat; black leather belt and hanger.

YARICO. — White and colored striped muslin dress, with colored feathers and ornaments; leopard's skin drapery across one shoulder; dark flesh-colored stockings and arms; sandals; various-colored feathers in head; a quantity of colored beads around the head, neck, wrists, arms, and ankles.

WOWSKI. — Black skin, arms and legs; sandals; plain white dress, with small skin hung across shoulder; beads, etc.

NARCISSA. — Handsome white trimmed dress, with ornamented head, satin hat, etc.

PATTY. — White muslin dress, trimmed with blue and pink ribbon; apron, hat. etc.

THE DECEIVED BRIDE.

From The Honeymoon, by John Tobin.

DRAMATIS PERSONÆ.

DUKE ARANZA.   JULIANA.   BALTHAZAR.

SCENE I: — *A Cottage. A table and two chairs. A door at 1. E. L. Enter the* DUKE, *leading in* JULIANA, L. D.

Duke. [*Brings a chair forward, c., and sits down*]
You are welcome home.

    Jul. [*Crosses,* R.] Home! You are merry. This retired spot
Would be a palace for an owl!

    Duke. 'T is ours.

    Jul. Ay, for the time we stay in it.

    Duke. By Heaven,
This is the noble mansion that I spoke of!

    Jul. This! — You are not in earnest, though you bear it
With such a sober brow. — Come, come, you jest.

    Duke. Indeed, I jest not. Were it ours in jest,
We should have none, wife.

Jul. Are you serious, sir?

Duke. I swear, as I'm your husband, and no duke.

Jul. No duke?

Duke. But of my own creation, lady.

Jul. Am I betrayed? — Nay, do not play the fool!
It is too keen a joke.

Duke. You'll find it true.

Jul. You are no duke, then?

Duke. None.

Jul. Have I been cozened?
And have you no estate, sir?
No palaces, nor houses?

Duke. None but this: —
A small, snug dwelling, and in good repair.

Jul. Nor money, nor effects?

Duke. None that I know of.

Jul. And the attendants who have waited on us —

Duke. They were my friends; who, having done
        my business,
Are gone about their own.

Jul. [Aside] Why, then, 't is clear. —
That I was ever born! — What are you, sir?

Duke. [Rises] I am an honest man; that may
        content you:
Young, nor ill-favored; should not that content you?
I am your husband; and that must content you.

Jul. I will go home!   [*Going,* L.

Duke. You are at home already.   [*Staying her.*

Jul. I'll not endure it! — But remember this,
Duke or no duke, I'll be a duchess, sir.   [*Crosses,* L.

Duke. A duchess! you shall be a queen — to all

Who, by the courtesy, will call you so.

Jul.   And I will have attendance.

Duke.   So you shall,
When you have learned to wait upon yourself.

Jul.   To wait upon myself! Must I bear this?
I could tear out my eyes, that bade you woo me,
And bite my tongue in two, for saying yes!

                                        [*Crosses,* R.

Duke.   And if you should, 't would grow again.—
I think, to be an honest yeoman's wife,
(For such, my would-be duchess, you will find me,)
You were cut out by nature.

Jul.   You will find, then,
That education, sir, has spoiled me for it.—
Why! do you think I'll work?

Duke.   I think 't will happen, wife.

Jul.   What! rub and scrub
Your noble palace clean?

Duke.   Those taper fingers
Will do it daintily.

Jul.   And dress your victuals
(If there be any)?—Oh, I could go mad! [*Crosses,* L.

Duke.   And mend my hose, and darn my night-
      caps neatly:
Wait, like an echo, till you're spoken to—

Jul.   Or, like a clock, talk only once an hour?

Duke.   Or like a dial; for that quietly
Performs its work, and never speaks at all.

Jul.   To feed your poultry and your hogs!—oh,
      monstrous!
And when I stir abroad, on great occasions,

Carry a squeaking tithe pig to the vicar;
Or jolt with higglers' wives the market trot,
To sell your eggs and butter!   [*Crosses*, L.

 Duke. Excellent!
How well you sum the duties of a wife!
Why, what a blessing I shall have in you!
 Jul. A blessing!
 Duke. When they talk of you and me,
Darby and Joan shall no more be remembered : —
We shall be happy.
 Jul. Shall we?
 Duke. Wondrous happy!
Oh, you will make an admirable wife!
 Jul. I 'll make a devil!
 Duke. What?
 Jul. A very devil!
 Duke. Oh, no; we 'll have no devils.
 Jul. I 'll not bear it!
I 'll to my father's! —
 Duke. Gently : you forget
You are a perfect stranger to the road.
 Jul. My wrongs will find a way, or make one.
 Duke. Softly!
You stir not hence, except to take the air;
And then I 'll breathe it with you.
 Jul. What, confine me?
 Duke. 'T would be unsafe to trust you yet abroad.
 Jul. Am I a truant schoolboy?
 Duke. Nay, not so;
But you must keep your bounds.
 Jul. And if I break them,

Perhaps you 'll beat me.

Duke.   Beat you!
The man that lays his hand upon a woman,
Save in the way of kindness, is a wretch
Whom 't were gross flattery to name a coward. —
I 'll talk to you, lady, but not beat you.

Jul.   Well, if I may not travel to my father,
I may write to him, surely! — and I will,
If I can meet, within your spacious dukedom,
Three such unhoped-for miracles at once,
As pens, and ink, and paper.

Duke.   You will find them
In the next room. — A word before you go:
You are my wife, by every tie that 's sacred;
The partner of my fortune and my bed —

Jul.   Your fortune!

Duke.   Peace! — No fooling, idle woman!
Beneath the attesting eye of Heaven, I 've sworn
To love, to honor, cherish, and protect you.
No human power can part us. What remains, then?
To fret and worry and torment each other,
And give a keener edge to our hard fate
By sharp upbraidings and perpetual jars? —
Or, like a loving and a patient pair,
(Waked from a dream of grandeur, to depend
Upon their daily labor for support,)
To soothe the taste of fortune's lowliness
With sweet consent, and mutual fond endearment? —
Now to your chamber — write whate'er you please;
But pause before you stain the spotless paper
With words that may inflame, but can not heal.

Jul. Why, what a patient worm you take me for!

Duke. I took you for a wife; and ere I've done,
I'll know you for a good one.

Jul. You shall know me
For a right woman, full of her own sex;
Who, when she suffers wrong, will speak her anger;
Who feels her own prerogative, and scorns,
By the proud reason of superior man,
To be taught patience when her swelling heart
Cries out revenge!   [*Exit at door in* c.

Duke. Why, let the flood rage on!
There is no tide in woman's wildest passion
But hath an ebb. I've broke the ice, however.
Write to her father! She may write a folio —
But if she send it! — 'T will divert her spleen —
The flow of ink may save her blood-letting.
Perchance she may have fits! — They are seldom
          mortal,
Save when the doctor's sent for.
Though I have heard some husbands say, and wisely,
A woman's honor is her safest guard,
Yet there's some virtue in a lock and key.
                              [*Locks the door.*
So, thus begins our honeymoon. 'T is well!
For the first fortnight, ruder than March winds
She'll blow a hurricane; the next, perhaps,
Like April, she may wear a changeful face
Of storm and sunshine; and, when that is past,
She will break glorious as unclouded May;
And where the thorns grew bare, the spreading
          blossoms

D. S.—13.

Meet with no lagging frost to kill their sweetness.
Whilst others, for a month's delirious joy,
Buy a dull age of penance, we, more wisely,
Taste first the wholesome bitter of the cup,
That after to the very lees shall relish;
And to the close of this frail life prolong
The pure delights of a well-governed marriage.

[*Exit*, R.

SCENE II:—*The Cottage. Two chairs.* JULIANA *sitting
    at her needle; the* DUKE *steals in behind, through*
    D. *in flat.*

Duke. Come, no more work to-night: [*sits by her*]
        it is the last
That we shall spend beneath this humble roof.
Our fleeting month of trial being past,
To-morrow you are free.
    Jul. Nay, now you mock me,
And turn my thoughts upon my former follies.
You know that, to be mistress of the world,
I would not leave you.
    Duke. No!
    Jul. No, on my honor.
    Duke. I think you like me better than you did:
And yet 't is natural. Come, come, be honest;
You have a sort of hankering — no wild wish,
Or vehement desire — yet a slight longing,
A simple preference, if you had your choice,
To be a duchess, rather than the wife
Of a low peasant?

Jul. No; indeed you wrong me.

Duke. I marked you closely at the palace, wife:
In the full tempest of your speech, your eye
Would glance to take the room's dimensions,
And pause upon each ornament; and then
There would break from you a half-smothered sigh,
Which spoke distinctly, "These should have been
 mine:"
And therefore, though with a well-tempered spirit,
You have some secret swellings of the heart
When these things rise to your imagination.

Jul. No, indeed: sometimes in my dreams, I own—
You know we can not help our dreams—

Duke. What then?

Jul. Why, I confess, that sometimes, in my dreams,
A noble house and splendid equipage,
Diamonds and pearls and gilded furniture,
Will glitter like an empty pageant by me;
And then I am apt to rise a little feverish:
But never do my sober waking thoughts—
As I 'm a woman worthy of belief—
Wander to such forbidden vanities.
Yet, after all, it was a scurvy trick—
Your palace and your pictures and your plate;
Your fine plantations; your delightful gardens,
That were a second Paradise — for fools;
And then your grotto, so divinely cool;
Your Gothic summer-house and Roman temple—
'T would puzzle much an antiquarian
To find out their remains.

Duke. No more of that!

Jul. You had a dozen spacious vineyards, too;
Alas! the grapes are sour; and, above all,
The Barbary courser that was breaking for me—
Duke. Nay, you shall ride him yet.
Jul. Indeed!
Duke. Believe me,
We must forget these things.
Jul. They are forgot;
And, by this kiss, we'll think of them no more,
But when we want a theme to make us merry.
Duke. It was an honest one, and spoke thy soul;
And by the fresh lip and unsullied breath,
Which joined to give it sweetness —

Enter BALTHAZAR, L.

Jul. [*Crosses*, c.] How! My father!
Duke. Signior Balthazar! You are welcome, sir,
To our poor habitation.
Bal. Welcome! Villain,
I come to call your dukeship to account,
And to reclaim my daughter.
Duke. [*Aside*] You will find her
Reclaimed already, or I have lost my pains.
Bal. Let me come at him!
Jul. Patience, my dear father!
Duke. Nay, give him room. Put up your weapon,
    sir —
'T is the worst argument a man can use;
So let it be the last. As for your daughter,

She passes by another title here,
In which your whole authority is sunk —
My lawful wife.

Bal. Lawful! — his lawful wife!
I shall go mad! Did not you basely steal her
Under a vile pretense?

Duke. What I have done
I 'll answer to the law.
Of what do you complain?

Bal. Why, are you not
A most notorious, self-confessed impostor?

Duke. True; I am somewhat dwindled from the
state
In which you lately knew me: nor alone
Should my exceeding change provoke your wonder;
You 'll find your daughter is not what she was.

Bal. How, Juliana?

Jul. 'T is, indeed, most true:
I left you, sir, a froward, foolish girl,
Full of capricious thoughts and fiery spirits,
Which, without judgment, I would vent on all:
But I have learned this truth indelibly —
That modesty in deed, in word, and thought,
Is the prime grace of woman; and with that,
More than by frowning looks and saucy speeches,
She may persuade the man that rightly loves her,
Whom she was ne'er intended to command.

Bal. Amazement! Why, this metamorphosis
Exceeds his own! What spells, what cunning witch-
craft
Has he employed?

Jul.   None: he has simply taught me
To look into myself: his powerful rhetoric
Hath with strong influence impressed my heart,
And made me see at length the thing I have been,
And what I am, sir.

Bal.   Are you, then, content
To live with him?

Jul.   Content? I am most happy.

Bal.   Can you forget your crying wrongs?

Jul.   Not quite, sir;
They sometimes serve to make us merry with.

Bal.   How like a villain he abused your father!

Jul.   You will forgive him that, for my sake.

Bal.   Never!

Duke.   Why, then, 'tis plain you seek your own
        revenge,
And not your daughter's happiness.

Bal.   No matter:
I charge you, on your duty as my daughter,
Follow me!

Duke.   On a wife's obedience,
I charge you, stir not!

Jul.   You, sir, are my father:
At the bare mention of that hallowed name,
A thousand recollections rise within me,
To witness you have ever been a kind one: —
This is my husband, sir.

Bal.   Thy husband; well —

Jul.   'Tis fruitless now to think upon the means
He used — I am irrevocably his:
And when he plucked me from my parent tree,

To graft me on himself, he gathered with me
My love, my duty, my obedience :
And, by adoption, I am bound as strictly
To do his reasonable bidding now
As once to follow yours.
    Duke. [*Aside*] Most excellent !
    Bal. · Yet I will be revenged !
    Duke. You would have justice?
    Bal. I will : so forthwith meet me at the duke's.
                          [*Crosses*, L.
    Duke. I am the duke.
    Bal. The jest is somewhat stale, sir.
    Duke. You'll find it true.
    Bal. Indeed !
    Jul. [*Aside*] Be still, my heart !
    Bal. I think you would not trifle with me now.
    Duke. I am the Duke Aranza !
[*Throws off a disguise, and appears in a splendid dress.*
And what's my greater pride, this lady's husband.
You now must see   [*Leads* JULIANA L. C.
The drift of what I have been lately acting,
And what I am. And though, being a woman
Giddy with youth and unrestrained fancy,
The domineering spirit of her sex
I have rebuked too sharply ; yet 't was done
As skillful surgeons cut beyond the wound,
To make the cure complete.
    Bal. You have done most wisely,
And all my anger dies in speechless wonder.
    Duke. What says my Juliana?
    Jul. I am lost, too,

In admiration, sir; my fearful thoughts
Rise, on a trembling wing, to that rash height
Whence, growing dizzy once, I fell to earth.
Yet since your goodness for the second time
Will lift me, though unworthy, to that pitch
Of greatness, there to hold a constant flight,
I will endeavor so to bear myself,
That in the world's eye and my friends' observance—
And what's far dearer, your most precious judg-
    ment—
I may not shame your dukedom.
   Duke. Bravely spoken!
Why, now you shall have rank and equipage—
Servants, for you can now command yourself—
Glorious apparel, not to swell your pride,
But to give luster to your modesty:
All pleasures, all delights that noble dames
Warm their chaste fancies with, in full abundance
Shall flow upon you;—and it shall go hard
But you shall ride the Barbary courser, too.

Tableau.   Curtain.

COSTUMES.

DUKE.—First dress—plain, rather coarse suit: second dress—
    splendid satin ducal vest; rich velvet robe, trimmed with
    green and silver; white silk pantaloons; white shoes, etc.
BALTHAZAR.—Plain suit.
JULIANA.—First dress—splendid bridal attire: second dress—
    neat white muslin.

THE GREEK GIRL AND THE BARBARIAN.

From Ingomar, as translated from the German by Maria Lovell.

DRAMATIS PERSONÆ.

INGOMAR, *leader of a band of Alemanni.*
PARTHENIA, *a Massilian girl.*

Scene : — *In the Cevennes. A Wood, densely arched with trees ; where the bushes are less thick, a mass of wild rock.* Ingomar *is seen, leaning upon a spear.*

Ingomar. With us is Freedom. She lives in the
    open air ;
In woods she dwells ; upon the rocks she breathes ;
Now here, now there ; not caring for to-day —
No, nor providing for to-morrow :
Freedom is hunting, feeding, fighting, danger :
That, that is freedom : that it is which makes
The veins to swell, the breast to heave and glow :
Ay, that is freedom ; that is pleasure — life !

Enter Parthenia, r. u. e.

Ah ! this must be the captive. Woman,
Thou seekest Ingomar : this is he.
They say thou 'rt come to treat for this man's ransom :
What is thy offer ?
    Par.   Jewels of more value
Than all the gold of earth : — a faithful wife's
Prayers to her latest breath ; a daughter's tears ;
A rescued household's deathless gratitude ;
The blessing of the gods, whose liberal hands
Recompense deeds of mercy thousand-fold.
Look : kneeling at your feet, a fainting child
Implores a gray-haired father's liberty.
He is infirm, old, valueless to you ;
But, oh ! how precious to his widowed home !
Give him, then, up — oh, give him up to me !

Ing. Woman, thy father is booty to our tribe:
Were he but mine, I 'd give him to thee freely,
If only to be rid of his tears and sighs.
But if thou hast deceived us, and dost dare —
Par. [*Suddenly rising*] Enough ! —
There need no threats. I but misunderstood you,
Thinking you had human hearts ; I 'll mend of that,
And speak now to your interests.
You ask gold for his ransom — he has none;
But he has strength and skill that yet may earn it,
With opportunity afforded him.
Here there is none — he can not pay a drachma.
Keep him, and slavery, gnawing his free heart,
In a few weeks shall leave you but his bones.
But, set him free, my mother and myself
Will labor with him ; we will live on crusts,
And all the surplus of our daily toil
Be yours, till the full ransom be accomplished.
    Ing. That 's not without some sense; but where
        is our surety
The compact should be kept?
    Par.   It shall not fail
For lack of that : I 'll leave with you a pledge
Dearer to him than liberty or life.
    Ing. Hast brought it with thee?
    Par. Ay.
    Ing.   Show it.
    Par.   Myself.
    Ing.   Thyself?
    Par. If you but knew
How precious to him is his child, you 'd not

Despise the hostage.

Ing.   It's a strange fancy; and yet — pshaw! no,
    no —

Burden us with a woman!

Par.   No — no burden;

I 'll be a help to you: these willing hands
Shall do more work than twenty pining slaves.
You do not guess my usefulness: I spin,
Can weave your garments, and prepare your meals,
Am skilled in music, and can tell brave tales,
And sing sweet songs to lull you to repose.
I am strong, too — healthy both in mind and body;
And when my heart's at ease, my natural temper
Is always joyous, happy, gay.   Oh, fear not!

Ing.   Troth, there's some use in that; thy father
    can

Only cry.

Par.   Say yes — say yes, and set him free!

Ing.   I'd counsel with my comrades. Stay thou
    here.   [*Exit* INGOMAR, L. PARTHENIA *gazes*
        anxiously after him.

Par.   Father, it must be so; my mother grieves—
Oh, dry her tears.   I am yet young and strong;
I could bear easily what would kill thee.
Father, thou shalt be free, thou shalt be free!

Re-enter INGOMAR, L. PARTHENIA *approaches him*
    eagerly.

Ing.   Woman, your wish is granted; we take thee
As hostage for the other, and he is free.

Par. Be thanked, ye gods!—My father, O farewell!

He is gone, and I shall never see him more!

> [*Clasping her hands before her face, sobbing.*

Ing. [*Standing on a rock, looking,* L., *at his followers*]

No violence! Ho, how he runs! and now

He stops and cries again! Poor, fearful fool!

It must be strange to fear. Now, by my troth,

I should like to feel, for once, what 't is to fear!—

But the girl. [*Leaning forward*] Ha! do I see right?

> [*To* PARTHENIA] You weep!

Is that the happy temper that you boast?

Par. Oh, I shall never see him more!

Ing. What! have we,

For a silly old man, got now a foolish

And timid, weeping girl? I have had enough

Of tears.

Par. Enough, indeed, since you but mock them.

I will not—no, I 'll weep no more!

> [*She quickly dries her eyes, and retires to the background.*

Ing. That 's good; come, that looks well.

She is a brave girl: she rules herself; and if

She keep her word, we have made a good exchange:

"I 'll weep no more." Aha! I like the girl.

And if—Ho! whither goest thou?

> [*To* PARTHENIA, *who is going off with two goblets.*

Par. Where should I go? to yonder brook, to
cleanse the cups.

Ing. No; stay and talk with me.

Par. I have duties to perform.   [*Going.*

Ing. Stay—I command you, slave!

Par. I am no slave! your hostage, but no slave.
I go to cleanse the cups.   [*Exit,* L.

   Ing.   Ho! here's a self-willed thing — here is a
      spirit!   [*Mimicking her.*
"I will not! I am no slave! I have duties to perform!
Take me for hostage!" and she flung back her head
As though she brought with her a ton of gold!
"I'll weep no more!"—Aha! an impudent thing:
She pleases me. I love to be opposed:
I love my horse when he rears, my dogs when they
      snarl,
The mountain torrent, and the sea, when it flings
Its foam up to the stars: such things as these
Fill me with life and joy. Tame indolence
Is living death! the battle of the strong
Alone is life!

      [*During this speech,* PARTHENIA *has returned
      with the cups and some field flowers. She sits on
      a rock in front.*

   Ing.   Ah! she is here again.   [*He approaches her.*
What art thou making there?

   Par.   I? garlands.

   Ing.   Garlands?
[*Musing*] It seems to me as I before had seen her,
In a dream. How! Ah, my brother!—he who died
A child — yes, that is it: my little Folko.
She has his dark brown hair, his sparkling eye:
Even the voice seems known again to me.
I'll not to sleep — I'll talk to her.   [*Returns to her.*
These you call garlands:
And wherefore do you weave them?

Par.   For these cups.

Ing.   How?

Par.   Is it not with you a custom?   With us
At home, we love to intertwine with flowers
Our cups and goblets.

Ing.   What use is such a plaything?

Par.   Use? they are beautiful; that is their use:
The sight of them makes glad the eye; their scent
Refreshes, cheers.   There!

                    [*Presents him the garland and cup.*
Is not that, now, beautiful?

Ing.   Ay, by the bright sun!   That dark green
        mixed up
With the gay flowers!   Thou must teach our women
To weave such garlands.

Par.   That is soon done: thy wife
Herself shall soon weave wreaths as well as I.

Ing. [*Laughing heartily*] My wife! my wife!   A
        woman,
Dost thou say?
I thank the gods, not I!   This is my wife:

                    [*Pointing to his accoutrements.*
My spear, my shield, my sword.   Let him who will
Waste cattle, slaves, or gold to buy a woman:
Not I — not I!

Par.   To buy a woman? — how?

Ing.   What is the matter?   why dost look so
        strangely?

Par.   How! did I hear aright? bargain for brides
As you would slaves? — buy them like cattle?

Ing.   Well, I think a woman fit only for a slave:

We follow our own customs, as you yours.
How do you in your city there?

  Par.   Consult our hearts.
Massilia's free-born daughters are not sold,
But bound by choice, with bands as light and sweet
As these I hold. Love only buys us there.

  Ing. Marry for love! What, do you love your
   husbands?

  Par. Why marry else?

  Ing. Marry for love! that's strange;
I can not comprehend. I love my horse,
My dogs, my brave companions — but no woman!
What dost thou mean by love? what is it, girl?

  Par. What is it? 'T is of all things the most
   sweet —
The heaven of life — or, so my mother says:
I never felt it.

  Ing.   Never?

  Par.   No, indeed. [*Looking at garland.*
Now look! How beautiful! Here would I weave
Red flowers, if I had them.

  Ing.   Yonder there,
In that thick wood they grow.

  Par.   How sayest thou? [*Looking off.*
Oh, what a lovely red! Go, pluck me some.

  Ing. [*Starting at the suggestion*] I go for thee! the
   master serve the slave!

     [*Gazing on her with increasing interest.*
And yet, why not? I'll go; the poor child's tired.

  Par. Dost thou hesitate?

  Ing. No; thou shalt have the flowers,

As fresh and dewy as the bush affords.   [*Goes off*, R.

Par. [*Holding out the wreath*] I never yet succeeded
    half so well:
It will be charming!—Charming? and for whom?
Here among savages! No mother here
Looks smiling on it: I am alone, forsaken!—
But no, I 'll weep no more! No, none shall say I fear!

Re-enter INGOMAR *with flowers for* PARTHENIA.

Ing. [*Aside*] The little Folko, when in his play he
    wanted
Flowers or fruit, would so cry, " Bring them to me;
Quick! I will have them: these I will have or none!"
Till somehow he compelled me to obey him:
And she, with the same spirit, the same fire —
Yes, there is much of the bright child in her.
Well, she shall be a little brother to me. —
There are the flowers.   [*He hands her the flowers.*

Par. Thanks, thanks! Oh, thou hast broken them
Too short off in the stem!
        [*She throws some of them on the ground.*
Ing. Shall I go and get thee more?
Par. No, these will do.
Ing. Tell me now about your home : I will sit here,
Near thee.
Par. Not there: thou art crushing all the flowers!
Ing. [*Seating himself at her feet*] Well, well; I will
    sit here, then. And now tell me,
What is your name?
Par.   Parthenia.
Ing.   Parthenia!

A pretty name! And now, Parthenia, tell me
How that which you call love grows in the soul;
And what love is.   'T is strange, but in that word
There's something seems like yonder ocean — fath-
    omless.
   Par.   How shall I say?   Love comes, my mother
    says,
Like flowers in the night — reach me those violets —
It is a flame a single look will kindle,
But not an ocean quench.
Fostered by dreams, excited by each thought,
Love is a star from heaven, that points the way
And leads us to its home — a little spot
In earth's dry desert, where the soul may rest —
A grain of gold in the dull sand of life –
A foretaste of Elysium : but when,
Weary of this world's woes, the immortal gods
Flew to the skies, with all their richest gifts,
Love stayed behind, self-exiled for man's sake.
   Ing.   I never yet heard aught so beautiful !
But still I comprehend it not.
   Par.   Nor I;
For I have never felt it : yet I know
A song my mother sang, an ancient song,
That plainly speaks of love, at least to me :
How goes it?   Stay —   [*Slowly, as trying to recollect.*

> *What love is, if thou wouldst be taught,*
>   *Thy heart must teach alone, —*
> *Two souls with but a single thought,*
>   *Two hearts that beat as one.*

And whence comes love?   Like morning's light,
It comes without thy call:
And how dies love?   A spirit bright,
Love never dies at all.

And when — and when —
        [*Hesitating, as unable to continue.*
Ing.   Go on.
Par.   I know no more.
Ing. [*Impatiently*] Try, try.
Par.   I can not now; but at some other time
I may remember.
Ing. [*Somewhat authoritatively*] Now go on, I say!
Par. [*Springing up in alarm*] Not now; I want
     more roses for my wreath:
Yonder they grow; I will fetch them for myself.
Take care of all my flowers and the wreath.
    [*Throws the flowers into* INGOMAR'S *lap and runs off.*
Ing. [*After a pause, without changing his position,*
    speaking to himself in deep abstraction]

Two souls with but a single thought,
    Two hearts that beat as one.

Curtain.

COSTUMES.

INGOMAR. — Leather breastplate, with copper bosses; brown,
    loose shirt; wolf's skin hung to back; helmet, shield, spear;
    fleshings and sandals.
PARTHENIA. — White merino dress, with Grecian trimming;
    amber Grecian drapery and trimming.

VENTIDIUS AND THE EMPEROR.

From Dryden's All for Love.

DRAMATIS PERSONÆ.

Marc Antony, *Emperor of Egypt.*
Ventidius, *his General.*
Two Roman Gentlemen.

Prologue.

The somewhat lengthy dialogue which we are about to render for your entertainment, is an extract from Dryden's best tragedy, entitled *All for Love.* The scene is laid in the Temple of Isis, at Alexandria, and the characters represented are Marc Antony and Ventidius, his lieutenant, than whom

> *A braver Roman never drew a sword;*
> *Firm to his prince, but as a friend, not slave.*

Antony, bound in the silken fetters of Cleopatra's love,

> *Shrunk from the vast extent of all his honors,*

had commanded that none should be admitted to his presence but the Egyptian Queen. It was Antony's birthday, and Cleopatra had proclaimed that labor should cease, and that Romans and Egyptians should give themselves over to general rejoicings. At this juncture Ventidius makes his appearance. He boldly accosts one of the queen's attendants:

> *Go tell thy queen,*
> *Ventidius is arrived to end her charms.*

He makes his way to Antony, regardless of orders to the contrary, and engages him in the scene which our actors will attempt to rehearse before you — a scene which Dryden himself preferred to any thing else he had written, of the dramatic kind.

SCENE : — *The Temple of Isis, at Alexandria. Enter* VENTIDIUS *and two* GENTLEMEN *of* MARC ANTONY.

2d Gent. The Emperor approaches, and commands, On pain of death, that none presume to stay.
1st Gent. I dare not disobey him.
       [*Exeunt the two* GENTLEMEN.
Vent. Well, I dare:
But I'll observe him first, unseen, and find
Which way his humor drives: the rest I'll venture.
       [*Withdraws.*

Enter ANTONY, *walking with a disturbed motion before he speaks.*

Ant. They tell me 't is my birthday; and I'll keep it
With double pomp of sadness.

'T is what the day deserves which gave me breath.
Why was I raised the meteor of the world,
Hung in the skies, and blazing as I traveled,
Till all my fires were spent, and then cast downward,
To be trod out by Cæsar?

    Vent. [*Aside*] On my soul,
'T is mournful — wondrous mournful!

    Ant. Count thy gains.
Now, Antony, wouldst thou be born for this?
Glutton of fortune, thy devouring youth
Has starved thy wanting age.

    Vent. [*Aside*] How sorrow shakes him!
So now the tempest tears him up by th' roots,
And on the ground extends the noble ruin.

    Ant. [*Having thrown himself down*] Lie there, thou
        shadow of an emperor!
The place thou pressest on thy mother earth,
Is all thy empire now: now it contains thee:
Some few days hence, and then 't will be too large;
When thou 'rt contracted in thy narrow urn,
Shrunk to a few cold ashes: then Octavia —
(For Cleopatra will not live to see it.)
Octavia then will have thee all her own,
And bear thee in her widowed hand to Cæsar;
Cæsar will weep — the crocodile will weep —
To see his rival of the universe
Lie still and peaceful there. I 'll think no more on 't.
Give me some music; look that it be sad:
I 'll sooth my melancholy, till I swell
And burst myself with sighing.   [*Soft music.*
'T is somewhat to my humor. Stay! I fancy

I'm now turned wild, a commoner of nature;
Of all forsaken, and forsaking all;
Live in a shady forest's sylvan scene;
Stretched at my length beneath some blasted oak,
I lean my head upon the mossy bark,
And look just of a piece, as I grew from it:
My uncombed locks, matted like mistletoe,
Hang o'er my hoary face; a murmuring brook
Runs at my foot.

    Vent. [*Aside*] Methinks I fancy
Myself there, too.

    Ant. The herd come jumping by me,
And fearless quench their thirst, while I look on,
And take me for their fellow-citizen.
More of this image, more; it lulls my thoughts.

                          [*Soft music again.*

    Vent. [*Aside*] I must disturb him; I can hold no
        longer.   [*Stands before him.*

    Ant. [*Starting up*] Art thou Ventidius?

    Vent. Are you Antony?
I'm liker what I was, than you to him
I left you last.

    Ant. I'm angry.

    Vent. So am I.

    Ant. I would be private: leave me.

    Vent. Sir, I love you;
And therefore will not leave you.

    Ant. Will not leave me?
Where have you learned that answer? Who am I?

    Vent. My emperor; the man I love next heaven.
If I said more, I think 't were scarce a sin:

You 're all that 's good and godlike.

Ant.   All that 's wretched.

You will not leave me, then?

Vent.   'T was too presuming
To say I would not; but I dare not leave you:
And 't is unkind in you to chide me hence
So soon, when I so far have come to see you.

Ant.   Now thou hast seen me, art thou satisfied?
For, if a friend, thou hast beheld enough;
And, if a foe, too much.

Vent.   Look, Emperor, this is no common dew:

                             [*Weeping.*

I have not wept these forty years: but now
My mother comes afresh into my eyes;
I can not help her softness.

Ant.   By Heaven, he weeps! poor, good old man,
       he weeps!
The big round drops course one another down
The furrows of his cheeks.   Stop them, Ventidius,
Or I shall blush to death: they set my shame,
That caused them, full before me.

Vent.   I 'll do my best.

Ant.   Sure, there 's contagion in the tears of friends:
See, I have caught it, too.   Believe me, 't is not
For my own griefs, but thine — nay, father!

Vent.   Emperor!

Ant.   Emperor! why, that 's the style of victory:
The conquering soldier, red with unfelt wounds,
Salutes his general so; but never more
Shall that sound reach my ears.

Vent.   I warrant you.

Ant. Actium, Actium! Oh!—

Vent. It fits too near you.

Ant. Here, here it lies: a lump of lead by day,
And, in my short, distracted, nightly slumbers,
The hag that rides my dreams—

Vent. Out with it; give it vent.

Ant. Urge not my shame:
I lost a battle!

Vent. So has Julius done.

Ant. Thou favor'st me, and speak'st not half thou
    think'st:
For Julius fought it out, and lost it fairly;
But Antony—

Vent. Nay, stop not.

Ant. Antony,
(Well, thou wilt have it,) like a coward, fled!
Fled while his soldiers fought; fled first, Ventidius!
Thou long'st to curse me, and I give thee leave:
I know thou cam'st prepared to rail.

Vent. I did.

Ant. I'll help thee. I have been a man, Ventidius.

Vent. Yes, and a brave one; but—

Ant. I know thy meaning:
But I have lost my reason; have disgraced
The name of soldier with inglorious ease:
In the full vintage of my flowing honors,
Sate still, and saw it pressed by other hands.
Fortune came smiling to my youth, and wooed it;
And purple greatness met my ripened years.
When first I came to empire, I was borne
On tides of people, crowding to my triumphs;

D. S.—15.

The wish of nations; and the willing world
Received me as its pledge of future peace:
I was so great, so happy, so beloved,
Fate could not ruin me; till I took pains
And worked against my fortune, chid her from me,
And turned her loose; yet still she came again:
My careless days, and my luxurious nights,
At length have wearied her, and now she 's gone —
Gone, gone; divorced forever! Help me, soldier,
To curse this madman, this industrious fool,
Who labored to be wretched! prithee, curse me!

 Vent. No.

 Ant. Why?

 Vent. You are too sensible already
Of what you 've done, too conscious of your failings;
And, like a scorpion, whipped by others first
To fury, sting yourself in mad revenge.
I would bring balm and pour it in your wounds,
Cure your distempered mind, and heal your fortunes.

 Ant. I know thou would'st.

 Vent. I will.

 Ant. Ha, ha, ha, ha!

 Vent. You laugh.

 Ant. I do, to see officious love
Give cordials to the dead.

 Vent. You would be lost, then.

 Ant. I am.

 Vent. I say you are not. Try your fortune.

 Ant. I have, to th' utmost. Dost thou think me
  desperate
Without just cause? No; when I found all lost

Beyond repair, I hid me from the world,
And learned to scorn it here; which now I do
So heartily, I think it is not worth
The cost of keeping.

Vent. Cæsar thinks not so:
He 'll thank you for the gift he could not take.
You would be killed, like Tully, would you? Do:
Hold out your throat to Cæsar, and die tamely.

Ant. No, I can kill myself; and so resolve.

Vent. I can die with you, too, when time shall
          serve;
But fortune calls upon us now to live,
To fight, to conquer.

Ant. Sure thou dream'st, Ventidius.

Vent. No, 't is you dream; you sleep away your
          hours
In desperate sloth, miscalled philosophy.
Up, up, for honor's sake! twelve legions wait you,
And long to call you chief. By painful journeys,
I led them, patient both of heat and hunger,
Down from the Parthian marshes to the Nile.
'T will do you good to see their sun-burned faces,
Their scarred cheeks, and chapped hands: there 's
          virtue in them:
They 'll sell those mangled limbs at dearer rates
Than yon trim bands can buy.

Ant. Where left you them?

Vent. I said, in lower Syria.

Ant. Bring them hither;
There may be life in these.

Vent. They will not come.

Ant. Why didst thou mock my hopes with prom-
     ised aids,
To double my despair? They are mutinous.
  Vent. Most firm and loyal.
  Ant. Yet they will not march
To succor me — O trifler!
  Vent. They petition
You would make haste to head them.
  Ant. I am besieged.
  Vent. There is but one way shut up. How came
     I hither?
  Ant. I will not stir.
  Vent. They would, perhaps, desire
A better reason.
  Ant. I have never used
My soldiers to demand a reason of
My actions. Why did they refuse to march?
  Vent. They said they would not fight for Cleopatra.
  Ant. What was it they said?
  Vent. They said they would not fight for Cleopatra.
Why should they fight, indeed, to make her conquer,
And make you more a slave? to gain you kingdoms,
Which, for a kiss, at your next midnight feast,
You'll sell to her? then she new names her jewels,
And calls this diamond such or such a tax;
Each pendant in her ear shall be a province.
  Ant. Ventidius, I allow your tongue free license
On all my other faults; but, on your life,
No word of Cleopatra! she deserves
More worlds than I can lose.
  Vent. Behold, you powers,

To whom you have intrusted humankind!
See Europe, Afric, Asia put in balance,
And all weighed down by one light, worthless woman!
I think the gods are Antonies, and give,
Like prodigals, this nether world away
To none but wasteful hands.

    Ant. You grow presumptuous.

    Vent. I take the privilege of plain love to speak.

    Ant. Plain love!—plain arrogance! plain inso-
      lence!

Thy men are cowards! thou, an envious traitor,
Who, under seeming honesty, hath vented
The burden of thy rank o'erflowing gall!
Oh, that thou wert my equal! great in arms
As the first Cæsar was, that I might kill thee
Without a stain to honor!

    Vent. You may kill me:
You have done more already — called me traitor!

    Ant. Art thou not one?

    Vent. For showing you yourself,
Which none else durst have done? But had I been
That name, which I disdain to speak again,
I needed not have sought your abject fortunes;
Come to partake your fate; to die with you.
What hindered me to 've led my conquering eagles
To fill Octavia's bands? I could have been
A traitor then — a glorious, happy traitor —
And not have been so called.

    Ant. Forgive me, soldier!
I 've been too passionate.

    Vent. You thought me false;

Thought my old age betrayed you. Kill me, sir;
Pray, kill me: yet you need not; your unkindness
Has left your sword no work.

 Ant. I did not think so;
I said it in my rage; prithee, forgive me:
Why did'st thou tempt my anger, by discovery
Of what I would not hear?

 Vent. No prince but you
Could merit that sincerity I used,   .
Nor durst another man have ventured it:
But you, ere love misled your wandering eye,
Were sure the chief and best of human race;
Framed in the very pride and boast of nature;
So perfect, that the gods who formed you wondered
At their own skill, and cried, "A lucky hit
Has mended our design." Their envy hindered,
Else you had been immortal, and a pattern,
When Heaven would work for ostentation's sake,
To copy out again.

 Ant. But Cleopatra —
Go on; for I can bear it now.

 Vent. No more.

 Ant. Thou darest not trust my passion, but thou
  mayest:
Thou only lovest; the rest have flattered me.

 Vent. Heaven's blessing on your heart for that
  kind word!
May I believe you love me? Speak again.

 Ant. Indeed I do. Speak this, and this, and this.
            [*Hugging him.*
Thy praises were unjust, but I'll deserve them,

And yet mend all. Do with me what thou wilt;
Lead me to victory; thou knowest the way.

Vent. And will you leave this —

Ant. Prithee, do not curse her,
And I will leave her; though, Heaven knows, I love
Beyond life, conquest, empire — all but honor:
But I will leave her.

Vent. That 's my royal master!
And shall we fight?

Ant. I warrant thee, old soldier,
Thou shalt behold me once again in iron;
And at the head of our old troops, that beat
The Parthians, cry aloud, "Come, follow me!"

Vent. Oh, now I hear my Emperor! in that word
Octavius fell. Gods, let me see that day!
And if I have ten years behind, take all:
I 'll thank you for the exchange.

Ant. Oh, Cleopatra!

Vent. Again!

Ant. I 've done; in that last sigh she went.
Cæsar shall know what 't is to force a lover
From all he holds most dear.

Vent. Methinks you breathe
Another soul; your looks are more divine;
You speak a hero, and you move a god.

Ant. Oh, thou hast fired me! My soul is up in
    arms,
And mans each part about me! Once again
That noble eagerness of fight has seized me;
That eagerness with which I darted upward
To Cassius' camp. In vain the steepy hill

Opposed my way; in vain a war of spears
Sung round my head, and planted all my shield:
I won the trenches, while my foremost men
Lagged on the plain below.

    Vent. Ye gods, ye gods,
For such another hour!

    Ant. Come on, my soldier!
Our hearts and arms are still the same. I long
Once more to meet our foes; that thou and I,
Like Time and Death, marching before our troops,
May taste fate to them; mow them out a passage,
And entering where the foremost squadrons yield,
Begin the noble harvest of the field.   [*Exeunt.*

COSTUMES.

Marc Antony.— Magnificent scarlet and gold Roman uniform,
    and toga.
Ventidius.— Roman general's armor.

WILLIAM TELL.

A Drama, in Three Acts.

Abridged from J. S. Knowles's William Tell.

DRAMATIS PERSONÆ.

AUSTRIANS.

GESLER, *Governor of the Waldstaetten.*
SARNEM, *his Lieutenant.*
RODOLPH,
LUTOLD, } *his Castellans.*
GERARD,
OFFICERS, ARCHERS, SOLDIERS, *etc.*

SWISS.

WILLIAM TELL.
ALBERT, *his son.*
MELCTHAL, *Erni's father.*
ERNI,
FURST, } *patriots in league with Tell:*
VERNER,
MICHAEL,
PIERRE, } *inhabitants of Altorf.*
THEODORE,
EMMA, *Tell's wife.*
SAVOYARDS, BURGHERS, MOUNTAINEERS, WOMEN, *etc.*

SCENE: — *Altorf and the neighboring mountains.*

ACT I.

SCENE I : — *The Field of Grütli; a Lake and Mountains. Enter* TELL *with a long bow.*

Tell. Ye crags and peaks, I'm with you once again!
I hold to you the hands you first beheld,
To show they still are free. Methinks I hear
A spirit in your echoes answer me,
And bid your truant welcome home again.
Hail! hail! Oh, sacred forms, how proud you look!
How high you lift your heads into the sky!
How huge you are, how mighty, and how free!
How do you look, for all your baréd brows,
More gorgeously. majestical than kings,
Whose loaded coronets exhaust the mine!
Ye are the things that tower, that shine; whose smile
Makes glad; whose frown is terrible; whose forms,
Robed or unrobed, do all the impress wear
Of awe divine; whose subject never kneels
In mockery, because it is your boast
To keep him free. Ye guards of liberty,
I'm with you once again! I call to you
With all my voice; I hold my hands to you,
To show they still are free; I rush to you,
As though I could embrace you.
    Erni. [*Without*] William! William!
    Tell. [*Looks out*] Here, Erni, here!

Enter ERNI.

Erni. Thou 'rt sure to keep the time,
That comest before the hour.

Tell. The hour, my friend,
Will soon be here. Oh, when will liberty
Be here? My Erni, that's my thought, which still
I find beside. Scaling yonder peak,
I saw an eagle wheeling near its brow:
O'er the abyss, his broad, expanding wings
Lay calm and motionless upon the air,
As if he floated there without their aid, —
By the sole act of his unlorded will,
That buoyed him proudly up. Instinctively
I strung my bow; yet kept he rounding still
His airy circles, as in the delight
Of measuring the ample range beneath,
And round about, absorbed, he heeded not
The death that threatened him. I could not shoot!
'T was liberty! I turned the shaft aside,
And let him soar away!
    Verner. [*Without*] Tell! Tell!

Enter VERNER.

Tell.   Here, Verner!
Furst. [*Without*] Tell!

Enter FURST.

Tell. Here, friends! well met. Do we go on?
Ver. We do.
Tell. Then you can reckon on the friends you
    named?
Ver. On every man of them.
Furst. And I on mine.

Erni.   Not one I sounded but did rate his blood
As water in the cause.   Then fix the day
Before we part.

Ver.   No, Erni; rather wait
For some new outrage to amaze and rouse
The common mind, which does not brood so much
On wrongs gone by, as it doth rankle with
The sense of present ones.

Tell.   [*To* VERNER] I wish with Erni,
But I think with thee.   Yet, when I ask myself
On whom the wrong shall light for which we wait,
Whose vineyard they 'll uproot, whose flocks they 'll
        ravage,
Whose threshold they 'll profane, whose hearth pol-
        lute,
Whose roof they 'll fire — when this I ask myself,
And think upon the blood of pious sons,
The tears of venerable fathers, and
The shrieks of pious mothers, fluttering round their
        spoiled
And nestless young — I almost take the part
Of generous indignation, that o'erboils
At such expense to wait on sober prudence.

Furst.   Yet it is best.

Tell.   On that we 're all agreed.
Who fears the issue, when the day shall come?

Ver.   Not I.

Furst.   Nor I.

Erni.   Nor I.

Tell.   I 'm not the man
To mar this harmony — Nor I, no more

Than any of you. You commit to me
The warning of the rest: remember, then,
My dagger sent to any one of you —
As time may press — is word enough; the others
I 'll see myself. Our course is clear. Dear Erni,
Remember me to Melcthal. Furst, provide
What store you can of arms. Do you the same.

[To ERNI and VERNER.

The next aggression of the tyrant is
The downfall of his power! — Remember me
To Melcthal, Erni, — to my father. Tell him
He has a son that was not born to him.
Farewell! When next we meet upon this theme,
All Switzerland shall witness what we do.

[Exeunt.

SCENE II : — TELL'S Cottage on the right of a mountain;
a distant view of a lake, backed by mountains of
stupendous height, their tops covered with snow,
and lighted at the very points by the rising sun,
the rest of the distance being yet in shade; on one
side, a vineyard. Enter EMMA, from the cottage.

Emma. (c.) Oh, the fresh morning! Heaven's kind
    messenger,
That never empty-handed comes to those
Who know to use its gifts. Praise be to Him
Who loads it still, and bids it constant run ·
The errand of His bounty! — Praise be to Him!
We need His care that on the mountain's cliff
Lodge by the storm, and can not lift our eyes,

But piles on piles of everlasting snows,
O'erhanging us, remind us of His mercy.

ALBERT *appears on an eminence,* L. U. E.

Alb.   My mother!
Emma.   Albert!
Alb. [*Descending and approaching* EMMA] Bless thee!
Emma.   Bless thee, Albert!
How early were you up?
Alb.   Before the sun.
Emma.   Ay, strive with him.   He never lies a-bed
When it is time to rise.   He ever is
The constant'st workman, that goes through his task,
And shows us how to work, by setting to 't
With smiling face; for labor 's light as ease
To him that toils with cheerfulness.   Be like
The sun.
Alb. (c.) What you would have me like, I 'll be like,
As far as will, to labor joined, can make me.
Emma.   Well said, my boy!   Knelt you when you
            got up
To-day?
Alb.   I did; and do so every day.
Emma.   I know you do.   And think you, when
            you kneel,
To whom you kneel?
Alb.   To Him who made me, mother.
Emma.   You have been early up, when I, that
            played
The sluggard in comparison, am up

Full early; for the highest peaks alone
As yet behold the sun. Now tell me what
You ought to think on, when you see the sun
So shining on the peak?

Alb. That as the peak
Feels not the pleasant sun, or feels it least,
So they who highest stand in fortune's smile
Are gladdened by it least, or not at all.

Emma. And what's the profit you should turn
this to?

Alb. Rather to place my good in what I have,
Than think it worthless, wishing to have more:
For more is not more happiness so oft
As less.

Emma. I'm glad you husband what you learn:
That is the lesson of content, my son;
He who finds which, has all; who misses, nothing.

Alb. Content is a good thing.

Emma. A thing the good
Alone can profit by.

Alb. My father's good.

Emma. What say'st thou, boy?

Alb. I say, my father's good.

Emma. Yes, he is good. What then?

Alb. I do not think
He is content — I'm sure he's not content;
Nor would I be content, were I a man,
And Gesler seated on the rock of Altorf!
A man may lack content and yet be good.

Emma. I did not say *all* good men find content.
I would be busy: leave me.

Alb.   You 're not angry?

Emma.   No, no, my boy.

Alb.   You 'll kiss me?

Emma.   Will I not?
The time will come you will not ask your mother
To kiss you.

Alb.   Never!

Emma.   Not when you 're a man?

Alb.   I would not be a man to see that time:
I 'd rather die, now that I am a child,
Than live to be a man and not love you!

    Emma. (c.) Live — live to be a man, and love your
      mother!

            [*They embrace.* ALBERT *enters cottage,* R.
Why should my heart sink? 't is for this we rear them;
Cherish their tiny limbs; pine if a thorn
But mar their tender skin; gather them to us
Closer than miser hugs his bag of gold;
Bear more for them than slave, who makes his flesh
A casket for the rich, purloinéd gem —
To send them forth into a wintry world,
To brave its flaws and tempests! — They must go:
Far better, then, they go with hearty will;
Be that my consolation.   Nestling as
He is, he is the making of a bird
Will own no cowering wing.   'T was fine —'t was fine
To see my eaglet on the verge o' the nest,
Ruffling himself at sight of the huge gulf
He feels anon he 'll have the wing to soar!

      [*Re-enter* ALBERT *from cottage, with bow, arrows,*
      and a target, which he sets up near R. U. E.

What have you there?

Alb. My bow and arrows, mother.

Emma. When will you use them like your father,
boy?

Alb. Some time, I hope.

Emma. You brag! There's not an archer
In all Helvetia can compare with him.

Alb. But I'm his son; and when I am a man,
I may be like him. Mother, do I brag,
To think I some time may be like my father?
If so, then is it he that teaches me;
For ever, as I wonder at his skill,
He calls me boy, and says I must do more
Ere I become a man.

Emma. May you be such
A man as he! — if Heaven wills, better! — I'll
Not quarrel with its work; yet 'twill content me,
If you are only such a man.

Alb. I'll show you
How I can shoot. [*Shoots*] Look, mother! there's
within
An inch!

Emma. Oh, fie! it wants a hand.
                    [*Going into the cottage,* R.

Alb. A hand's
An inch for me. I'll hit it yet. Now for it!
         [*Shoots again. While he continues to shoot, the
         light gradually approaches the base of the mount-
         ains in the distance, and spreads itself over the
         lake and valley.*

Enter TELL, L., *watching* ALBERT *some time in silence.*

Tell. [*Aside*] That's scarce a miss, that comes so
    near the mark.
Well aimed, young archer! With what ease he draws
The bow! To see those sinews, who'd believe
Such vigor lodged in them? Well aimed again!
There plays the skill will thin the chamois' herd,
And bring the lammergeir from the cloud
To earth. Perhaps do greater feats — perhaps
Make man its quarry, when he dares to tread
Upon his fellow-man! That little arm,
His mother's palm can span, may help, anon,
To pull a sinewy tyrant from his seat,
And from their chains a prostrate people lift
To liberty! I'd be content to die,
Living to see that day! — [*Aloud*] What, Albert!
    Alb. (C.) Ah!
My father!   [*Running to* TELL, *who embraces him.*
    Emma. [*Running from the cottage,* R.] William! —
    Welcome, welcome, William!
I did not look for you till noon.
Joy is double joy
That comes before the time: it is a debt
Paid ere 't is due, which fills the owner's heart
With gratitude, and yet 't is but his own.
And are you well? And has the chase proved good?
How has it fared with you? Come in; I'm sure
You want refreshment.
    Tell. No; I shared
A herdsman's meal, upon whose lonely chalet

I chanced to light. I 've had bad sport. My track
Lay with the wind, which to the startlish game
Betrayed me still. One only prize; and that
I gave mine humble host.
[*To* ALBERT, *who has returned to his practice*] You raise
    the bow
Too fast. Bring it slowly to the eye. [ALBERT *shoots*.
You 've missed.
How often have you hit the mark to-day?
   Alb. Not once yet.
   Tell. You 're not steady; I perceived
You wavered now. Stand firm! Let every limb
Be braced as marble, and as motionless.
Stand like the sculptor's statue on the gate
Of Altorf, that looks life, yet neither breathes
Nor stirs. [ALBERT *shoots*] That 's better!
   Emma. William, William! Oh!
To be the parents of a boy like that!
Why speak you not? and wherefore do you sigh?
What 's in your heart, to keep the transport out
That fills up mine, when looking on our child,
Till it o'erflows mine eye?   [ALBERT *shoots*.
   Tell. You 've missed again!
Dost see the mark? Rivet your eye to it!
There let it stick, fast as the arrow would,
Could you but send it there.
   Emma. Why, William, do n't
You answer me?   [ALBERT *shoots*.
   Tell. (c.) Again! How would you fare,
Suppose a wolf should cross your path, and you
Alone with but your bow, and only time

To fix a single arrow!   'T would not do
To miss the wolf!   You said, the other day,
Were you a man, you'd not let Gesler live.
'T was easy to say that.   Suppose you, now,
Your life or his depended on that shot! —
Take care! that's Gesler! — Now for liberty!
Right to the tyrant's heart! [ALBERT *shoots*] Well
  done, my boy!
Come here! — Now, Emma, I will answer you:
Do I not love you? do I not love our child?
Is not that cottage dear to me, where I
Was born?   How many acres would I give
That little vineyard for, which I have watched
And tended since I was a child!   Those crags
And peaks — what spired city would I take
To live in, in exchange for them? — Yet what
Are these to me?   What is this boy to me?
What art thou, Emma, to me, when a breath
Of Gesler's can take all?   [*Crosses*, R.
  [*While* TELL *speaks these last lines*, EMMA *draws*
  ALBERT *fondly to her.*
 Emma.   Oh, William!
 Tell.   Emma, let the boy alone;
Don't clasp him so — 't will soften him.   Go, sir:
See if the valley sends us visitors
To-day.   Some friend, perchance, may need thy
  guidance.
Away! [*Exit* ALBERT, L.] He's better from thee,
  Emma: the time
Is come, a mother on her breast should fold
Her arms, as they had done with such endearments;

And bid her children go from her to hunt
For danger, which will presently hunt them, —
The less to heed it.

Emma. (c.) William, you are right:
The task you set me I will try to do.
I would not live myself to be a slave —
I would not be the dam of one!
No! woman as I am, I would not, William!
Then choose my course for me: whate'er it is,
I will say ay, and do it, too: suppose
To dress my little stripling for the war,
And take him by the hand to lead him to 't!
Yes, I would do it at thy bidding, William,
Without a tear: I say that I would do it —
But, now I only talk of doing it,
I can't help shedding one!

Tell. When I wedded thee,
The land was free. Oh, with what pride I used
To walk these hills, and look up to my God,
And bless Him that it was so! It was free —
From end to end, from cliff to lake 't was free!
Free as our torrents are that leap our rocks,
And plow our valleys without asking leave;
Or as our peaks, that wear their caps of snow
In very presence of the regal sun!
How happy was I in it then! I loved
Its very storms! Yes, Emma, I have sat
In my boat at night, when, midway o'er the lake,
The stars went out, and down the mountain gorge
The wind came roaring: I have sat and eyed
The thunder breaking from his cloud, and smiled

To see him shake his lightnings o'er my head,
And think I had no master save his own.
You know the jutting cliff, round which a track
Up hither winds, whose base is but the brow
To such another one, with scanty room
For two abreast to pass? O'ertaken there
By the mountain blast, I 've laid me flat along,
And while gust followed gust more furiously,
As if to sweep me o'er the horrid brink:
And I have thought of other lands, whose storms
Are summer flaws to those of mine, and just
Have wished me there — the thought that mine was
     free,
Has checked that wish, and I have raised my head,
And cried in thralldom to that furious wind,
Blow on! This is the land of liberty! [*Crosses*, R.

Emma. I almost see thee on that fearful pass;
And yet, so seeing thee, I have a feeling
Forbids me wonder that thou didst so.

Tell. 'T is
A feeling must not breathe where Gesler breathes,
But may within these arms. List, Emma, list!
A league is made to pull the tyrant down,
E'en from his seat upon the rock of Altorf!
Four hearts have staked their blood upon the cast,
And mine is one of them!

Emma. I did not start: —
Tell me more, William.

Tell. I will tell thee all —

Alb. [*Without*] Oh, father!

Old Melcthal. [*Without*] Tell! Tell! — William!

Emma. Do n't you know
That voice?

Enter OLD MELCTHAL, L., *blind, led by* ALBERT.

Old M. Where art thou, William?
Tell. Who is it?
Emma. Do you not know him?
Tell. No!—It can not be
The voice of Melcthal!
Alb. Father, it is Melcthal.
Emma. What ails you, Tell?
Alb. Oh, father, speak to him!
Emma. What passion shakes you thus?
Tell. His eyes — where are they? —
Melcthal has eyes.
Old M. Tell! Tell!
Tell. 'T is Melcthal's voice:
Where are his eyes? Have they put out his eyes?
Has Gesler turned the little evening of
The old man's life to night before its time?
To such black night as sees not with the day
All round it! Father, speak! Pronounce the name
Of Gesler!
Old M. Gesler!
Tell. (c.) Gesler has torn out
The old man's eyes!—Support thy mother!—Erni—
Where's Erni? Where's thy son? Is he alive?
And are his father's eyes torn out?
Old M. He lives, my William,
But knows it not.

Tell.   When he shall know it! — Heavens!
When he shall know it! — I am not thy son,
Yet —

    Emma. [*Alarmed at his increasing vehemence*] Wil-
        liam! William!

    Alb.   Father!

    Tell.   Could I find
Something to tear — to rend — were worth it! some-
        thing
Most ravenous and bloody! — something like
Gesler! — a wolf! — no, no! a wolf's a lamb
To Gesler!   'T is a natural hunger makes
The wolf a savage : and, savage as he is,
Yet with his kind he gently doth consort.
'T is but his lawful prey he tears; and that
He finishes — not mangles, and then leaves
To live!
I'd let the wolf go free for Gesler! — Water!
My tongue cleaves to its roof!   [EMMA *goes out,* R.

    Old M.   What ails thee, William?
I pray thee, William, let me hear thy voice:
That's not thy voice.

    Tell.   I can not speak to thee!

    Emma. [*Returning,* R., *with a cup of water*] Here,
        William!

    Tell. • Emma!

    Emma.   Drink!

    Tell.   I can not drink!

    Emma.   Your eyes are fixed!

    Tell.   Melcthal — he has no eyes! [*Bursts into tears.*
The poor old man!   [*Falls on* MELCTHAL's *neck.*

Old M. I feel thee, Tell! I care not
That I have lost my eyes. I feel thy tears —
They 're more to me than eyes! When I had eyes,
I never knew thee, William, as I know
Thee now without. I do not want my eyes!

Tell. How came it, father? briefly, father! quick
And briefly! Action! action! I 'm in such glee
For work — so eager to be doing — have
Such stomach for a task, I 've scarcely patience
To wait to know what 't is! — Here, here; sit down.
Now, father!

> [OLD MELCTHAL *sits down,* C.; TELL *kneels,* L.;
> EMMA *and* ALBERT, R.

Old M. Yesterday, when I and Erni
Went to the field, to bring our harvest home,
Two soldiers of the tyrant came upon us;
And, without cause alleged, or interchange
Of word, proceeded to unyoke the oxen.

Tell. Go on.

Old M. As one stunned by a thunder-clap
Stands sudden still, nor for a while bethinks him
Of taking shelter from the storm, so we,
Confounded by an act so bold, a while
Looked on in helpless silence; till, at length,
Erni, as sudden as the hurricane,
That lays the oak uprooted ere you see
Its branches quiver, bounding on the spoilers,
Wrenched from their grasp the yoke, and would have
    smote
Them dead, had they not ta'en to instant flight.

Tell. Did he pursue them?

Old M.   No : I threw myself
Between.

Tell.   Why didst thou save them?

Old M.   'T was my son
I saved!   I clasped his knees ; I calmed his rage :
I forced him from me to the caverns of
Mount Faigel, William, till the tyrant's wrath
Might cool or be diverted.   'T was my son
I saved ; for, scarcely was he out of sight,
And I within my cottage, when the cries
Of Gesler's bands beset it, calling for
The blood of Erni !   William, he was safe —
Clear of their fangs !   My son was safe !   Oh, think —
Think, William, what I felt to see his lair,
His very lair beset, and know my boy,
My lion boy was safe !   Enough : they seized me,
And dragged me before Gesler.

Tell.   Say no more !
His life cost you your eyes   'T is worth a pair
Of eyes, but not your eyes, old man.   No, no;
He would have given it ten times over for
But one of them. — But one !   but for a hair
Of the lash ! — My bow and quiver !   [EMMA *obeys his*
      directions]   He was by?

Old M.   Was by.

Tell.   More arrows for my quiver.—
And looking on?

Old M.   And looking on.

Tell.   [*Putting arrows into his quiver*]   'T will do !
He would dine after that, and say a grace —
He would ! to tear a man's eyes out, and then

Thank God! — My staff! — He 'd have his wine, too.
      How
The man could look at it, and drink it off,
And not grow sick at the color on 't!

  [EMMA's *expression, as she equips him, catches his eye.*
Emma, I thank thee for that look!
Now seem'st thou like some kind, o'erseeing angel,
Smiling as he prepares the storm, that, while it
Shakes the earth, and makes its tenants pale,
Doth smite a pestilence. Thou wouldst not stay me?
  Emma. No.
  Tell. Nor thy boy, if I required his service?
  Emma. No, William.
  Tell. Make him ready, Emma.
  Old M. No;
Not Albert, William.
  Emma. Yes; even Albert, father.
Thy cap and wallet, boy — thy mountain staff —
Where hast thou laid it? Find it — haste! Do n't
     keep   [*Leading* ALBERT *up to* TELL.
Thy father waiting. He is ready, William.
  Tell. (L.) Well done — well done! I thank you,
    love, I thank you!
Now mark me, Albert: dost thou fear the snow,
The ice-field, or the hail-flaw? Carest thou for
The mountain mist, that settles on the peak
When thou 'rt upon it? Dost thou tremble at
The torrent roaring from the deep ravine,
Along whose shaking ledge thy track doth lie?
Or faint'st thou at the thunder-clap, when on
The hill thou art o'ertaken by the cloud,

And it doth burst around thee? Thou must travel
All night.

 Alb. I'm ready. Say all night again.

 Tell. The mountains are to cross; for thou must
  reach

Mount Faigel by the dawn.

 Alb. Not sooner shall

The dawn be there than I.

 Tell. Heaven speeding thee!

 Alb. Heaven speeding me!

 Tell. Show me thy staff. Art sure

Of the point? I think 't is loose. No — stay — 't will
  do!

Caution is speed when danger's to be passed.
Examine well the crevice; do not trust
The snow! 'T is well there is a moon to-night.
You are sure of the track?

 Alb. Quite sure.

 Tell. The buskin of

That leg's untied: stoop down and fasten it.
You know the point where you must round the cliff?

 Alb. I do.

 Tell. Thy belt is slack: draw it tight.

Erni is in Mount Faigel: take this dagger,
And give it him. You know its caverns well:
In one of them you'll find him. Bid thy mother
Farewell. Come, boy; we go a mile together.
Father, thy hand. [*Shakes hands with* OLD MELCTHAL.

 Old M. How firm thy grasp is, William!

 Tell. There is a resolution in it, father,
Will keep.

Old M. I can not see thine eye, but I know
How it looks.

Tell. I 'll tell thee how it looks. List, father,
List. Father, thou shalt be revenged! My Emma,
Melethal 's thy father: that is his home till I
Return. Yes, father, thou shalt be revenged!
Lead him in, Emma, lead him in; the sun
Grows hot; the old man 's weak and faint. Mind,
    father,
Mind, thou shalt be revenged! In, wife; in, in!—
Thou shalt be sure revenged! Come, Albert.

[EMMA *and* MELCTHAL *enter the cottage,* R.—
    Exeunt TELL *and* ALBERT *hastily,* L.

End of Act I.

ACT II.

SCENE I:—*A Mountain with mist.* GESLER *is seen
descending the mountain with a hunting pole,* R. U. E.

Ges. (c.) Alone, alone! and every step the mist
Thickens around me! On these mountain tracks
To lose one's way, they say, is sometimes death.
What, ho! hollo!—No tongue replies to me!
No thunder hath the horror of this silence!
I dare not stop! The day, though not half run,
Is not less sure to end in night; and night,
Dreary when through the social haunts of men

Her solemn darkness walks, in such a place
As this, comes wrapped in most appalling fear!
I dare not stop; nor dare I, yet, proceed,
Begirt with hidden danger.   If I take
This hand, it carries me still deeper into
The wild and savage solitudes I 'd shun,
Where once to faint with hunger is to die;
If this, it leads me to the precipice,
Whose brink with fatal horror rivets him
That treads upon it, till, drunk with fear, he reels
Into the gaping void, and headlong down
Plunges to still more hideous death!   Cursed slaves!
To let me wander from them! [*Thunder*] Ho! hollo!
My voice sounds weaker to mine ear: I 've not
The strength to call I had; and through my limbs
Cold tremor runs, and sickening faintness seizes
On my heart!   Oh, Heaven, have mercy!   Do not see
The color of the hands I lift to thee!
Look only on the strait wherein I stand,
And pity it!   Let me not sink!   Uphold —
Support me!   Mercy! mercy!   I shall die!

> [*He leans against a rock, exhausted; it grows
> darker; the rain pours down in torrents, and a
> furious wind arises.* ALBERT *is seen descending
> by the side of one of the streams, which he crosses
> with the help of his pole,* L.

Alb.   I 'll breathe upon this level, if the wind
Will let me.   Ha! a rock to shelter me!
Thanks to it! — A man, and fainting! — Courage,
    friend,
Courage! — A stranger that has lost his way! —

Take heart, take heart; you're safe. How feel you
    now?   [*Gives him drink from a flask.*

  Ges. Better.

  Alb. (L. C.) You 've lost your way upon the hill?

  Ges. I have.

  Alb. And whither would you go?

  Ges. To Altorf.

  Alb. I 'll guide you thither.

  Ges. You 're a child.

  Alb. I know

The way. The track I 've come is harder far
To find.

  Ges. (R. C.) The track you 've come! What mean
    you? Sure

You have not been still farther in the mountains?

  Alb. I 've traveled from Mount Faigel.

  Ges. No one with thee?

  Alb. No one but God.

  Ges. Do you not fear these storms?

  Alb. God 's in the storm.

  Ges. And there are torrents, too,

That must be crossed.

  Alb. God 's by the torrent, too.

  Ges. You 're but a child.

  Alb. God will be with a child.

  Ges. You 're sure you know the way?

  Alb. 'T is but to keep

The side of yonder stream.

  Ges. But guide me safe,

I 'll give thee gold.

  Alb. I 'll guide thee safe without.

Ges. Here 's earnest for thee. [*Offers gold*] Here.
   I 'll double that —
Yea, treble it — but let me see the gate
Of Altorf. Why do you refuse the gold?
Take it.
   Alb. No.
   Ges. You shall.
   Alb. I will not.
   Ges. Why?
   Alb. Because
I do not covet it; and, though I did,
It would be wrong to take it as the price
Of doing one a kindness.
   Ges. Ha! who taught
Thee that?
   Alb. My father.
   Ges. Does he live in Altorf?
   Alb. No; in the mountains.
   Ges. How! — a mountaineer?
He should become a tenant of the city:
He 'd gain by it.
   Alb. Not so much as he might lose by it.
   Ges. What might he lose by it?
   Alb. Liberty.
   Ges. Indeed!
He also taught thee that?
   Alb. He did.
   Ges. His name?
   Alb. This is the way to Altorf, sir.
   Ges. I 'd know
Thy father's name.

Alb. The day is wasting : we
Have far to go.

Ges. Thy father's name, I say?

Alb. I will not tell it thee.

Ges. Not tell it me?
Why?

Alb. You may be an enemy of his.

Ges. May be a friend.

Alb. May be : but should you be
An enemy, although I would not tell you
My father's name, I'd guide you safe to Altorf.
Will you follow me?

Ges. Ne'er mind thy father's name :
What would it profit me to know it? Thy hand!
We are not enemies.

Alb. I never had
An enemy.

Ges. Lead on.

Alb. Advance your staff
As you descend, and fix it well. Come on.

Ges. What, must we take that steep?

Alb. 'T is nothing. Come,
I'll go before. Ne'er fear. Come on! come on!
[*Exeunt, L.*

SCENE II :— *The Gate of Altorf.* *Enter* GESLER *and*
ALBERT, R.

Alb. You're at the gate of Altorf. [*Returning,* R.

Ges. Tarry, boy!

Alb. I would be gone — I'm waited for

Ges. Come back!

Who waits for thee? Come, tell me; I am rich
And powerful, and can reward.

Alb. (R.) 'T is close
On evening: I have far to go: I 'm late.

Ges. (C.) Stay! I can punish, too.

Alb. I might have left you,
When on the hill I found you fainting, with
The mist around you: but I stopped and cheered you.
Till to yourself you came again. I offered
To guide you, when you could not find the way;
And I have brought you to the gate of Altorf.

Ges. Boy, do you know me?

Alb. No.

Ges. Why fear you, then,
To trust me with your father's name?—Speak.

Alb. Why
Do you desire to know it?

Ges. You have served me,
And I would thank him, if I chanced to pass
His dwelling.

Alb. 'T would not please him that a service
So trifling should be made so much of.

Ges. Trifling?
You 've saved my life.

Alb. Then do not question me,
But let me go.

Ges. When I have learned from thee
Thy father's name. What, ho! [*Knocks at gate*, C. F.

Sentinel [*Within*] Who 's there?

Ges. Gesler! [*The gate is opened.*

Alb. Ha, Gesler!

Ges. [*To* SOLDIERS] Seize him!—Wilt thou tell me
Thy father's name!

Alb. No!

Ges. I can bid them cast thee
Into a dungeon! Wilt thou tell it now?

Alb. No!

Ges. I can bid them strangle thee! Wilt tell it?

Alb. Never!

Ges. Away with him! Send Sarnem to me.

[SOLDIERS *take off* ALBERT *through the gate.*

Behind that boy I see the shadow of
A hand must wear my fetters, or 't will try
To strip me of my power. I have felt to-day
What 't is to live at others' mercy. I
Have tasted fear to very sickness, and
Owed to a peasant boy my safety — ay,
My life! and there does live the slave can say
Gesler's his debtor! How I loathed the free
And fearless air with which he trod the hill!
Yea, though the safety of his steps was mine,
Oft as our pathway brinked the precipice,
I wished to see him miss his footing, and
Roll over! But he's in my power! — Some way
To find the parent nest of this fine eaglet,
And harrow it! I'd like to clip the broad
And full-grown wing that taught his tender pinion
So bold a flight!

Enter SARNEM *through the gate,* C. F.

Ho, Sarnem! Have the slaves
Attended me, returned?

Sar. They have.

Ges. You'll see

That every one of them be laid in chains!

Sar. I will.

Ges. Didst see the boy?

Sar. That passed me?

Ges. Yes.

Sar. A mountaineer.

Ges. You'd say so, saw you him

Upon the hills: he walks them like their lord!

I tell thee, Sarnem, looking on that boy,

I felt I was not master of those hills.

He has a father! Neither promises

Nor threats could draw from him his name — a father

Who talks to him of liberty! I fear

That man.

Sar. He may be found.

Ges. He must; and, soon

As found, disposed of. I can see the man!

He is as palpable to my sight as if

He stood like you before me. I can see him

Scaling that rock; yea, I can feel him, Sarnem,

As I were in his grasp, and he about

To hurl me o'er yon parapet! I live

In danger till I find that man. Send parties

Into the mountains, to explore them far

And wide; and if they chance to light upon

A father who expects his child, command them

To drag him straight before us. Sarnem, Sarnem,

They are not yet subdued! Some way to prove

Their spirit! — Take this cap, and have it set

Upon a pole in the market-place, and see
That one and all do bow to it: whoe'er
Resists, or pays the homage sullenly,
Our bonds await him! Sarnem, see it done.

             [*Exit* SARNEM *through the gate,* C.

We need not fear the spirit that would rebel,
But dares not. That which dares, we will not fear.

[*Exit, accompanied by* SOLDIERS, *through the gate,* C.

SCENE III:—*The Market-place.* BURGHERS *and* PEAS-
ANTS, *with* PIERRE, THEODORE, *and* SAVOYARDS,
discovered.

CHORUS.

Pierre. (C.) Come, come, another strain.
The. (R.) A cheerful one.
Sav. (L.) What shall it be?
The. No matter, so 't is gay.
Begin!
Sav. You 'll join the burden?
The. Never fear.
Go on!

    [SAVOYARD *plays and sings, during which* TELL
    and VERNER *enter,* L. S. E. TELL *leans upon his*
    bow, and listens gloomily.

    The Savoyard, from clime to clime,
    Tunes his strain and sings his rhyme;
    And still, whatever clime he sees,
    His eye is bright, his heart 's at ease:

For gentle, simple —all reward
The labors of the Savoyard.

The rich forget their pride, the great
Forget the splendor of their state,
Whene'er the Savoyard they meet,
And list his song, and say 't is sweet;
For titled, wealthy — none regard
The fortune of the Savoyard.

But never looks his eye so bright,
And never feels his heart so light,
As when in beauty's smile he sees
His strain is sweet, his rhyme doth please:
Oh, that 's the praise doth best reward
The labors of the Savoyard.

But though the rich retained their pride,
And though the great their praise denied,
Though beauty pleased his song to slight,
His heart would smile, his eye be bright:
His strain itself would still reward
The labors of the Savoyard.

[*They shout, and laughingly accompany the* SA-
VOYARDS *to* R. U. E.

Tell.   What 's the heart worth that lends itself to
          glee,
With argument like theirs for bitterness?
Or is it the melancholy sport of grief
To look on pleasures, and to handle them,
That, when it lays the precious jewels down,
It may perceive its poverty the more?   [*A laugh.*

Methinks those cheeks are not exactly dressed
, To please the hearts that own them.

Ver. Doubt it not:
They feel their thralldom.

Tell. (L.) So they should — that's hope:
I'd have it gall them — eat into their flesh!
Long as they fester, there's a remedy:
But for your callous slave I know no cure!
To-morrow brings the test will surely prove them.
You'll not forget the hour? [*Crosses,* c.

Ver. Be sure I will not.

Tell. Erni is warned ere this; and Furst, I've said,
Is ready. Fare you well. [*Going,* R.

Ver. Stay, William! Now
Observe the people.

> [*The people have gathered to one side, and look
> in the opposite direction with apprehension and
> trouble; those who had gone off, return,* R. U. E.

Tell. Ha! they please me now:
That's honest — that's sincere. I still preferred
The seasons like themselves. Let summer laugh,
But give me winter with a hearty scowl:
None of your hollow sunshine — fogs and clouds
Become it best. I like them now: their looks
Are just in season. There has surely been
Some shifting of the wind, upon such brightness
To bring so sudden lowering.

Ver. We shall see.

Pierre. 'T is Sarnem!

The. [*Looking out,* R. U. E.] What is that he brings
    with him?

Pierre.   A pole; and on the top of it, a cap
That looks like Gesler's.   I could pick it from
A hundred!
  The.   So could I: my heart hath oft
Leaped at the sight of it!   What comes he now
To do?

Enter SARNEM, R. U. E., *with* SOLDIERS, *bearing* GES-
  LER'S *cap upon a pole, which he fixes into the
  ground,* C., *the people looking on in silence and
  amazement.   The guards station themselves behind
  the pole.*

  Sar.   Ye men of Altorf!
Behold the emblem of your master's power
And dignity!   This is the cap of Gesler,
Your Governor.   Let all bow down to it
Who owe him love and loyalty.   To such
As shall refuse this lawful homage, or
Accord it sullenly, he shows no grace,
But dooms them to the penalty of bondage,
Till they're instructed.   'T is no less their gain
Than duty to obey their master's mandate.
Conduct the people hither, one by one,
To bow to Gesler's cap.
  Tell.   Have I my hearing?
  [PEASANTS *pass from* L. *to* R., *taking off their hats
    and bowing to* GESLER'S *cap as they pass.*
  Ver.   Away! away!
  Tell. (R.) Or sight?—They do it, Verner,
They do it!—Look!—Ne'er call me man again!

I 'll herd with baser animals! They keep
Their stations: still the dog 's a dog; the reptile
Doth know his proper rank, and sinks not to
The uses of the grade below him. — Man!
Man! that exalts his head above them all,
Doth ape them all! He 's man and he 's the reptile!
Look! — Look! Have I the outline of that caitiff,
Who to the tyrant's feather bends his crown,
The while he loathes the tyrant?

   Ver. Come away,
Before they mark us.

   Tell. No! no! Since I 've tasted,
I 'll e'en feed on.
I 'gin, methinks, to like it.

     [PIERRE *passes the cap, smiles, and bows slightly.*

   Sar. (L.) What smiled you at?

   Pierre. I bowed as low as he did.

   Sar. Nay, but you smiled. How dared you smile?
Take that!   [*Striking him.*
Remember, when you do smile again, to do it
In season.

   Tell. Good, good!

   Ver. [*Takes hold of* TELL's *arm*] Come away.

   Tell. Not yet — not yet.
Why would you have me quit. The feast, methinks,
Grows richer and richer?

   Ver. You change color.

   Tell. Do I?
And so do you.

   Sar. [*Striking another*] Bow lower, slave!

   Tell. Do you feel
    D. S.—18.

That blow? My flesh doth tingle with it. Well done!
How pleasantly the rascal lays it on!
Well done! well done! I would it had been I!

    Ver. You tremble, William. Come, you must not
       stay.

    Tell. Why not? What harm is there? I tell thee,
       Verner,

I know no difference 'twixt enduring wrong,
And living in the fear on 't. I wear
The tyrant's fetters, when it only wants
His nod to put them on; and bear his stripes,
When, that I suffer them, he needs but hold
His finger up. Verner, you 're not the man
To be content because a villain's mood
Forbears. You 're right — you 're right! Have with
    you, Verner.   [*Going,* R.

          Enter MICHAEL, L.

    Sar. Bow, slave!   [TELL *stops and turns.*
    Mic. For what?   [*Laughs.*
    Sar. Obey, and question then.
    Mic. I 'll question now; perhaps not then obey.
    Tell. A man! a man!
    Sar. 'T is Gesler's will that all
Bow to that cap.
    Mic. Were it thy lady's cap,
I 'd courtesy to it.
    Sar. Do you mock us, friend?
    Mic. Not I. I 'll bow to Gesler, if you please,
But not his cap; nor cap of any he
In Christendom!   [*Crosses,* C.

Sar. I see you love a jest; but jest not now,
Else you may make us mirth, and pay for it, too.
Bow to the cap! Do you hear?
   Mic. I do.
   Tell. Well done! A man! I swear, a man!
The lion thinks as much of cowering
As he does.
   Sar. Once for all, bow to that cap!
   Tell. Verner, let go my arm!
   Sar. Do you hear me, slave?
   Mic. Slave!
   Tell. Let me go!
   Ver. He is not worth it, Tell:
A wild and idle gallant of the town.
   Tell. A man!—I 'll swear, a man!—Do n't hold
      me, Verner!
Verner, let go my arm! Do you hear me, man?
You must not hold me, Verner.
   Sar. Villain, bow
To Gesler's cap!
   Mic. No—not to Gesler's self!   [*Crosses*, L.
   Sar. Seize him!
   Tell. [*Rushing forward*, c.] Off, off, you base and
      hireling pack!
Lay not your brutal touch upon the thing
God made in his own image! Crouch yourselves!
'T is your vocation, which you should not call
On free-born men to share with you, who stand
Erect, except in presence of their God
Alone!
   Sar. What! shrink you, cowards? Must I do

Your duty for you?

   Tell.   Let them but stir! — I 've scattered
A flock of hungry wolves outnumbering them —
For sport I did it — sport! I scattered them
With but a staff not half so thick as this.

      [*Wrests* Sarnem's *weapon from him.* Sarnem
        and Soldiers *fly,* R. U. E.

What! Ha! beset by hares! Ye men of Altorf,
What fear ye? See what things you fear — the
    shows
And surfaces of men! Why stand you wondering
    there?
Why look you on a man that 's like yourselves,
And see him do the deeds yourselves might do,
And act them not? Or know you not yourselves?
Why gaze you still with blanchéd cheeks upon me?
Lack you the manhood even to look on,
And see bold deeds achieved by others' hands?
Or is it that cap still holds you thralls to fear?
Be free, then! There! Thus do I trample on
The insolence of Gesler!   [*Throws down the pole.*
   Sar. [*Suddenly entering with* Soldiers, R.] Seize
    him!

      [*All the people, except* Verner *and* Michael, *fly.*
   Tell. Surrounded!
   Mic. Stand! — I 'll back thee!
   Ver. Madman!   [*Forces* Michael *off,* L.
   Sar. Upon him, slaves! — upon him all at once!
    [Tell, *after a struggle, is secured and thrown to
      the ground, where they chain him, breathless
      with indignation.*

Tell. (c.) Slaves!

Sar. Rail on: thy tongue has yet its freedom.

Tell. Slaves!

Sar. On to the castle with him — forward!

Tell. Slaves!

Sar. Away with him!

Tableau.

End of Act II.

ACT III.

Scene I: — *A Chamber in the Castle. Enter* Gesler, *with* Rodolph, Lutold, Gerard, *and Officers,* R.

Ges. (c.) [*To* Rodolph] Double the guards! —
    Stay! Place your trustiest men
At the postern! — Stop! You'd go with half your
    errand:
I'll tell you when to go. Let every soul
Within the walls be under arms! the sick
That do not keep their beds, or can rise from them,
Must take a weapon; can they only raise
A hand, we've use for them. Away, now!
Tumult   [*Exit* Rodolph, c. d. f.
Under our very brows! The slaves will come
In torrents from the hills, and, like a flood,
O'erwhelm us! [*To* Lutold] Lutold, 'tis our final
    order,

On pain of death, no quarter shall be given!
Another word: let them be men this once,
I promise them the sacking of the town!
Without reserve, I give it them — of property
Or soul! I 've nothing further, sir.

      I 'll raze   [*Exit* LUTOLD, C. D. F.
Their habitations, hunt them from their hills,
Exterminate them, ere I 'll live in fear!
What word now? [*To* RODOLPH, *who re-enters,* C. D. F.

    Rod. (R. C.) 'T was a false alarm. The people
Paid prompt submission to your order: one
Alone resisted, whom they have secured,
And bring in chains before you.

    Ges. (L. C.) So! — I breathe
Again! 'T was false, then, that our soldiers fled?

    Rod. 'T was but a party of them fled, my lord;
Which, reïnforced, returned and soon o'erpowered
The rash offender.

    Ges. What! fled they from one —
A single man? How many were there?

    Rod. Four,
With Sarnem.

    Ges. Sarnem! Did he fly?

    Rod. He did;
But 't was for succor.

    Ges. Succor! — One to four,
And four need succor! I begin to think
We 're sentineled by effigies of men,
Not men themselves. And Sarnem, too! What kind
Of man is he can make a tiger cower?
Yea, and with backers! I should like to see

That man.

    Rod   He's here.   [*Door in* F. *opens.*

    Ges. I'm on the hills again!

I see their bleak tops looking down upon me,

And think I hear them ask me, with a scowl,

If I would be their master. Do not sheathe

Your swords!—Stand near me!—Beckon some of
      those

About me: I would be attended. If

He stirs, dispatch him!

    Rod. He's in chains, my lord.

    Ges. I see — I see he is.

Enter SARNEM *and* SOLDIERS, *with* TELL *in chains,*
                 C. D. F.

    Sar. Down, slave!

Behold the Governor! Down! down! and beg

For mercy!

    Ges. [*Seated,* R.] Does he hear?

    Sar. Debate it not:

Be prompt. Submission, slave! Thy knee! thy knee!

Or with thy life thou playest!

    Rod. (R.) Let's force him to

The ground.

    Ges. Can I believe my eyes? He smiles!

    Rod. Why don't you smite him for that look?

    Ges. He grasps

His chains, as he would make a weapon of them

To lay the smiter dead!

Behold!

He has brought them to a pause; and there they
　　　stand
Like things entranced by some magician's spell.
They must not see me　　　　　　　　[*Rises.*
So lost.　Come, draw thy breath with ease.　Thou 'rt
　　　Gesler —
Their lord; and he's a slave thou look'st upon!
Why speak'st thou not?

　　Tell. (c.) For wonder.

　　Ges.　Wonder?

　　Tell.　Yes:
That thou shouldst seem a man.

　　Ges.　What should I seem?

　　Tell.　A monster!

　　Ges.　Ha! beware!　Think on thy chains.

　　Tell.　Though they were doubled, though they
　　　weighed me down
Prostrate to the earth, methinks I could rise up
Erect, with nothing but the honest pride
Of telling thee, usurper, to the teeth,
Thou art a monster!　Think upon my chains!
Show me the link of them, which, could it speak,
Would give its evidence against my word.
Think on my chains! think on my chains!
How came they on me?

　　Ges.　Darest thou question me?

　　Tell.　Darest thou not answer?

　　Ges.　Do I hear?

　　Tell.　Thou dost.

　　Ges.　Beware my vengeance!

　　Tell.　Can it more than kill?

Ges. Enough — it can do that.

Tell. No, not enough:
It can not take away the grace of life,
Its comeliness of port that virtue gives,
Its head erect with consciousness of truth,
Its rich attire of honorable deeds,
Its fair report that's rife on good men's tongues;
It can not lay its hands on these, more
Than it can pluck his brightness from the sun,
Or with polluted finger tarnish it.

Ges. But it can make thee writhe

Tell. It may.

Ges. And groan.

Tell. It may; and I may cry:
Go on, though it should make me groan again.

Ges. Whence comest thou?

Tell. From the mountains. Wouldst thou learn
What news from them?

Ges. Canst tell me any?

Tell. Ay:
They watch no more the avalanche.

Ges. Why so?

Tell. Because they look for thee! The hurricane
Comes unawares upon them: from its bed,
The torrent breaks and finds them in its track—

Ges. What do they then?

Tell. Thank Heaven, it is not thou!
Thou hast perverted nature in them. The earth
Presents her fruits to them, and is not thanked;
The harvest sun is constant, and they scarce
Return his smile; their flocks and herds increase,

D. S.—19.

And they look on as men who count a loss;
They hear of thriving children born to them,
And never shake the teller by the hand;
While those they have, they see grow up and flourish,
And think as little of caressing them,
As they were things a deadly plague had smit: —
There's not a blessing Heaven vouchsafes them, but
The thought of thee converts into a curse;
As something they must lose, and richer were
Forever to have lacked.

 Ges. That pleases me! I'd have them like their
   peaks
That never smile, though joyous summer tempt
Them e'er so much.

 Tell. Nay, but they sometimes smile.
 Ges. Ay! when is that?   [*Crosses*, L.
 Tell. When they discourse of vengeance!
 Ges. Vengeance! Dare
They talk of that?

 Tell. Ay, and expect it, too.
 Ges. From whence?
 Tell. From Heaven!
 Ges From Heaven?
 Tell. And from the hands
Which they lift up to it on every hill,
For justice on thee.

 Ges. Where's thy abode?
 Tell. I told thee: in the mountains.
 Ges. How lies it — north or south?
 Tell. Nor north, nor south.
 Ges. Is it to the east or west, then?

Tell. Where it lies,
Concerns thee not.

Ges. It does.

Tell. And if it does, thou shalt not learn.

Ges. Art married?

Tell. Married! — Yes.

Ges. And hast a family?

Tell. A son.

Ges. A son!   [*Crosses,* R., *and sits.*
Sarnem!   [*Calls* SARNEM, *who crosses to him.*

Sar. My lord! The boy?

    [GESLER *signs* SARNEM *to keep silence, and, whispering, sends him off,* L.

Tell. [*Aside*] The boy! — What boy?
Is it mine? and have they netted my young fledgeling?
Now Heaven support me, if they have! He'll own me,
And share his father's ruin! But a look
Would put him on his guard; yet how to give it!
Now, heart, thy nerve! Forget thou 'rt flesh — be rock!
They come — they come! That step —
That step — so light upon the ground,
How heavy does it fall upon my heart!
I feel my child! — 't is he!
We can but perish.

Enter SARNEM *with* ALBERT, *whose eyes are riveted on* TELL's *bow, which* SARNEM *carries,* L.

Alb. [*Aside*] I was right: it is my father's bow;
For there's my father. I'll not own him, though.

Sar. See!

Alb. What?   •

Sar. Look there!

Alb. What would you have
Me see?

Sar. Thy father.

Alb. That is not my father, sir.

Tell. [*Aside*] My boy! my boy! — my own brave
   boy! He's safe!

Sar. [*Aside to* GESLER] They're like each other.

Ges. Yet I see no sign
Of recognition to betray the tie
That binds a father and his child.

Sar. My lord,
I'm sure it is his father. Look at them:
The boy did spring from him, or never cast
Came from the mold it fitted. It may be
A preconcerted thing 'gainst such a chance,
That they survey each other coldly thus.
Besides, with those who lead the mountain life.
The passions are not taken by surprise
As ready as with us.

Ges. [*Rises*] We shall try.
Lead forth the caitiff.

Sar. To a dungeon?

Ges. No:
Into the court.

Sar. The court, my lord?

Ges. And tell
The headsman to make ready. — Quick! He dies!
The slave shall die! — You marked the boy?

Sar. I did:

He started. — 'T is his father!

Ges. We shall see. —

Away with him!

Tell. Stop! — stay!

Ges. What would you?

Tell. Time —

A little time, to call my thoughts together.

Ges. Thou shalt not have a minute!

Tell. Some one, then,

To speak with.

Ges. Hence with him!

Tell. A moment — stop!

Let me speak to the boy.

Ges. Is he thy son?

Tell. And if

He were, art thou so lost to nature as

To send me forth before his face to die?

Ges. Well, speak with him. — Now, Sarnem, mark

them well.   [ALBERT *goes to* TELL.

Tell. Thou dost not know me, boy; and well for

thee

Thou dost not. I am the father of a son

About thy age. I dare not tell thee where

To find him, lest he should be found of those

'T were not so safe for him to meet with. Thou,

I see, wast born, like him, upon the hills.

If thou shouldst 'scape thy present thralldom, thou

May'st chance to cross him: if thou should'st, I pray

thee,

Relate to him what has been passing here,

And say I laid my hand upon thy head,
And said to thee — if he were here, as thou art —
Thus would I bless him : May'st thou live, my boy,
To see thy country free, or die for her,
As I do!   [*Crosses*, L.

   Sar.   Mark! — He weeps!

   Tell.   Were he my son,
He would not shed a tear : he would remember
The cliff where he was bred, and learned to scan
A thousand fathoms' depth of nether air;
Where he was trained to hear the thunder talk,
And meet the lightning eye to eye! where last
We spoke together — when I told him death
Bestowed the brightest gem that graces life,
Embraced for virtue's sake. — He shed a tear!

                              [*Crosses*, C.

Now, were he by, I'd talk to him; and his cheek
Should never blanch, nor moisture dim his eye:
I'd talk to him —

   Sar.   He falters.

   Tell. [*Aside*] 'T is too much!
And yet it must be done! — I'd talk to him —

   Ges.   Of what?

   Tell. [*Turns to* GESLER] The mother, tyrant, whom
     thou dost make
A widow of!   I'd talk to him of her.

                         [*Turns to* ALBERT.
I'd bid him tell her, next to liberty,
Her name was the last word my lips pronounced:
And I would charge him never to forget
To love and cherish her, as he would have

His father's dying blessing rest upon him!

Sar. You see, what one suggests, the other acts.

Tell. [*Aside*] So well he bears it, I almost give way.
My boy! my boy! — Oh, for the hills — the hills!
To see him bound along their tops again,
With liberty, so light upon his heel,
That, like the chamois, he flings behind him —

Sar. Was there not all the father in that look?

Ges. Yet 't is against nature.

Sar. Not if he believes
Owning the boy, the son belike might share
The father's fate.

Ges. I did not think of that.
I thank thee, Sarnem, for the thought. — 'T is well
The boy is not thy son: he is about
To die along with thee.

Tell. To die! for what?

Ges. For having braved my power, as thou hast.
Lead them forth!

Tell. He 's but a child.

Ges. (R.) Away with them!

Tell. (R. C.) Perhaps an only child.

Ges. No matter.

Tell. He
May have a mother.

Ges. So the viper hath;
And yet who spares it for the mother's sake?

Tell. I talk to stone! I talk to it as though
'T were flesh, yet know 't is none. No wonder: I 've
An argument might turn as hard a thing
To flesh — to softest, kindliest flesh that e'er

Sweet Pity chose to lodge her fountain in —
But still 't is nought but stone.   I 'll talk to it
No more. — Come, my boy!
I taught thee how to live, I 'll show thee how
To die!

 Ges. He is thy child?

 Tell. [*Embraces* ALBERT] He is my child!

 Ges. I 've wrung a tear from him! — Thy name.

 Tell. My name!
[*Aside*] It matters not to keep it from him now. —
My name is Tell.

 Ges. What! William Tell?

 Tell. The same.

 Ges. What! he so famed 'bove all his countrymen,
For guiding o'er the stormy lake the boat?
And such a master of his bow, 't is said
His arrows never miss! — Indeed, I 'll take
Exquisite vengeance! — Mark! I 'll spare thy life,
Thy boy's, too — both of you are free — on one
Condition.

 Tell. Name it.

 Ges. I would see you make
A trial of your skill with that same bow
You shoot so well with.

 Tell. Please you name the trial
You would have me make. [*Looks on* ALBERT.

 Ges. You look upon your boy,
As though instinctively you guessed it.

 Tell. Look
Upon my boy! What mean you? Look upon
My boy as though I guessed it! Guessed the trial

You would have me make? Guessed it instinctively?
Instinctively! You do not mean — No, no —
You would not have me make a trial of
My skill upon my child! Impossible!
I do not guess your meaning.

   Ges. ' I would see
Thee hit an apple at the distance of
A hundred paces.

   Tell. Is my boy to hold it?

   Ges. No.

   Tell. No! — I'll send the arrow through the core!

   Ges. It is to rest upon his head.

   Tell. Oh, Nature!
Thou hearest him!

   Ges. Thou dost hear the choice I give:
Such trial of the skill thou 'rt master of,
Or death to both of you, not otherwise
To be escaped.

   Tell. Oh, monster!

   Ges. Wilt thou do it?

   Alb. He will! he will!

   Tell. Ferocious monster! Make
A father murder his own child!

   Ges. Take off
His chains, if he consents.

   Tell. With his own hand!

   Ges. Does he consent?

   Alb. He does!

    [GESLER *signs to his* OFFICERS, *who take off* TELL'S
     chains; TELL *unconscious of what they do.*

   Tell. (c.) With his own hand!

Murder his child with his own hand!
The hand I 've led him, when an infant, by!
'T is beyond horror — 't is most horrible! —
Amazement! — 'T is too much for flesh and blood
To bear — I should be made of steel to stand it:
And I believe I am almost about
To turn to some such thing; for feeling grows
Benumbed within me.   [*His chains fall off.*
Villains! [*To the* GUARDS] put on my chains again!
      My hands
Are free from blood, and have no gust for it,
That they would drink my child's! — Here! here!
      I 'll not
Murder my boy for Gesler!
    Alb. Father — father!
You will not hit me, father!
    Tell. Hit thee! send
The arrow through thy brain! or, missing that,
Shoot out an eye! or, if thine eye escapes,
Mangle the cheek I 've seen thy mother's lips
Cover with kisses! — Hit thee! hit a hair
Of thee, and cleave thy mother's heart! Who is he
That bids me do it? Show him me — the monster!
Make him perceptible unto my reason
And heart! In vain my senses vouch for it:
I hear he lives — I see it — but it is
A prodigy that nature can't believe!
    Ges. (R.) Dost thou consent?
    Tell. Give me my bow and quiver.
    Ges. For what?
    Tell. To shoot my boy!

Alb. No, father! no:
To save me! You 'll be sure to hit the apple.
Will you not save me, father?

Tell. Lead me forth —
I 'll make the trial!

Alb. Thank you!

Tell. Thank me! Do
You know for what? — I will not make the trial,
To take him to his mother in my arms,
And lay him down a corse before her! [*Crosses*, L.

Ges. Then
He dies this moment; and you certainly
Murder the child whose life you have a chance
To save, and will not use it.

Tell. Well, I 'll do it:
I 'll make the trial.

Alb. [*Runs to* TELL *and embraces him*] Father!

Tell. Speak not to me!
Let me not hear thy voice — thou must be dumb!
And so should all things be: earth should be dumb,
And Heaven, unless its thunders muttered at
The deed, and sent a bolt to stop it! Give me
My bow and quiver.

Ges. When all is ready.

Tell. Well!
Lead on!

       [*Exeunt* GESLER *and* SARNEM, R.; TELL, ALBERT,
        and GUARDS, C. D. F.

SCENE II : — *Without the Castle. Enter, slowly, several* CITIZENS, *as if observing something following them,* VERNER *and* THEODORE, L. U. E.

Ver. (c.) The pace they 're moving at is that of men
About to do the work of death.   Some wretch
Is doomed to suffer.   Should it be my friend —
Should it be Tell!

The. (L. C.) No doubt 't is some good man.

Ver. Poor Switzerland! poor country! Not a son
Is left thee now that 's worth the name of one!
'T is not a common man, with such parade,
They lead to death : I count four castellans
Already.

The. There 's a fifth.

Ver. And Sarnem, too.
Do you see him?

The. Yes; and Gesler follows him.
Who can it be?

Ver. We 'll see.   He 's coming now. —
'T is William Tell!

The. Verner, do you know the boy
That follows him?

Ver. A boy!   It is his son!
What horror is to be acted?   Do you see
The headsman?

The. No, I see no headsman there;
No apparatus for the work of death.
Perhaps they 're not to suffer.

Ver. Lo you how
The women clasp their hands, and now and then

Look up to Heaven! You see that some do weep.
No headsman is there; but Gesler's at no loss
For means of cruelty, because there lacks
A headsman.

Enter PIERRE, R. U. E.

Pierre. [*Rushing in*] Horrible! — most horrible
Decree! — To save his own and Albert's life,
Tell is to hit an apple resting on the head
Of his own child!

Enter, slowly, BURGHERS *and* WOMEN, LUTOLD, RO-
DOLPH. GERARD, SARNEM, GESLER, TELL, ALBERT,
and a SOLDIER *bearing* TELL'S *bow and quiver,*
another with a basket of apples; SOLDIERS, *etc.,* R.
The SOLDIERS *form on* R., *the* VILLAGERS *on* L.

Ges. (L. C.) That is your ground. Now shall they
    measure thence
A hundred paces. Take the distance.
Tell. [*Advancing to the front,* R.] Is
The line a true one?
Ges. True or not, what is it
To thee?
Tell. What is it to me? A little thing,
A very little thing; a yard or two
Is nothing here or there, were it a wolf
I shot at. Never mind.
Ges. Be thankful, slave,
Our grace accords thee life on any terms.
Tell. I will be thankful, Gesler! — Villain, stop!

You measure to the sun.

    Ges. And what of that?
What matter, whether to or from the sun?

    Tell. I'd have it at my back. The sun should
        shine
Upon the mark, and not on him that shoots.
I can not see to shoot against the sun —
I will not shoot against the sun!

    Ges. Give him his way. Thou hast cause to bless
        my mercy.

    Tell. I shall remember it. I'd like to see
The apple I'm to shoot at.

    Ges. (c.) Show me
The basket. — There!   [*Gives a very small apple.*

    Tell. (L. c.) You've picked the smallest one.

    Ges. I know I have.

    Tell: Oh! do you? But you see
The color on it is dark : I'd have it light,
To see it better.

    Ges. Take it as it is :
Thy skill will be the greater if thou hit'st it.

    Tell. True, true ; I did n't think of that : I wonder
I did not think of that. — Give me some chance
To save my boy! [*Throws away the apple with all his
        force*] I will not murder him,
If I can help it! — for the honor of
The form thou wearest, if all the heart is gone.

    Ges. Well, choose thyself.
        [*Hands a basket of apples;* TELL *takes one.*

    Tell. Have I a friend among
The lookers-on?

Ver. Here, Tell!

Tell. I thank thee, Verner!
He is a friend that does not mind a storm
To shake a hand with us. I must be brief:
When once the bow is bent, we can not take
The shot too soon. Verner, whatever be
The issue of this hour, the common cause
Must not stand still. Let not to-morrow's sun
Set on the tyrant's banner. — Verner — Verner!
The boy — the boy! Think'st thou he has the courage
To stand it?

Ver. Yes.

Tell. Does he tremble?

Ver. No.

Tell. Art sure?

Ver. I am.

Tell. How looks he?

Ver. Clear and smilingly.
If you doubt it, look yourself.

Tell. No, no, my friend!
To hear it is enough.

Ver. He bears himself
So much above his years —

Tell. I know — I know!

Ver. With constancy so modest —

Tell. I was sure
He would —

Ver. And looks with such relying love
And reverence upon you —

Tell. Man! man! man!
No more! Already I'm too much the father

To act the man. — Verner, no more, my friend!
I would be flint — flint — flint! do n't make me feel
I 'm not. You do not mind me. Take the boy
And set him, Verner, with his back to me:
Set him upon his knees; and place the apple
Upon his head so that the stem may front me —
Thus, Verner. Charge him to keep steady: tell him
I 'll hit the apple. Verner, do all this
More briefly than I tell it thee.

    Ver. Come, Albert.   [*Leading him behind.*
    Alb. May I not speak with him before I go?
    Ver. No —
    Alb. I would only kiss his hand.
    Ver. You must not.
    Alb. I must! I can not go from him without!
    Ver. It is his will you should.
    Alb. (L. C.) His will, is it?
I am content, then. Come!

    Tell. My boy!   [*Holding out his arms to him.*
    Alb. My father!   [*Running into* TELL'S *arms.*
    Tell. If thou canst bear it, should not I? Go, now,
My son, and keep in mind that I can shoot.
Go, boy — be thou but steady: I shall hit
The apple. [*Kisses him*] Go! — God bless thee! — go.
      My bow!   [SARNEM *gives the bow.*
Thou wilt not fail thy master, wilt thou? Thou
Hast never failed him yet, old servant. No,
I 'm sure of thee; I know thy honesty:
Thou 'rt stanch — stanch! I 'd deserve to find thee
    treacherous,
Could I suspect thee so. Come, I will stake

My all upon thee!—Let me see my quiver.

Ges. Give him a single arrow.

Tell. Do you shoot?

Lut. I do.

Tell. Is it so you pick an arrow, friend?
The point, you see, is blunt; the feather jagged:
That's all the use 't is fit for.   [*Breaks it.*

Ges. Let him have
Another.   [**TELL** *examines another.*

Tell. Why, 't is better than the first,
But yet not good enough for such an aim
As I'm to take. 'T is heavy in the shaft:
I'll not shoot with it! [*Throws it away*] Let me see
            my quiver;
Bring it! 't is not one arrow in a dozen
I'd take to shoot with at a dove, much less
A dove like that! What is it you fear? I'm but
A naked man — a wretched, naked man!
Your helpless thrall, alone in the midst of you;
With every one of you a weapon in
His hand! What can I do, in such a strait,
With all the arrows in that quiver? Come,
Will you give it me or not?

Ges. It matters not:
Show him the quiver. You're resolved, I see,
Nothing shall please you.

                [**TELL** *kneels and picks out an arrow.*

Tell. Am I so? That's strange —
That's very strange! — Is the boy ready?
    [*While* **TELL**, *unobserved, secures an arrow in his
    breast,* **LUTOLD** *goes out,* L., *and returns immediately.*

Lut. The boy is ready.

Tell. I'm ready, too! — Keep silence, every one!
And stir not, for my child's sake: and let me have
Your prayers — your prayers: and be my witnesses,
That if his life's in peril from my hand,
'T is only for the chance of saving it.

> [TELL *raises the bow as if to shoot, but, overcome*
> *with agitation, he lets the bow fall.*

Ges. Go on! go on!

Tell. I will! I will!
Now friends, for mercy's sake, keep motionless
And silent! [*Shoots from* R. C., *and a shout of exulta-*
> *tion bursts from the crowd.* TELL *drops on the*
> *stage.* VERNER *rushes in with* ALBERT, L.

Ver. Thy boy is safe! no hair of him is touched!

Alb. Father, I'm safe! your Albert's safe! Dear
   father,
Speak to me — speak to me!

Ver. He can not, boy.

Alb. [*To* GESLER] You grant him life?

Ges. I do.

Alb. And we are free?

Ges. You are. [*Crossing angrily behind to* L. C.

Alb. Thank Heaven! thank Heaven!

Ver. Open his vest,
And give him air.

> [ALBERT *opens his father's vest, and an arrow drops*
> *out.* TELL *starts. fixes his eyes on* ALBERT, *and*
> *clasps him to his breast.*

Tell. (C.) My boy! my boy!

Ges. For what

Hid you that arrow in your breast? Speak, slave!

Tell. To kill thee, tyrant, had I slain my son!
And now, beware! [*Suddenly takes aim at* GESLER.
Stir thou, or any stir,
This shaft is in thy heart!

> [TELL *retreats slowly, while* VERNER *removes* AL-
> BERT; GESLER *and the rest, following* TELL *with
> their eyes, remain in breathless and motionless
> suspense.*

Sar. He shoots!

Ges. Oh! [*Falls dead, transfixed with the arrow.*

Sar. Pursue him!—Hold! A host of friends
    have joined him,
And all in arms! They now advance!

Lut. On this side
Another speeds!

Sar. Back to the castle!

Lut. Look!

> [MICHAEL *and his friends appear on the ramparts.*

The castle is betrayed!

Mic. We thank you, friends,
For changing quarters with us!

Sar. Ha! Shut out!
Surrounded!

> [*Enter, on one side,* SWISS, *led by* TELL, *etc., and,
> on the other,* EMMA, *followed by* SWISS, *led by*
> ERNI.

Tell. Yield! Resistance now is hopeless!
Your lives are spared: the tyrant's will suffice!
Emma, your child!—We are free, my countrymen!
Our country is free!—Austrians, you'll quit the land

You never had a right to! And remember,
The country's never lost that's left a son
To struggle with the foe that would enslave her!

COSTUMES.

Gesler. — Green velvet tunic and cloak, trimmed with ermine; flesh legs and sandals; black cap and feathers.

Sarnem. — Russet-colored body, cloak, and trunks, trimmed with yellow, and brass buttons; white leggings and russet boots; black cap and feathers.

Lutold. — Same — green.

Melcthal. — Light brown tunic and cloak; flesh legs and sandals; gray hair; hat to match suit.

Pierre. — Brown tunic; blue hose; russet shoes; black cap.

Theodore. — Same — gray.

Officers. — Red tunics; flesh-colored legs and arms; sandals; caps with bright rims round them; swords and bands.

Archers, Soldiers. — Same — green and red.

Savoyards. — Plum-colored jackets and trunks, trimmed with red binding; white shirts; Swiss braces and hats.

Peasants. — Different-colored tunics; gray and red or blue hose; blue-black hats; russet shoes.

William Tell. — Dark brown jacket and trunks; flesh legs and sandals; loose cloak to throw across his shoulders; white shirt to draw close round the throat; cap to match suit.

Verner. — Light gray tunic; cloak to throw across shoulders; cap of same; flesh legs and sandals; white shirt.

Erni. — Same — light blue.

Furst. — Same — dark brown.

Albert. — Same — drab-colored.

Emma. — Slate-colored body and petticoat, trimmed with fur; sandals, flesh stockings, etc.

JAFFIER AND BELVIDERA.

From Otway's Venice Preserved.

DRAMATIS PERSONÆ.

BELVIDERA.	PRIULI.
JAFFIER.	PIERRE.
THE DUKE OF VENICE.	SENATORS.
GUARDS.	

SCENE I:—*A Street.* *Enter* BELVIDERA *and* JAFFIER, L.

Jaf. Where dost thou lead me? Every step I move,
Methinks I tread upon some mangled limb
Of a racked friend. Oh, my dear, charming ruin!
Where are we wandering?

Bel. (R. C.) To eternal honor!
To do a deed shall chronicle thy name
Among the glorious legends of those few
That have saved sinking nations. Every street
Shall be adorned with statues to thy honor;
And at thy feet this great inscription written:
" Remember him that propped the fall of Venice!"

Jaf. Rather, remember him who, after all
The sacred bonds of oaths and holier friendship,
In fond compassion to a woman's tears,
Forgot his manhood, virtue, truth, and honor,
To sacrifice the bosom that relieved him!
Why wilt thou damn me?

Bel. Oh, inconstant man!
How will you promise! how will you deceive!
Do return back; replace me in my bondage;
Tell all thy friends how dangerously thou lov'st me;
And let thy dagger do its bloody office!
Or, if thou think'st it nobler, let me live
Till I'm a victim to the hateful will
Of that infernal devil!
Last night, my love —

Jaf. Name — name it not again!
Destruction, swift destruction,
Fall on my coward head, if
I forgive him!

Bel. Delay no longer, then, but to the senate,

And tell the dismalest story ever uttered;
Tell them what bloodshed, rapines, desolations
Have been prepared; how near is the fatal hour.
Save thy poor country; save the reverend blood
Of all its nobles, which to-morrow's dawn
Must else see shed!

Jaf. Oh!

Bel. Think what then may prove
My lot: the ravisher may then come safe,
And, 'midst the terror of the public ruin,
Do a black deed.

Jaf. By all Heaven's powers, prophetic truth
  dwells in thee!
For every word thou speakest strikes through my
  heart
Like a new light, and shows it how it has wandered.
Just what thou 'st made me, take me, Belvidera,
And lead me to the place where I 'm to say
This bitter lesson; where I must betray
My truth, my virtue, constancy, and friends.
Must I betray my friends? Ah! take me quickly,
Secure me well, before that thought is renewed:
If I relapse once more, all 's lost forever.

Bel. Hast thou a friend more dear than Belvidera?

Jaf. No: thou 'rt my soul itself — wealth, friend-
  ship, honor!
All present joys, and earnest of all future,
Are summed in thee.   [*Going*, R.

Enter CAPTAIN *and* GUARDS, R. S. E.

Capt. Stand! — Who goes there?

Bel. Friends.

Capt. But what friends are you?

Bel. Friends to the senate and the state of Venice.

Capt. My orders are to seize on all I find
At this late hour, and bring them to the council,
Who are now sitting.

Jaf. Sir, you shall be obeyed.
Now the lot is cast, and, Fate, do what thou wilt.

        [*Exeunt* JAFFIER *and* BELVIDERA, *guarded.*

SCENE II : —*The Senate House. The* DUKE OF VENICE,
    PRIULI, *and other* SENATORS *discovered, sitting.*

Duke. Antony, Priuli, senators of Venice,
Speak : why are we assembled here this night?
What have you to inform us of, concerns
The state of Venice's honor or its safety?

Priuli. (R.) Could words express the story I've to
        tell you,
Fathers, these tears were useless — these sad tears
That fall from my old eyes : but there is cause
We all should weep, tear off these purple robes,
And wrap ourselves in sackcloth, sitting down
On the sad earth, and cry aloud to Heaven.
Heaven knows if yet there be an hour to come
Ere Venice be no more!

Duke. How!

Priuli. Nay, we stand
Upon the very brink of gaping ruin!
Within this city is formed a dark conspiracy

To massacre us all — our wives and children,
Kindred and friends; our palaces and temples
To lay in ashes: nay, the hour, too, fixed;
The swords, for aught I know, drawn even this
    moment,
And the wild waste begun. From unknown hands
I had this warning. But, if we are men,
Let's not be tamely butchered, but do something
That may inform the world, in after ages,
Our virtue was not ruined, though we were.

                    [A noise within, L.

    Capt. [*Within*] Room, room! make room there for
    some prisoners!

           Enter OFFICER, L.

    Duke. Speak, speak, there! What disturbance?
    Officer. A prisoner have the guards seized in the
    street,
Who says he comes to inform this reverend council
About the present danger.

  Enter OFFICER, JAFFIER, CAPTAIN, *and* GUARDS, L.

    All. Give him entrance. [*Exit* OFFICER] Well, who
    are you?
    Jaf. (L.) A villain!
Would every man that hears me -
Would deal so honestly, and own his title!
    Duke. 'T is rumored that a plot has been contrived
Against the state, and you 've a share in it, too.
    D. S.—21.

If you 're a villain, to redeem your honor,
Unfold the truth, and be restored with mercy.

Jaf. Think not that I to save my life came hither;
I know its value better; but in pity
To all those wretches whose unhappy dooms
Are fixed and sealed. You see me here before you,
The sworn and covenanted foe of Venice:
But use me as my dealings may deserve,
And I may prove a friend.

Duke. The slave capitulates!
Give him the tortures!

Jaf. That you dare not do;
Your fears won't let you, nor the longing itch
To hear a story which you dread the truth of:
Truth, which the fear of smart shall ne'er get from
 me.
Cowards are scared with threat'nings; boys are
 whipped
Into confessions; but a steady mind
Acts of itself—ne'er asks the body counsel.
Give him the tortures! Name but such a thing
Again, by Heaven, I 'll shut these lips forever!
Nor all your racks, your engines, or your wheels
Shall force a groan away that you may guess at!
         [*Crosses,* R.

Duke. Name your conditions.

Jaf. For myself full pardon,
Besides the lives of two-and-twenty friends,
Whose names I have enrolled. Nay, let their crimes
Be ne'er so monstrous, I must have the oaths
And sacred promise of this reverend council,

That, in a full assembly of the senate,
The thing I ask be ratified.   Swear this,
And I'll unfold the secrets of your danger.

Duke.   Propose the oath.

Jaf. (c.)   By all the hopes
You have of peace and happiness hereafter,
Swear!

Duke.   We swear!

Jaf.   And, as ye keep the oath,
May you and your posterity be blessed
Or cursed forever!

Duke.   Else be cursed forever!

Jaf.   Then here's the list, and with it the full dis-
closure [*Delivers two papers to the* OFFICER, *who*
Of all that threaten you.   *hands them to the* DUKE.
Now, Fate, thou hast caught me!

Duke.   Give order that all diligent search be made
To seize these men: their characters are public.
The paper intimates their rendezvous
To be at the house of the famed Grecian courtesan,
Called Aquilina: see that place secured.
You, Jaffier, must with patience bear till morning
To be our prisoner.

Jaf.   Would the chains of death
Had bound me fast ere I had known this minute!

Duke.   Captain, withdraw your prisoner.

Jaf. [*To* OFFICER] Sir, if possible,
Lead me where my own thoughts themselves may
lose me;
Where I may doze out what I've left of life;
Forget myself and this day's guilt and falsehood.

Cruel remembrance! how shall I appease thee?

                         [*Exit, guarded*, R.

Officer. [*Without*] More traitors! Room, room,
    room! make room there!

Duke. How is this?
The treason is
Already at the doors!

Enter OFFICER *and* CAPTAIN, L.

Officer. My lords, more traitors!
Seized in the very act of consultation;
Furnished with arms and instruments of mischief.—
Bring in the prisoners!

Enter PIERRE *and other* PRISONERS *in chains*, L.

Pierre. (L.) You, my lords and fathers,
(As you are pleased to call yourselves,) of Venice!
If you set here to guide the course of justice,
Why these disgraceful chains upon the limbs
That have so often labored in your service?
Are these the wreaths of triumph you bestow
On those that bring you conquest home, and honors?

Duke. Go on: you shall be heard, sir.

Pierre. (L. C.) Are these the trophies I've deserved
    for fighting
Your battles with confederated powers?
When winds and seas conspired to overthrow you,
And brought the fleets of Spain to your own harbors;

When you, great duke, shrunk trembling in your
    palace,
Stepped not I forth and taught your loose Venetians
The task of honor and the way to greatness?
Raised you from your capitulating fears,
To stipulate the terms of sued-for peace?
And this my recompense! If I 'm a traitor,
Produce my charge; or show the wretch that 's base
And brave enough to tell me I 'm a traitor!

       [*Goes to the table.*

 Duke. Know you one Jaffier?
 Pierre. Yes, and know his virtue.
His justice, truth, his general worth, and sufferings
From a hard father, taught me first to love him.
 Duke. See him brought forth.

  Enter Captain *with* Jaffier *in chains,* R.

 Pierre. My friend, too, bound! Nay, then,
Our fate has conquered us, and we must fall.
Why droops the man whose welfare's so much mine,
They 're but one thing? These reverend tyrants,
    Jaffier,
Do call us traitors. Art thou one, my brother?
 Jaf. (R. C.) To thee I am the falsest, veriest slave
That e'er betrayed a generous, trusting friend,
And gave up honor to be sure of ruin.
All our fair hopes, which morning was to 've crowned,
Has this cursed tongue o'erthrown.
 Pierre. (C.) So, then, all 's over!
Venice has lost her freedom, I my life.

No more! [*Crosses*, L.

Duke. Say, will you make confession
Of your vile deeds, and trust the senate's mercy?

Pierre. [*Returns to* C.] Cursed be your senate!
cursed your constitution!
The curse of growing factions and divisions
Still vex your councils, shake your public safety,
And make the robes of government you wear
Hateful to you as these base chains to me!

Duke. Pardon or death!

Pierre. Death!—honorable death!

Prisoner. Death's the best thing we ask or you
can give.

Duke. Break up the council. Captain, guard your
prisoners.
Jaffier, you 're free; but these must wait for judgment.

[*Exeunt* DUKE, SENATORS, CONSPIRATORS, *and*
OFFICER.

Pierre. (C.) Come, where 's my dungeon? Lead
me to my straw:
It will not be the first time I 've lodged hard
To do your senate service.

Jaf. (R. C.) Hold—one moment!

Pierre. Who 's he disputes the judgment of the
senate?
Presumptuous rebel!—on!— [*Strikes* JAFFIER.

Jaf. (C.) By Heaven, you stir not!

[*Exeunt* CAPTAIN *and* GUARDS, R.

I must be heard! I must have leave to speak!
Thou hast disgraced me, Pierre, by a vile blow:
Had not a dagger done thee nobler justice?

But use me as thou wilt, thou canst not wrong me,
For I am fallen beneath the basest injuries:
Yet look upon me with an eye of mercy,
And as there dwells a godlike nature in thee,
Listen with mildness to my supplications.

    Pierre. (R. C.) What whining monk art thou? what
        holy cheat,
That wouldst encroach upon my credulous ears,
And cantest thus vilely? Hence! I know thee not!

    Jaf. Not know me, Pierre!

    Pierre. No — know thee not! What art thou?

    Jaf. Jaffier, thy friend — thy once-loved, valued
        friend;
Though now deservedly scorned and used most
        hardly.

    Pierre. Thou Jaffier! thou my once-loved, valued
        friend!
By Heavens, thou liest! the man so called my friend
Was generous, honest, faithful, just, and valiant;
Noble in mind, and in his person lovely;
Dear to my eyes and tender to my heart:
But thou, a wretched, base, false, worthless coward;
Poor even in soul, and loathsome in thy aspect;
All eyes must shun thee, and all hearts detest thee.
Prithee, avoid, nor longer cling thus round me,
Like something baneful that my nature's chilled at.

    Jaf. I have not wronged thee; by these tears, I
        have not!

    Pierre. Hast thou not wronged me? Dar'st thou
        call thyself
That once-loved, honest, valued friend of mine,

And swear thou hast not wronged me? Whence
    these chains?
Whence the vile death which I may meet this mo-
    ment?
Whence this dishonor, but from thee, thou false one?
    Jaf. All's true: yet grant one thing, and I've
    done asking.
    Pierre. What's that?
    Jaf. To take thy life on such conditions
The council have proposed. Thou and thy friends
May yet live long, and to be better treated.
    Pierre. Life! — ask my life! — confess! — record
    myself
A villain for the privilege to breathe,
And carry up and down this cursèd city
A discontented and repining spirit,
Burdensome to itself, a few years longer!
To lose it, may be, at last, in a lewd quarrel
For some new friend, treacherous and false as thou
    art!
No! this vile world and I have long been jangling,
And can not part on better terms than now,
When only men like thee are fit to live in it.
    Jaf. By all that's just —
    Pierre. Swear by some other power;
For thou hast broke that sacred oath too lately.
    Jaf. Then by that hell I merit, I'll not leave thee
Till to thyself, at least, thou 'rt reconciled,
However thy resentments deal with me.
    Pierre. Not leave me!
    Jaf. No: thou shalt not force me from thee.

Use me reproachfully and like a slave;
Tread on me, buffet me, heap wrongs on wrongs
On my poor head: I'll bear it all with patience;
Shall weary out thy most unfriendly cruelty;
Lie at thy feet, [*falls on his knees*] and kiss them
      though they spurn me;
Till, wounded by my sufferings, thou relent,
And raise me to thy arms with dear forgiveness.
    Pierre. Art thou not —
    Jaf. What?
    Pierre. A traitor?
    Jaf. Yes.
    Pierre. A villain?
    Jaf. Granted.
    Pierre. A coward — a most scandalous coward?
Spiritless? void of honor? one who has sold
Thy everlasting fame for shameless life?
    Jaf. [*Rising and turning*, R.] All, all, and more,
    much more; my faults are numberless.
    Pierre. And wouldst thou have me live on terms
    like thine?
Base as thou 'rt false —
    Jaf. [*Returning*] No; 't is to me that 's granted.
The safety of thy life was all I aimed at,
In recompense for faith and trust so broken.
    Pierre. I scorn it more because preserved by thee;
And as when first my foolish heart took pity
On thy misfortunes, sought thee in thy miseries,
Relieved thy wants, and raised thee from the state
Of wretchedness in which thy fate had plunged thee,
To rank thee in my list of noble friends;

All I received in surety for thy truth
Were unregarded oaths, and this, this dagger,
Given with a worthless pledge thou since hast stolen:
So I restore it back to thee again,
Swearing by all those powers which thou hast vio-
    lated,
Never, from this cursed hour, to hold communion,
Friendship, or interest with thee, though our years
Were to exceed those limited the world!
Take it — farewell — for now I owe thee nothing.

    Jaf. Say thou wilt live, then.

    Pierre. For my life, dispose it
Just as thou wilt, because 't is what I 'm tired with.

    Jaf. Oh, Pierre!

    Pierre. No more.   [*Going,* R.

    Jaf. My eyes won't lose the sight of thee,
                        [*Following.*
But languish after thine, and ache with gazing.

    Pierre. Leave me! Nay, then, thus, thus I throw
    thee from me!
And curses, great as is thy falsehood, catch thee!
                [*Drives him back. Exit,* R.

    Jaf. [*Pausing*] He's gone — my father, friend,
    preserver;
And here's the portion he has left me —
This dagger. Well remembered! with this dagger
I gave a solemn vow of dire importance:
Parted with this and Belvidera together.
Have a care, memory! drive that thought no farther!
No, I 'll esteem it as a friend's last legacy;
Treasure it up within this wretched bosom

Where it may grow acquainted with my heart,
That, when they meet, they start not from each other.
So, now for thinking. — A blow — called traitor, villain,
Coward, dishonorable coward — faugh!
Oh, for a long, sound sleep, and so forget it!—
Down, busy devil!

Enter BELVIDERA, L.

Bel. (L.) Whither shall I fly?
Where hide me and my miseries together?
Where's now the Roman constancy I boasted?
Sunk into trembling fears and desperation;
Not daring to look up to that dear face
Which used to smile even on my faults; but down,
Bending these miserable eyes to earth,
Must move in penance and implore much mercy.

Jaf. (R. C.) Mercy! kind Heaven has surely endless stores
Hoarded for thee of blessings yet untasted:
Let wretches loaded hard with guilt as I am,
Bow with the weight, and groan beneath the burden,
Before the footstool of that Heaven they've injured.
Oh, Belvidera! I'm the wretchedest creature
E'er crawled on earth!

Bel. (L. C.) Alas! I know thy sorrows are most mighty.

Jaf. My friend, too, Belvidera, that dear friend
Who, next to thee, was all my heart rejoiced in,
Has used me like a slave — shamefully used me:

'Twould break thy pitying heart to hear the story.

Bel. What has he done?

Jaf. Oh, my dear angel! in that friend I've lost
All my soul's peace; for every thought of him
Strikes my sense hard, and deads it in my brain!
Wouldst thou believe it?
Before we parted,
Ere yet his guards had led him to his prison,
Full of severest sorrows for his sufferings,
As at his feet I kneeled and sued for mercy,
With a reproachful hand he dashed a blow —
He struck me, Belvidera! by Heaven, he struck me,
Buffeted, called me traitor, villain, coward!
Am I a coward? am I a villain? tell me:
Thou 'rt the best judge, and mad'st me, if I am so!
Coward!

Bel. Oh, forgive him, Jaffier!
And if his sufferings wound thy heart already,
What will they do to-morrow?

Jaf. Ah!

Bel. To-morrow,
When thou shalt see him stretched in all the agonies
Of a tormenting and a shameful death!
What will thy heart do then? Oh, sure 't will stream
Like my eyes now!

Jaf. What means thy dreadful story?
Death and to-morrow!

Bel. (c.) The faithless senators, 't is they've de-
creed it:
They say, according to our friends' request,
They shall have death, and not ignoble bondage;

Declare their promised mercy all as forfeited:
False to their oaths, and deaf to intercession,
Warrants are passed for public death to-morrow.

Jaf. Death! doomed to die! condemned unheard,
unpleaded!

Bel. Nay, cruelest racks and torments are pre-
paring,
To force confession from their dying pangs!
Oh, do not look so terribly upon me!
How your lips shake, and all your face disordered!
What means my love?

Jaf. Leave me—I charge thee, leave me! Strong
temptations
Wake in my heart!

Bel. (L.) For what?

Jaf. No more, but leave me!

Bel. Why?

Jaf. (L. C.) Oh, by Heaven, I love thee with that
fondness,
I would not have thee stay a moment longer
Near these cursed hands!

[*Pulls the dagger half out of his bosom, and puts it
back again.*

Art thou not terrified?

Bel. No.

Jaf. Call to mind
What thou hast done, and whither thou hast brought
me.

Bel. Ha!

Jaf. Where's my friend — my friend, thou smiling mischief?

Nay, shrink not, now 't is too late; for dire revenge
Is up, and raging for my friend!—He groans!
Hark, how he groans! His screams are in my ears!
Already, see, they 've fixed him on the wheel!
And now they tear him!—Murder! perjured senate!
Murder—oh! Hark thee, traitoress, thou hast done
    this!
Thanks to thy tears and false, persuading love.
How her eyes speak! Oh, thou bewitching creature!
Madness can't hurt thee! Come, thou little trembler,
Creep even into my heart, and there lie safe;
'T is thy own citadel—ha! yet stand off! [*Going,* R.
Heaven must have justice, and my broken vows
Will sink me else beneath its reaching mercy.
I 'll wink, and then 't is done!—

    Bel. (C.) What means the lord
Of me, my life, and love? What is in thy bosom
Thou graspest at so?

      [JAFFIER *draws the dagger, and offers to stab her.*
Ah! do not kill me, Jaffier!

    Jaf. (R. C.) Know, Belvidera, when we parted last,
I gave this dagger, with thee, as in trust,
To be thy portion if I e'er proved false:
On such condition was my truth believed;
But now 't is forfeited, and must be paid for. .

        [*Offers to stab her again.*

    Bel. Oh! mercy!
    Jaf. Nay, no struggling!
    Bel. Now, then, kill me,
        [*Falls on his neck and kisses him.*
While thus I cling about thy cruel neck,

Kiss thy revengeful lips, and die in joys
Greater than any I can guess hereafter.

Jaf. I am, I am a coward! witness, Heaven,
Witness it, earth, and every being witness!
'T is but one blow; yet, by immortal love,
I can not longer bear the thought to harm thee!
           [*Throws away the dagger and embraces her.*
The seal of Providence is sure upon thee,
And thou wast born for yet unheard-of wonders:
Oh, thou wert born either to save or damn me!
By all the power that is given thee o'er my soul,
By thy resistless tears and conquering smiles,
By the victorious love that still waits on thee,
Fly to thy cruel father, save my friend,
Or all our future quiet's lost forever!
Fall at his feet, cling round his reverend knees,
Speak to him with thy eyes, and with thy tears
Melt his hard heart, and wake dead nature in him;
Nor, till thy prayers are granted, set him free,
But conquer him, as thou hast vanquished me.
          [*Exeunt* JAFFIER, R., BELVIDERA, L.

COSTUMES.

DUKE. — Crimson velvet dress, with purple robe, richly embroidered with gold.

PRIULI. — Purple velvet dress; scarlet mantle; black trunks, puffed with black satin; black silk stockings; shoes and roses; black sword; round black hat, and black plumes.

JAFFIER. — Same as Priuli, except mantle.

PIERRE. — White doublet and blue Venetian fly, embroidered;

white pantaloons; russet boots; black sword; round black
hat, and scarlet plumes.

SENATORS. — Black gowns, trimmed with ermine, and black caps.

CONSPIRATORS. — Rich Venetian dresses.

GUARDS. — Gray doublets, breeches, and hats.

BELVIDERA. — First dress — white satin, trimmed with silver;
long purple robe, richly embroidered with gold: second
dress — white muslin.

THE DUTIFUL SON.

From The Rivals, by Sheridan.

DRAMATIS PERSONÆ.

SIR ANTHONY ABSOLUTE.	CAPTAIN ABSOLUTE, *his son.*
FAG.	ERRAND-BOY.

SCENE I : — CAPTAIN ABSOLUTE's *Lodgings.* *Enter* CAPTAIN ABSOLUTE *and* FAG, R.

Fag. Sir, there is a gentleman below desires to see you. Shall I show him into the parlor?

Capt. A. Ay, you may. — Stay! who is it, Fag?

Fag. Your father, sir.

Capt. A. You puppy! why did n't you show him up directly? [*Exit* FAG, R.] Now for a parental lecture. I hope he has heard nothing of the business that has brought me here. I wish the gout had held him fast in Devonshire, with all my soul!

Enter SIR ANTHONY, R.

Sir, I am delighted to see you here, and looking so well! Your sudden arrival at Bath made me apprehensive for your health.

D. S.—22.

Sir A. Very apprehensive, I dare say, Jack!—
What, you are recruiting here, hey?

Capt. A. Yes, sir; I am on duty.

Sir A. Well, Jack, I 'm glad to see you, though I
did not expect it; for I was going to write to you on
a little matter of business. Jack, I have been con·
sidering that I grow old and infirm, and shall proba·
bly not trouble you long.

Capt. A. Pardon me, sir, I never saw you look
more strong and hearty; and I pray fervently that
you may continue so.

Sir A. I hope your prayers may be heard, with
all my heart. Well, then, Jack, I have been considering that I am so strong and hearty, I may continue
to plague you a long time. Now, Jack, I am sensible
that the income of your commission, and what I have
hitherto allowed you, is but a small pittance for a lad
of your spirit.

Capt. A. Sir, you are very good.

Sir A. And it is my wish, while yet I live, to have
my boy make some figure in the world. I have resolved, therefore, to fix you at once in a noble independence.

Capt. A. Sir, your kindness overpowers me. Yet,
sir, I presume you would not wish me to quit the
army?

Sir A. Oh, that shall be as your wife chooses.

Capt. A. My wife, sir!

Sir A. Ay, ay; settle that between you — settle
that between you.

Capt. A. A wife, sir, did you say?

Sir A. Ay, a wife! Why, did not I mention her before?

Capt. A. Not a word of her, sir.

Sir A. Odd so! I mus'n't forget her, though. — Yes, Jack, the independence I was talking of, is by a marriage — the fortune is saddled with a wife: but I suppose that makes no difference?

Capt. A. Sir, sir, you amaze me!

Sir A. Why, what the deuce is the matter with the fool? Just now you were all gratitude and duty.

Capt. A. I was, sir: you talked to me of independence and a fortune, but not a word of a wife.

Sir A. Why, what difference does that make? Odds life, sir! if you have the estate, you must take it with the live-stock on it, as it stands.

Capt. A. Pray, sir, who is the lady?

Sir A. What's that to you, sir? — Come, give me your promise to love and to marry her directly.

Capt. A. Sure, sir, this is not very reasonable — to summon my affections for a lady I know nothing of!

Sir A. I am sure, sir, 'tis more unreasonable in you, to object to a lady you know nothing of.

Capt. A. You must excuse me, sir, if I tell you, once for all, that in this point I can not obey you.

Sir A. Hark ye, Jack! I have heard you for some time with patience; I have been cool — quite cool; but take care! You know I am compliance itself — when I am not thwarted; no one more easily led — when I have my own way; — but do n't put me in a frenzy!

Capt. A. Sir, I must repeat it: in this, I can not obey you.

Sir A. Now, confound me if ever I call you Jack again while I live!

Capt. A. Nay, sir, but hear me.

Sir A. Sir, I won't hear a word — not a word! not one word! so give me your promise by a nod. And I'll tell you what, Jack — I mean, you dog — if you do n't, by —

Capt. A. What, sir, promise to link myself to some mass of ugliness!

Sir A. Zounds, sirrah! the lady shall be as ugly as I choose! She shall have a hump on each shoulder; she shall be as crooked as the crescent; her one eye shall roll like the bull's in the museum; she shall have a skin like a mummy, and the beard of a Jew! She shall be all this, sirrah, yet I'll make you ogle her all day, and sit up all night to write sonnets on her beauty!

Capt. A. This is reason and moderation, indeed!

Sir. A. None of your sneering, puppy! — no grinning, jackanapes!

Capt. A. Indeed, sir, I never was in a worse humor for mirth in my life.

Sir A. 'T is false, sir! I know you are laughing in your sleeve! I know you'll grin when I am gone, sirrah!

Capt. A. Sir, I hope I know my duty better.

Sir A. None of your passion, sir! none of your violence, if you please! — it won't do with me, I promise you.

Capt. A. Indeed, sir, I never was cooler in my life.

Sir A. 'T is a confounded lie! I know you are in a passion in your heart! I know you are, you hypocritical young dog! — but it won't do.

Capt. A. Nay, sir, upon my word —

Sir A. So, you will fly out! Can't you be cool, like me? What good can passion do? Passion is of no service, you impudent, insolent, overbearing reprobate! — There, you sneer again! Don't provoke me! But you rely upon the mildness of my temper — you do, you dog! you play upon the meekness of my disposition! Yet, take care! the patience of a saint may be overcome at last. But, mark! I give you six hours and a half to consider of this: if you then agree, without any condition, to do every thing on earth that I choose, why, confound you, I may in time forgive you; if not — zounds! don't enter the same hemisphere with me! don't dare to breathe the same air or use the same light with me, but get an atmosphere and a sun of your own! I'll strip you of your commission! I'll lodge a five-and-threepence in the hands of trustees, and you shall live on the interest! I'll disown you — I'll disinherit you — and, hang me, if ever I call you Jack again!

[*Exit,* R.

Capt. A. Mild, gentle, considerate father, I kiss your hands!

Enter FAG. R.

Fag. Assuredly, sir, our father is wroth to a degree. He comes down stairs eight or ten steps

at a time, muttering, growling, and thumping the
banisters all the way. I and the cook's dog stand
bowing at the door — rap! he gives me a stroke on
the head with his cane — bids me carry that to my
master; then, kicking the poor turnspit into the area,
damns us all for a puppy triumvirate! Upon my
credit, sir, were I in your place, and found my father
such very bad company, I should certainly drop his
acquaintance.

Capt. A. Cease your impertinence, sir! did you
come in for nothing more? Stand out of the way!

[*Pushes him aside, and exit,* R.

Fag. So! — Sir Anthony trims my master; he is
afraid to reply to his father, then vents his spleen on
poor Fag! When one is vexed by one person, to revenge one's self on another, who happens to come in
the way, shows the worst of temper, the basest —

Enter Errand-boy, R.

Boy. Mr. Fag! Mr. Fag! your master calls you.

Fag. Well, you little, dirty puppy! you need n't
bawl so — the meanest disposition, the —

Boy. Quick, quick, Mr. Fag!

Fag. Quick, quick — you impudent jackanapes!
Am I to be commanded by you, too, you little, impertinent, insolent kitchen-bred! [*Kicks him off,* R.

SCENE II: — *The Same. Enter* CAPTAIN ABSOLUTE, L.

Capt. A. 'T is just as Fag told me, indeed — whim-
sical enough, faith! My father wants to force me to

marry the very girl I am plotting to run away with! He must not know of my connection with her yet awhile; he has too summary a method of proceeding in these matters. However, I'll read my recantation instantly. My conversion is something sudden, indeed; but I can assure him it is very sincere. So, so; here he comes. He looks plaguy gruff!

[*Steps aside*, L.

Enter SIR ANTHONY, R.

Sir A. No — I'll die sooner than forgive him! Die, did I say? I'll live these fifty years to plague him! At our last meeting, his impudence had almost put me out of temper — an obstinate, passionate, self-willed boy! Who can he take after? This is my return for putting him, at twelve years old, into a marching regiment, and allowing him fifty pounds a year, besides his pay, ever since. But I have done with him; he's any body's son for me; I never will see him more — never, never, never, never!

Capt. A. Now for a penitential face!

[*Comes forward on the* L.

Sir A. Fellow, get out of my way! [*Crosses*, R.

Capt. A. Sir, you see a penitent before you.

Sir A. I see an impudent scoundrel before me!

Capt. A. A sincere penitent. I am come, sir, to acknowledge my error, and to submit entirely to your will.

Sir A. What's that?

Capt. A. I have been revolving and reflecting and

considering on your past goodness and kindness and condescension to me.

Sir A. Well, sir?

Capt. A. I have been likewise weighing and balancing what you were pleased to mention concerning duty and obedience and authority.

Sir A. Why, now you talk sense, absolute sense: I never heard any thing more sensible in my life. Confound you, you shall be Jack again!

Capt. A. I am happy in the appellation.

Sir A. Why, then, Jack — my dear Jack — I will now inform you who the lady really is. Nothing but your passion and violence, you silly fellow, prevented me telling you at first. Prepare, Jack, for wonder and rapture — prepare! What think you of Miss Lydia Languish?

Capt. A. Languish! What, the Languishes of Worcestershire?

Sir A. Worcestershire! — no. Did you never meet Mrs. Malaprop, and her niece, Miss Languish, who came into our country just before you were last ordered to your regiment?

Capt. A. Malaprop! — Languish! I don't remember ever to have heard the name before. — Yet, stay! I think I do recollect something. Languish! — Languish! She squints, don't she? — A little red-haired girl?

Sir A. Squints! — A red-haired girl! Zounds! — no!

Capt. A. Then I must have forgot: it can't be the same person.

Sir A. Jack, Jack! what think you of blooming, love-breathing seventeen?

Capt. A. As to that, sir, I am quite indifferent: if I can please you in the matter, 't is all I desire.

Sir A. Nay, but Jack, such eyes! such eyes! — so innocently wild! so bashfully irresolute! — not a glance but speaks and kindles some thought of love! Then, Jack, her cheeks! — her cheeks, Jack! so deeply blushing at the insinuations of her tell-tale eyes! Then, Jack, her lips! — Oh, Jack, lips smiling at their own discretion! and, if not smiling, more sweetly pouting — more lovely in sullenness! Then, Jack, her neck! — Oh, Jack! Jack!

Capt. A. And which is to be mine, sir — the niece or the aunt?

Sir A. Why, you unfeeling, insensible puppy! — I despise you! When I was of your age, such a description would have made me fly like a rocket! — The aunt, indeed! Odds life! When I ran away with your mother, I would not have touched any thing old or ugly to gain an empire!

Capt. A. Not to please your father, sir?

Sir A. To please my father! — zounds! not to please — Oh! my father? Odd so! yes, yes! if my father, indeed, had desired — that 's quite another matter. Though he was n't the indulgent father that I am, Jack.

Capt. A. I dare say not, sir.

Sir A. But, Jack, you are not sorry to find your mistress is so beautiful?

Capt. A. Sir, I repeat it — if I please you in this

affair, 't is all I desire. Not that I think a woman
the worse for being handsome; but, sir, if you please
to recollect, you before hinted something about a
hump or two, one eye, and a few more graces of that
kind. Now, without being very nice, I own I should
rather choose a wife of mine to have the usual number of limbs, and a limited quantity of back: and
though one eye may be very agreeable, yet, as the
prejudice has always run in favor of two, I would
not wish to affect a singularity in that article.

Sir A. What a phlegmatic sot it is! Why, sirrah,
you are an anchorite! — a vile, insensible stock!
You a soldier! you 're a walking block, fit only to
dust the company's regimentals on! — Odds life!
I 've a great mind to marry the girl myself!

Capt. A. I am entirely at your disposal, sir. If
you should think of addressing Miss Languish yourself, I suppose you would have me marry the aunt;
or, if you should change your mind, and take the
old lady, 't is the same to me — I 'll marry the niece.

Sir A. Upon my word, Jack, thou art either a
very great hypocrite, or — but, come; I know your
indifference on such a subject must be all a lie — I 'm
sure it must. Come, now — come, confess, Jack:
you have been lying, ha'n't you? you have been
playing the hypocrite, hey? I 'll never forgive you,
if you ha'n't been lying and playing the hypocrite.

Capt. A. I am sorry, sir, that the respect and
duty which I bear to you should be so mistaken.

Sir A. Hang your respect and duty! — But come
along with me. [*Crosses to* L.] I 'll write a note to

Mrs. Malaprop, and you shall visit the lady directly. Her eyes shall be the Promethean torch to you. Come along: I'll never forgive you, if you don't come back stark mad with rapture and impatience! If you don't, egad, I'll marry the girl myself!

[*Exeunt*, L.

COSTUMES.

Sir Anthony Absolute. — Light brown cloth suit, lined with crimson silk, and gold buttons; a brown great-coat, black silk plush cuffs and collar, and gold vellum button-holes; cocked hat, gold loop and cockade; white silk stockings; square-toed shoes, and buckles.

Captain Absolute. — Scarlet regimental full-dress coat; white breeches; silk stockings; cocked hat.

Fag. — Dark livery frock; buff waistcoat and breeches; glazed hat, with cockade and silver band; top boots.

THE POUND OF FLESH.

From Shakespeare's Merchant of Venice.

DRAMATIS PERSONÆ.

THE DUKE OF VENICE.
MAGNIFICOES OF VENICE.
ANTONIO, *the Merchant of Venice.*
BASSANIO, *his friend.*
GRATIANO, *friend to Antonio and Bassanio.*
SHYLOCK, *a Jew.*
PORTIA, *a rich heiress.*
NERISSA, *her waiting-maid.*
OFFICERS OF THE COURT OF JUSTICE,
JAILER, SERVANTS, AND OTHER ATTENDANTS.

SCENE:— *A Court of Justice in Venice.* The DUKE, *the* MAGNIFICOES, ANTONIO, BASSANIO, GRATIANO, *and* ATTENDANTS, *discovered.*

Duke. [*Seated,* c.] What, is Antonio here?
Ant. Ready, so please your grace.
Duke. I am sorry for thee: thou art come to an-
    swer
A stony adversary, an inhuman wretch

Incapable of pity, void and empty
From any dram of mercy.

Ant.   I have heard
Your grace hath ta'en great pains to qualify
His rigorous course; but since he stands obdurate,
And that no lawful means can carry me
Out of his envy's reach, I do oppose
My patience to his fury, and am armed
To suffer, with a quietness of spirit,
The very tyranny and rage of his.

Duke. Go one, and call the Jew into the court.

Servant. He is ready at the door: he comes, my
lord.

Enter SHYLOCK, R.

Duke. Make room, and let him stand before our
face.
Shylock, the world thinks, and I think so, too,
That thou but lead'st this fashion of thy malice
To the last hour of act, and then, 't is thought,
Thou 'lt show thy mercy and remorse, more strange
Than is thy strange apparent cruelty;
And where thou now exact'st the penalty,
Which is a pound of this poor merchant's flesh,
Thou wilt not only loose the forfeiture,
But, touched with human gentleness and love,
Forgive a moiety of the principal;
Glancing an eye of pity on his losses,
That have of late so huddled on his back,
Enow to press a royal merchant down,

And pluck commiseration of his state
From brassy bosoms and rough hearts of flint;
From stubborn Turks and Tartars, never trained
To offices of tender courtesy. —
We all expect a gentle answer, Jew.

 Shy. (R.) I have possessed your grace of what I
   purpose;
And by our holy Sabbath have I sworn
To have the due and forfeit of my bond:
If you deny it, let the danger light
Upon your charter and your city's freedom.
You'll ask me why I rather choose to have
A weight of carrion flesh, than to receive
Three thousand ducats. I'll not answer that;
But say, it is my humor: is it answered?
What if my house be troubled with a rat,
And I be pleased to give ten thousand ducats
To have it baned? What, are you answered yet?
Some men there are love not a gaping pig;
Some that are mad if they behold a cat:
Masters of passion sway it to the mood
Of what it likes or loathes. Now for your answer:
As there is no firm reason to be rendered
Why he can not abide a gaping pig,
Why he, a harmless, necessary cat,
So can I give no reason, nor I will not,
More than a lodged hate and a certain loathing
I bear Antonio, that I follow thus
A losing suit against him. Are you answered?

 Bass. (L. C.) This is no answer, thou unfeeling man,
To excuse the current of thy cruelty.

Shy. I am not bound to please thee with my answers.

Bass. Do all men kill the things they do not love?

Shy. Hates any man the thing he would not kill?

Bass. Every offense is not a hate at first.

Shy.. What, wouldst thou have a serpent sting thee twice?

Ant. (L. C.) I pray you, think you question with the Jew.

You may as well go stand upon the beach,
And bid the main flood bate his usual height;
You may as well use question with the wolf,
Why he hath made the ewe bleat for the lamb;
You may as well forbid the mountain pines
To wag their high tops, and to make no noise,
When they are fretten with the gusts of Heaven:
You may as well do any thing most hard,
As seek to soften that — than which, what harder —
His Jewish heart. Therefore, I do beseech you,
Make no more offers, use no farther means;
But with all brief and plain conveniency,
Let me have judgment, and the Jew his will.

Bass. For thy three thousand ducats, here is six.

Shy. If every ducat in six thousand ducats
Were in six parts, and every part a ducat,
I would not draw them; I would have my bond.

Duke How shalt thou hope for mercy, rendering none?

Shy. What judgment shall I dread, doing no wrong?

You have among you many a purchased slave,

Which, like your asses and your dogs and mules,
You use in abject and in slavish parts,
Because you bought them : shall I say to you,
Let them be free, marry them to your heirs?
Why sweat they under burdens? let their beds
Be made as soft as yours, and let their palates
Be seasoned with such viands. — You will answer,
The slaves are ours. So do I answer you :
The pound of flesh, which I demand of him,
Is dearly bought; 't is mine, and I will have it.
If you deny me, fie upon your law !
There is no force in the decrees of Venice.
I stand for judgment: answer, shall I have it?

    Duke. Upon my power I may dismiss this court,
Unless Bellario, a learned doctor
Whom I have sent for to determine this,
Come here to-day.

    Gra.   My lord, here stays without
A messenger with letters from the doctor,
New come from Padua.

    Duke. Bring us the letters; call the messenger.

                    [*Exit* GRATIANO, R.

    Bass. Good cheer, Antonio! What, man, courage
        yet!
The Jew shall have my flesh, blood, bones, and all,
Ere thou shalt lose for me one drop of blood.

    Ant. I am a tainted wether of the flock,
Meetest for death. The weakest kind of fruit
Drops earliest to the ground ; and so let me.
You can not better be employed, Bassanio,
Than to live still and write mine epitaph.

Enter GRATIANO *with* NERISSA, *dressed like a Lawyer's Clerk,* R., *and goes to the* DUKE.

Duke. Came you from Padua, from Bellario?

Ner. From both, my lord. Bellario greets your
    grace. [*Presents a letter.* SHYLOCK *kneels on
    one knee, and whets his knife on his shoe.*

Bass. Why dost thou whet thy knife so earnestly?

Shy. To cut the forfeiture from that bankrupt
    there.

Gra. Not on thy sole, but on thy soul, harsh Jew,
Thou mak'st thy knife keen. But no metal can —
No, not the hangman's ax — bear half the keenness
Of thy sharp envy. Can no prayers pierce thee?

Shy. [*Gets up*] No, none that thou hast wit enough
    to make.

Gra. (R. C.) Oh, be thou damned, inexorable dog!
And for thy life let justice be accused!
Thou almost mak'st me waver in my faith,
To hold opinion with Pythagoras,
That souls of animals infuse themselves
Into the trunks of men. Thy currish spirit
Governed a wolf, who, hanged for human slaughter,
Even from the gallows did his fell soul fleet;
And whilst thou lay'st in thy unhallowed dam,
Infused itself in thee; for thy desires
Are wolfish, bloody, starved, and ravenous!

Shy. (R. C.) [*Holding up the bond, and tapping it with
    the knife*] Till thou canst rail the seal from off
    my bond,
Thou but offend'st thy lungs to speak so loud.

Repair thy wit, good youth, or it will fall
To endless ruin. — I stand here for law.

Duke. This letter from Bellario doth commend
A young and learned doctor to our court.
Where is he?

Ner. He attendeth here hard by,
To know your answer, whether you 'll admit him.

Duke. With all my heart. — Some three or four
     of you
Go give him courteous conduct to this place.

     [*Exit* Gratiano *and others*, R.
Meantime, the court shall hear Bellario's letter.

Ner. [*Reads*] " Your grace shall understand, that
at the receipt of your letter I am very sick : but in
the instant that your messenger came, in loving
visitation was with me a young doctor of Rome ;
his name is Balthazar. I acquainted him with the
cause in controversy between the Jew and Antonio,
the merchant : we turned o'er many books together :
he is furnished with my opinion, which, bettered
with his own learning, the greatness whereof I can
not enough commend, comes with him, at my impor-
tunity, to fill up your grace's request in my stead.
I beseech you, let his lack of years be no impediment,
to let him lack a reverend estimation ; for I never
knew so young a body with so old a head. I leave
him to your gracious acceptance, whose trial shall
better publish his commendation."

Duke. You hear the learned Bellario, what he
     writes ;
And here, I take it, is the doctor come.

Enter Portia, *dressed like a Doctor of Laws:* Gratiano,
  R. Portia, *advancing to* c., *bows to the Court, and
  then approaches toward the* Duke.

Give me your hand. Came you from old Bellario?
Por. I did, my lord.
Duke.   You are welcome. Take your place.
                         [Portia *sits.*
Are you acquainted with the difference
That holds this present question in the court?
Por. I am informed thoroughly of the cause.
Which is the merchant here, and which the Jew?
Duke. Antonio and old Shylock, both stand forth.
        [*They stand forth.* Portia *in* c. *of stage.*
Por. Is your name Shylock?
Shy.   Shylock is my name.
Por. Of a strange nature is the suit you follow;
Yet in such rule, that the Venetian law
Can not impugn you as you do proceed. —
[*To* Ant.] You stand within his danger, do you not?
Ant. Ay, so he says.   .
Por.   Do you confess the bond?
Ant. I do.
Por.   Then must the Jew be merciful.
Shy. On what compulsion must I? tell me that.
Por. The quality of mercy is not strained;
It droppeth as the gentle rain from heaven
Upon the place beneath: it is twice blest —
It blesseth him that gives and him that takes:
'T is mightiest in the mightiest: it becomes
The throned monarch better than his crown:

His scepter shows the force of temporal power,
The attribute to awe and majesty,
Wherein doth sit the dread and fear of kings.
But mercy is above this sceptered sway:
It is enthroned in the hearts of kings:
It is an attribute to God himself;
And earthly power doth then show likest God's,
When mercy seasons justice. Therefore, Jew,
Though justice be thy plea, consider this,
That, in the course of justice, none of us
Should see salvation: we do pray for mercy,
And that same prayer doth teach us all to render
The deeds of mercy. I have spoke thus much
To mitigate the justice of thy plea,
Which, if thou follow, this strict court of Venice
Must needs give sentence 'gainst the merchant there.

 Shy. My deeds upon my head! I crave the law;
The penalty and forfeit of my bond.

 Por. Is he not able to discharge the money?

 Bass. Yes: here I tender it for him in the court —
Yea, twice the sum: if that will not suffice,
I will be bound to pay it ten times o'er,
On forfeit of my hands, my head, my heart:
If this will not suffice, it must appear
That malice bears down truth; and, I beseech you,
Wrest once the law to your authority:
To do a great right, do a little wrong,
And curb this cruel devil of his will.

 Por. It must not be: there is no power in Venice
Can alter a decree established.
'T will be recorded for a precedent,

And many an error, by the same example,
Will rush into the state. It can not be.

Shy. [*In ecstasy*] A Daniel come to judgment! —
yea, a Daniel!
Oh, wise young judge, how do I honor thee!

Por. . I pray you, let me look upon the bond.

Shy. Here 't is, most reverend doctor; here it is.
[*Gives it.*

Por. Shylock, there 's thrice thy money offered
thee.

Shy. An oath, an oath: I have an oath in Heaven.
Shall I lay perjury upon my soul?
No, not for Venice!

Por. Why, this bond is forfeit;
And lawfully by this the Jew may claim
A pound of flesh, to be by him cut off
Nearest the merchant's heart. — Be merciful:
Take thrice thy money; bid me tear the bond.

Shy. When it is paid according to the tenor.
It doth appear you are a worthy judge:
You know the law; your exposition
Hath been most sound. I charge you by the law,
Whereof you are a well-deserving pillar,
Proceed to judgment. By my soul I swear,
There is no power in the tongue of man
To alter me! I stay here on my bond.

Ant. Most heartily I do beseech the court
To give the judgment.

Por. Why, then, thus it is:
You must prepare your bosom for his knife; —

Shy. O noble judge! O excellent young man!

Por. — For the intent and purpose of the law
Hath full relation to the penalty
Which here appeareth due upon the bond.

Shy.   'T is very true, O wise and upright judge!
How much more elder art thou than thy looks!

Por.   Therefore, lay bare your bosom.

Shy.   Ay, his breast;
So says the bond : — doth it not, noble judge? —
Nearest his heart : those are the very words.

Por.   It is so.   Are there balance here to weigh
The flesh?

Shy.   I have them ready.

Por.   Have by some surgeon, Shylock, on your
        charge,
To stop his wounds, lest he should bleed to death.

Shy.   It is not nominated in the bond.

Por.   It is not so expressed ; but what of that?
'T were good you do so much for charity.

Shy.   I can not find it : 't is not in the bond.

Por.   Come, merchant, have you any thing to say?

Ant.   But little : I am armed and well prepared.
Give me your hand, Bassanio : fare you well!
Grieve not that I am fallen to this for you ;
For herein Fortune shows herself more kind
Than is her custom : it is still her use
To let the wretched man outlive his wealth ;
To view with hollow eye and wrinkled brow
An age of poverty : from which lingering penance
Of such misery doth she cut me off.
Commend me to your honorable wife ;
Tell her the process of Antonio's end ;

Say how I loved you; speak me fair in death:
And, when the tale is told, bid her be judge
Whether Bassanio had not once a love.
Repent not you that you shall lose your friend;
And he repents not that he pays your debt:
For if the Jew do cut but deep enough,
I'll pay it instantly with all my heart.

Bass. Antonio, I am married to a wife
Which is as dear to me as life itself;
But life itself, my wife, and all the world,
Are not with me esteemed above thy life:
I would lose all, ay, sacrifice them all
Here to this devil, to deliver you.

Por. Your wife would give you little thanks for
that,
If she were by, to hear you make the offer.

Gra. I have a wife, whom, I protest, I love:
I would she were in Heaven, so she could
Entreat some power to change this currish Jew.

Ner. 'T is well you offer it behind her back:
The wish would make, else, an unquiet house.

Shy. [*Aside*] These be the Christian husbands! I
have a daughter:
Would any of the stock of Barrabas
Had been her husband, rather than a Christian!
[*To* PORTIA] We trifle time: I pray thee, pursue
sentence.

Por. A pound of that same merchant's flesh is
thine:
The court awards it, and the law doth give it.

Shy. Most rightful judge!

Por. And you must cut this flesh from off his
    breast :
The law allows it, and the court awards it.
    Shy. Most learned judge ! — A sentence ! — Come,
    prepare !
    Por. Tarry a little : there is something else.
This bond doth give thee here no jot of blood :
The words expressly are, a pound of flesh.
Take, then, thy bond — take thou thy pound of flesh :
But, in the cutting it, if thou dost shed
One drop of Christian blood, thy lands and goods
Are, by the laws of Venice, confiscate
Unto the state of Venice.
    Gra. (R.) O upright judge ! — Mark, Jew ! — O
    learned judge !
    Shy. Is that the law ?
    Por.   Thyself shalt see the act :
For, as thou urgest justice, be assured
Thou shalt have justice — more than thou desirest.
    Gra. O learned judge ! — Mark, Jew ! — A learned
    judge !
    Shy. I take this offer, then : pay the bond thrice,
And let the Christian go.
    Bass.   Here is the money.
    Por. Soft !
The Jew shall have all justice ; — soft ! — no haste :
He shall have nothing but the penalty.
    Gra. O Jew ! — An upright judge ! a learned judge !
    Por. Therefore, prepare thee to cut off the flesh.
Shed thou no blood ; nor cut thou less nor more
But just a pound of flesh : if thou tak'st more

Or less than a just pound, be it so much
As makes it light or heavy in the substance
Or the division of the twentieth part
Of one poor scruple — nay, if the scale do turn
But in the estimation of a hair —
Thou diest, and all thy goods are confiscate.

Gra. A second Daniel! — a Daniel, Jew!
Now, infidel, I have thee on the hip!

Por. Why doth the Jew pause? — Take thy forfeiture.

Shy. Give me my principal, and let me go.

Bass. I have it ready for thee: here it is.

Por. He hath refused it in the open court:
He shall have merely justice, and his bond.

Gra. A Daniel, still say I — a second Daniel!
I thank thee, Jew, for teaching me that word.

Shy. Shall I not have barely my principal?

Por. Thou shalt have nothing but the forfeiture,
To be so taken at thy peril, Jew.

Shy. Why, then, the devil give him good of it!
I 'll stay no longer question.

Por.   Tarry, Jew:
The law hath yet another hold on you.
It is enacted in the laws of Venice,
If it be proved against an alien,
That, by direct or indirect attempts,
He seek the life of any citizen,
The party 'gainst the which he doth contrive
Shall seize one-half his goods; the other half
Comes to the privy coffer of the state;
And the offender's life lies in the mercy

Of the duke only, 'gainst all other voice.
In which predicament, I say, thou stand'st:
For it appears, by manifest proceeding,
That indirectly, and directly, too,
Thou hast contrived against the very life
Of the defendant; and thou hast incurred
The danger formerly by me rehearsed.
Down, therefore, and beg mercy of the duke!

 Gra. Beg that thou mayst have leave to hang
  thyself:
And yet, thy wealth being forfeit to the state,
Thou hast not left the value of a cord;
Therefore, thou must be hanged at the state's charge.

 Duke. · That thou shalt see the difference of our
  spirit,
I pardon thee thy life before thou ask it.
For half thy wealth, it is Antonio's;
The other half comes to the general state,
Which humbleness may drive unto a fine.

 Por. Ay, for the state; not for Antonio.

 Shy. Nay, take my life and all; pardon not that:
You take my house when you do take the prop
That doth sustain my house; you take my life
When you do take the means whereby I live.

 Por. What mercy can you render him, Antonio?

 Ant. So please my lord the duke and all the court,
To quit the fine for one-half of his goods
I am content, so he will let me have
The other half in use, to render it,
Upon his death, unto the gentleman
That lately stole his daughter:

Two things provided more — that, for this favor,
He presently become a Christian;
The other, that he do record a gift,
Here in the court, of all he dies possessed,
Unto his son Lorenzo and his daughter.
  Duke. He shall do this, or else I do recant
The pardon that I late pronounced here.
  Por. Art thou contented, Jew? what dost thou say?
  Shy. I am content.
  Por.   Clerk, draw a deed of gift.
  Shy. I pray you, give me leave to go from hence:
I am not well. Send the deed after me,
And I will sign it.
  Duke.   Get thee gone, but do it.

        [*As* SHYLOCK *slowly leaves the stage,* R., *the
        curtain descends.*

COSTUMES.

DUKE. — Crimson velvet jacket and breeches; purple robe;
    ermine cape; white shoes with crimson rosettes.
ANTONIO. — Black velvet trunks, puffed with black satin; black
    silk stockings; shoes and rosettes; round black hat, and
    black plumes.
BASSANIO. — White tunic, trimmed with silver; blue satin waist-
    coat, embroidered; blue sash belt; white silk stocking pan-
    taloons; white shoes with rosettes.
GRATIANO. — Green velvet coat; white waistcoat; buff worsted
    pantaloons; russet boots.
SHYLOCK. — Black cloth gabardine, or long, flowing cloak; scarlet
    sash; blue stockings; black shoes with buckles.
PORTIA. — Black silk stockings, black tunic, and lawyer's gown.
NERISSA. — Same as Portia, but no gown.

THE BEQUEST.

From Bulwer's Money.

DRAMATIS PERSONÆ.

ALFRED EVELYN.	GRAVES.
SIR JOHN VESEY.	CAPTAIN DUDLEY SMOOTH.
LORD GLOSSMORE.	SHARP.
SIR FREDERICK BLOUNT.	CLARA DOUGLAS.
STOUT.	LADY FRANKLIN.
GEORGINA.	

SCENE I: — *A drawing-room in* SIR JOHN VESEY'S *house; folding doors at the back, which open on another drawing-room. To the right, a table with newspapers, books, etc.; to the left, a sofa and writing-table.* SIR JOHN *and* GEORGINA, R. C.

Sir J. [*Reading a letter edged with black*] Yes, he says at two precisely. — "Dear Sir John: As since the death of my sainted Maria" — hum! that's his wife: she made him a martyr, and now he makes her a saint!

Geor. Well, as since her death? —

Sir J. [*Reading*] "I have been living in chambers,

where I can not so well invite ladies, you will allow me to bring Mr. Sharp, the lawyer, to read the will of the late Mr. Mordaunt, (to which I am appointed executor,) at your house — your daughter being the nearest relation. I shall be with you at two precisely. HENRY GRAVES."

Geor. And you really feel sure that poor Mr. Mordaunt has made me his heiress?

Sir J. Ay, the richest heiress in England. Can you doubt it? are you not his nearest relation? — niece by your poor mother, his own sister. I feel that I may trust you with a secret. You see this fine house, our fine servants, our fine plate, our fine dinners: — every one thinks Sir John Vesey a rich man.

Geor. And are you not, papa?

Sir J. Not a bit of it — all humbug, child; all humbug, upon my soul! There are two rules in life: first, men are valued not for what they *are*, but what they *seem* to be; secondly, if you have no merit or money of your own, you must trade on the merits and money of other people. My father got the title by services in the army, and died penniless. On the strength of his services, I got a pension of £400 a year; on the strength of £400 a year, I took credit for £800; on the strength of £800 a year, I married your mother, with £10,000; on the strength of £10,000, I took credit for £40,000, and paid Dickey Gossip three guineas a week to go about everywhere calling me "Stingy Jack."

Geor. Ha! ha! — a disagreeable nickname.

Sir J. But a valuable reputation. When a man is called stingy, it is as much as calling him rich; and when a man's called rich, why, he's a man universally respected. On the strength of my respectability, I wheeled a constituency, changed my politics, resigned my seat to a minister, who, to a man of such stake in the country, could offer nothing less in return than a patent office of £2,000 a year. That's the way to succeed in life. Humbug, my dear!—all humbug, upon my soul!

Geor. I must say that you —

Sir J. Know the world?—to be sure. Now, for your fortune, as I spend all that I have, I can have nothing to leave you: yet, even without counting your uncle, you have always passed for an heiress, on the credit of your expectations from the savings of "Stingy Jack." The same with your education: I never grudged any thing to make a show; never stuffed your head with histories and homilies; but you draw, you sing, you dance, you walk well into a room; and that's the way young ladies are educated, nowadays, in order to become a pride to their parents and a blessing to their husband—that is, when they have caught him. Apropos of a husband, you know we thought of Sir Frederick Blount.

Geor. Ah, papa, he is charming!

Sir J. He *was* so, my dear, before we knew your poor uncle was dead; but an heiress, such as you will be, should look out for a duke.—Where the deuce is Evelyn this morning?

Geor. I've not seen him, papa. What a strange

character he is!—so sarcastic! and yet he can be agreeable.

Sir J. A humorist—a cynic! one never knows how to take him. My private secretary; a poor cousin; has not got a shilling; and yet, hang me, if he does not keep us all at a sort of a distance.

Geor. But why do you take him to live with us, papa, since there's no good to be got by it?

Sir J. There you are wrong: he has a great deal of talent:—prepares my speeches, writes my pamphlets, looks up my calculations. Besides, he *is* our cousin—he has no salary. Kindness to a poor relation always tells well in the world; and benevolence is a useful virtue—particularly when you can have it for nothing. With our other cousin, Clara, it was different: her father thought fit to leave me her guardian, though she had not a penny—a mere useless incumbrance: so, you see, I got my half-sister, Lady Franklin, to take her off my hands.

Geor. How much longer is Lady Franklin's visit to be?

Sir J. I don't know, my dear: the longer, the better; for her husband left her a good deal of money at her own disposal.—Ah! here she comes.

Enter LADY FRANKLIN *and* CLARA, R.

My dear sister, we were just loud in your praise. But how's this?—not in mourning?

Lady F. Why should I go into mourning for a man I never saw?

Sir J. Still there may be a legacy.

Lady F. Then there 'll be less cause for affliction.

[*Retires up a little.*

Sir J. [*Aside*] Very silly woman!—But, Clara, I see you are more attentive to the proper decorum: yet you are very, *very*, VERY distantly connected with the deceased—a third cousin, I think.

Clara. Mr. Mordaunt once assisted my father, and these poor robes are all the gratitude I can show him.

Sir J. [*Aside*] Gratitude! humph! I am afraid the minx has got expectations.

Lady F. So, Mr. Graves is the executor: the will is addressed to him? The same Mr. Graves who is always in black—always lamenting his ill fortune and his sainted Maria, who led him the life of a dog?

Sir J. The very same. His liveries are black; his carriage is black; he always rides a black galloway; and, faith, if he ever marry again, I think he will show his respect to the sainted Maria by marrying a black woman!

Lady F. Ha, ha! we shall see. [*Aside*] Poor Graves! I always liked him: he made an excellent husband.

Enter EVELYN, *who seats himself,* R. C., *and takes up a book, unobserved.*

Sir J. What a crowd of relations this will brings to light: Mr. Stout, the political economist; Lord Glossmore—

Lady F. Whose grandfather kept a pawnbroker's

shop, and who, accordingly, entertains the profoundest contempt for every thing popular, *parvenu*, and plebeian.

Sir J. Sir Frederick Blount —

Lady F. Sir Fwedewick Blount, you mean, who objects to the letter *r* as being too *w*ough, and therefore d*w*ops its acquaintance : — one of the new class of prudent young gentlemen, who, not having spirits and constitution for the hearty excesses of their predecessors, entrench themselves in the dignity of a lady-like languor. A man of fashion, in the last century, was riotous and thoughtless; in this, he is tranquil and egotistical : he never does any thing that is silly, or says any thing that is wise. — [*To* GEORGINA] I beg your pardon, my dear! I believe Sir Frederick is an admirer of yours. — Then, too, our poor cousin, the scholar — Oh, Mr. Evelyn, there you are !

[*Crosses to* L. *corner.*

Sir J. Evelyn ! the very person I wanted : where have you been all day? Have you seen to those papers ? have you written my epitaph on poor Mordaunt? — Latin, you know; have you reported my speech at Exeter Hall? have you looked out the debates on the customs? and, oh ! have you mended up all the old pens in the study?

Geor. And have you brought me the black floss silk ? have you been to Storr's for my ring? and, as we can not go out on this melancholy occasion, did you call at Hookham's for the last *H. B.* and the *Comic Annual?*

Eve. [*Always reading*] Certainly, Paley is right
D. S.—25.

upon that point; for, put the syllogism thus — [*looking up*] Ma'am — Sir — Miss Vesey — you want something of me? — Paley observes, that to assist even the undeserving, tends to the better regulation of our charitable feelings. — No apologies: I am quite at your service.

Sir J. Now he's in one of his humors.

Lady F. You allow him strange liberties, Sir John.

Eve. You will be the less surprised at that, madam, when I inform you that Sir John allows me nothing else. I am now about to draw on his benevolence.

Lady F. I beg your pardon, sir, and like your spirit. Sir John, I'm in the way, I see; for I know your benevolence is so delicate, that you never allow any one to detect it!   [*Walks aside a little*, L.

Eve. I could not do your commissions to-day: I have been to visit a poor woman who was my nurse and mother's last friend. She is very poor, *very* — sick — dying — and she owes six months' rent!

Sir J. You know I should be most happy to do any thing for yourself: but the nurse — [*aside*] some people's nurses are always ill! — there are so many impostors about. We'll talk of it to-morrow. This most mournful occasion takes up all my attention. [*Looking at his watch*] Bless me, so late! I've letters to write, and — none of the pens are mended! [*Exit*, R.

Geor. [*Taking out her purse*] I think I will give it to him : — and yet, if I do n't get the fortune, after all! — papa allows me so little! — then I *must* have those ear-rings. [*Puts up the purse*] Mr. Evelyn, what is the address of your nurse?

Eve. [*Writes and gives it*] She has a good heart, with all her foibles.—Ah! Miss Vesey, if that poor woman had not closed the eyes of my lost mother, Alfred Evelyn had not been this beggar to your father!　　　　　[CLARA *looks over the address.*

Geor. . I will certainly attend to it—[*aside*] if I get the fortune.

Sir J. [*Calling without*] Georgy, I say!

Geor. Yes, papa!　　　　　　　　　[*Exit*, R.

　　　[EVELYN *has seated himself again at the table*, R.,
　　　　and leans his face on his hands.

Clara. His noble spirit bowed to this! Ah! at least here I may give him comfort. [*Sits down to write*] But he will recognize my hand.

Lady F. [*Looking over her shoulder*] What bill are you paying, Clara?—Putting up a bank-note?

Clara. Hush!—Oh, Lady Franklin, you are the kindest of human beings! This is for a poor person. I would not have her know whence it came, or she would refuse it. Would you?—No: he knows *her* handwriting, also.

Lady F. Will I—what? give the money myself? with pleasure! Poor Clara! why, this covers all your savings! and I am so rich.

Clara. Nay, I would wish to do all myself: it is a pride—a duty—it is a joy; and I have so few joys!—But, hush!—this way.

　　　[*They retire into the inner room, and converse in
　　　　dumb-show.*

Eve. And thus must I grind out my life forever! I am ambitious, and Poverty drags me down! I have

learning, and Poverty makes me the drudge of fools.
I love, and Poverty stands like a specter before the
altar. — But, no! if, as I believe, I am but loved
again, I will — will — what? — turn opium-eater, and
dream of the Eden I may never enter.

Lady F. [*To* CLARA] Yes, I will get my maid to
copy and direct this: she writes well, and *her* hand
will never be discovered. I will have it done and
sent instantly. [*Exit*, R.

[CLARA *advances to the front of the stage and
seats herself.* EVELYN, *reading.*

Enter SIR FREDERICK BLOUNT, R. C.

Blount. No one in the woom. — Oh, Miss Douglas!
Pway, don't let me disturb you. Where is Miss
Vesey—Georgina? [*Taking* CLARA'S *chair as she rises.*

Eve. [*Looking up, gives* CLARA *a chair, and re-seats
himself*] [*Aside*] Insolent puppy!

Clara. Shall I tell her you are here, Sir Frederick?

Blount. Not for the world! [*Aside*] Vewy pwetty
girl, this companion.

Clara. What did you think of the panorama, the
other day, cousin Evelyn?

Eve. [*Reading*]

> *I can not talk with civet in the room :*
> *A fine puss gentleman that 's all perfume.*

Rather good lines these.

Blount. Sir!

Eve. [*Offering the book*] Do n't you think so?—
Cowper.

Blount. [*Declining the book*] Cowper!

Eve. Cowper.

Blount. [*Shrugging his shoulders, to* CLARA] Stwange
person, Mr. Evelyn — quite a chawacter! — Indeed,
the panowama gives you no idea of Naples — a delightful place! I make it a wule to go there evewy
second year. I am vewy fond of twaveling. You 'd
like Wome — bad inns, but vewy fine wuins: — gives
you quite a taste for that sort of thing.

Eve. [*Reading*]

> *How much a dunce that has been sent to Rome,*
> *Excels a dunce that has been kept at home!*

Blount. [*Aside*] That fellow Cowper says vewy
odd things! Humph! it is beneath me to quawwel.
[*Aloud*] It will not take long to wead the Will, I
suppose. Poor old Mordaunt! I am his neawest
male welation. He was vewy eccentwic. [*Draws
his chair nearer*] By the way, Miss Douglas, did you
wemark my cuwicle? It is bwinging cuwicles into
fashion. — I should be most happy, if you would
allow me to dwive you out — nay, nay, I should,
upon my word.   [*Trying to take her hand.*

Eve. [*Starting up*] A wasp! a wasp! — just going
to settle! Take care of the wasp, Miss Douglas!

Blount. A wasp! — where? — do n't bwing it this
way! Some people do n't mind them. I 've a paw-
ticular dislike to wasps: they sting feawfully!

Eve. I beg pardon — it 's only a gad-fly!

Enter SERVANT, R.

Serv. Sir John will be happy to see you in his study, Sir Frederick.   [*Exit* SERVANT.

Blount. Vewy well.—Upon my word, there is something vewy nice about this girl. To be sure, I love Georgina; but if this one would take a fancy to me—[*thoughtfully*] well, I don't see what harm it could do me.—*Au plaisir!*   [*Exit*, R.

Eve. Clara!

Clara. Cousin!

Eve. And you, too, are a dependent!

Clara. But on Lady Franklin, who seeks to make me forget it.

Eve. Ay, but can the world forget it? This insolent condescension—this coxcombry of admiration—more galling than the arrogance of contempt! Look you, now: robe Beauty in silk and cashmere; hand Virtue into her chariot; lackey their caprices; wrap them from the winds; fence them round with a golden circle—and Virtue and Beauty are as goddesses, both to peasant and to prince. Strip them of the adjuncts: see Beauty and Virtue poor, dependent, solitary; walking the world defenseless!—oh, *then* the devotion changes its character: the same crowd gather eagerly around—fools, fops, libertines—not to worship at the shrine, but to sacrifice the victim!

Clara. My cousin, you are cruel.

Eve. Forgive me! There is a something, when a man's heart is better than his fortunes, that makes even affection bitter.

Clara. I can smile at the pointless innocence --

Eve. Smile!—and he took your hand! Oh, Clara, you know not the tortures that I suffer hourly! When others approach you — young, fair, rich, the sleek darlings of the world — I accuse you of your very beauty ;. I writhe beneath every smile that you bestow. [CLARA *about to speak*] No — speak not! my heart has broken its silence, and you shall hear the rest. For you I have endured the weary bondage of this house — the fool's gibe, the hireling's sneer, the bread purchased by toils that should have led to loftier ends: yes, to see you — hear you: for this — for this I have lingered, suffered, and forborne. Oh, Clara, we are orphans both! friendless both! you are all in the world to me! [*She turns away*] Turn not away: my very soul speaks in these words — I LOVE YOU!

Clara. No, Evelyn — Alfred — no! Say it not — think it not! It were madness!

Eve. Madness! — Nay, hear me yet. I *am* poor — penniless — a beggar for bread to a dying servant. True: but I have a heart of iron; I have knowledge, patience, health; and my love for you gives me, at last, ambition. I have trifled with my own energies till now; for I despised all things till I loved thee. With you to toil for, your step to support, your path to smooth, and I — I. poor Alfred Evelyn — promise at last to win for you even fame and fortune. Do not withdraw your hand — *this* hand — shall it not be mine? [*Kneels.*

Clara. Ah, Evelyn, never — never!

Eve. Never!   [*Rises.*

Clara. Forget this folly: our union is impossible; and to talk of love were to deceive both.

Eve. [*Bitterly*] Because I am poor!

Clara. And I, *too.* — A marriage of privation, of penury, of days that dread the morrow! I have seen such a lot. Never return to this again.   [*Crosses,* R.

Eve. Enough — you are obeyed. I deceived myself — ha, ha! I fancied that I, too, was loved — I, whose youth is already half gone with care and toil; whose mind is soured; whom no body *can* love; who ought to have loved no one!

Clara. [*Aside*] And if it were only *I* to suffer, or, perhaps, to starve! Oh, what shall I say?—Evelyn— cousin!

Eve. Madam!

Clara. Alfred, I — I —

Eve. Reject me?

Clara. Yes! It is past!   [*Exit,* R.

Eve. Let me think. It was yesterday her hand trembled when mine touched it: and the rose I gave her — yes, she pressed her lips to it once, when she seemed as if she saw me not. But it was a trap — a trick; for I was as poor then as now. This will be a jest for them all! Well — courage! it is but a poor heart that a coquette's contempt can break. And, now that I care for no one, the world is but a great chess-board; and I will sit down in earnest, and play with Fortune.   [*Retires up to the table,* R.

Enter Lord Glossmore, *preceded by* Servant, r.

Serv. I will tell Sir John, my lord.   [*Exit*, r.

          [Evelyn *takes up the newspaper.*

Gloss. The secretary — hum! [*To* Evelyn] Fine day, sir! Any news from the East?

Eve. (r.) Yes: — all the wise men have gone back there!

Gloss. Ha, ha! — not all; for here comes Mr. Stout, the great political economist.

Enter Stout, r.

Stout. (r. c.) Good morning, Glossmore!

Gloss. (l.) [*Aside*] Glossmore! — the *parvenu!*

Stout. Afraid I might be late: been detained at the vestry. Astonishing how ignorant the English poor are! Took me an hour and a half to beat it into the head of a stupid old widow, with nine children, that to allow her three shillings a week was against all the rules of public morality!

Eve. (r.) Excellent! — admirable! Your hand, sir!

Gloss. What! you approve such doctrines, Mr. Evelyn! Are old women only fit to be starved?

Eve. Starved! — popular delusion! Observe, my lord: to squander money upon those who starve, is only to afford encouragement to starvation!

Stout. [*Aside*] A very superior person that.

Gloss. Atrocious principles! Give me the good old times, when it was the duty of the rich to succor the distressed.

Eve. On second thoughts, *you* are right, my lord. I, too, know a poor woman — ill, dying, in want. Shall *she*, too, perish?

Gloss. Perish! — horrible! — in a Christian country! Perish! Heaven forbid!

Eve. [*Holding out his hand*] What, then, will you give her?

Gloss. Ahem! Sir, the parish ought to give.

Stout. [*With vehemence*] No, no, no! — certainly not!

Enter SIR JOHN, ·BLOUNT, LADY FRANKLIN, *and* GEORGINA, R.

Sir J. How d' ye do? — Ah! how d' ye do, gentlemen? This is a most melancholy meeting! The poor deceased — what a man he was!

Blount. I was chwistened Fwedewick, after him. He was my first cousin.

Sir J. And Georgina, his own niece — next of kin. An excellent man, though odd : a kind heart, but no liver. I sent him, twice a year, thirty dozen of the Cheltenham waters. It's a comfort to reflect on these little attentions, at such a time.

Stout. And I, too, sent him the parliamentary debates regularly, bound in calf. He was my second cousin — sensible man, and a follower of Malthus : never married to increase the surplus population, and fritter away his money on his own children. And now —

Eve. He reaps the benefit of celibacy in the

prospective gratitude of every cousin he had in the world!

Lady F. Ha, ha, ha!

Sir J. Hush, hush! Decency, Lady Franklin! decency!

Enter SERVANT, R.

Serv. Mr. Graves, Mr. Sharp!

Sir J. Oh, here's Mr. Graves. That's Sharp, the lawyer, who brought the Will from Calcutta.

Enter GRAVES *and* SHARP, R.

Chorus of SIR J., GLOSS., BLOUNT, STOUT. Ah, sir! Ah, Mr. Graves!   [GEORGINA *holds her hand-*
Sir J. A sad occasion!   *kerchief to her eyes.*

Graves. But every thing in life is sad. — Be comforted, Miss Vesey. True, you have lost an uncle; but I — I have lost a wife — such a wife! — the first of her sex — and the second cousin of the defunct! Excuse me, Sir John : at the sight of your mourning, my wounds bleed afresh.

[SERVANTS *hand round refreshments.*

Sir J. Take some refreshment — a glass of wine.

Graves. Thank you! — Very fine sherry! — My poor, sainted Maria! sherry was *her* wine. Every thing reminds me of Maria. — Ah, Lady Franklin! *you* knew her. Nothing in life can charm me now. [*Aside*] A monstrous fine woman that!

Sir J. And now to business. Evelyn, you may retire.

Sharp. [*Looking at his notes*] Evelyn — any relation to Alfred Evelyn?

Eve. The same.

Sharp. Cousin to the deceased, seven times removed. — Be seated, sir: there may be some legacy, though trifling. All the relations, however distant, should be present.

Lady F. Then Clara is related: I will go for her.
[*Exit,* R.

Geor. Ah, Mr. Evelyn, I hope you will come in for something — a few hundreds, or even more.

Sir J. Silence! hush! whugh — ugh! Attention!
[*While the* LAWYER *opens the Will, re-enter* LADY FRANKLIN *and* CLARA.

Sharp. The Will is very short, being all personal property. He was a man that always came to the point.

Sir J. I wish there were more like him.
[*Chorus groan and shake their heads.*

Sharp. [*Reading*] "I, Frederick James Mordaunt, of Calcutta, being, at the present date, of sound mind, though infirm body, do hereby give, will, and bequeath, *imprimis*, to my second cousin, Benjamin Stout, Esq., of Pall Mall, London — [*Chorus exhibit lively emotion*] — being the value of the parliamentary debates, with which he has been pleased to trouble me for some time past — deducting the carriage thereof, which he always forgot to pay — the sum of 14l. 2s. 4d." [*Chorus breathe more freely.*

Stout. Eh! what! 14l.? Oh, hang the old miser!

Sir J. Decency — decency! Proceed, sir.

Sharp. [*Reading*] " Item : To Sir Frederick Blount,
Baronet, my nearest male relative " —

[*Chorus exhibit lively emotion.*

Blount. Poor old boy !

[GEORGINA *puts her arm over* BLOUNT'S *chair.*

Sharp. [*Reading*] " Being, as I am informed, the
best dressed young gentleman in London, and in
testimony to the only merit I ever heard he possessed,
the sum of £500, to buy a dressing-case."

[*Chorus breathe more freely.* GEORGINA *catches
her father's eye, and removes her arm.*

Blount. [*Laughing confusedly*] Ha, ha, ha ! vewy
poor wit ! — low ! — vewy — vewy low !

Sir J. Silence, now, will you ?

Sharp. [*Reading*] " Item : To Charles Lord Glossmore — who asserts that he is my relation — my collection of dried butterflies, and the pedigree of the
Mordaunts from the reign of King John."

[*Chorus as before.*

Gloss. Butterflies ! — pedigree ! I disown the
plebeian !

Sir J. [*Angrily*] Upon my word, this is too revolting ! Decency ! — Go on.

Sharp. [*Reading*] " Item : To Sir John Vesey,
Baron, Knight of the Guelph, F.R.S., F.S.A., etc."—

[*Chorus as before.*

Sir J. Hush ! *Now* it is really interesting.

Sharp. [*Reading*] " Who married my sister, and
who sends me, every year, the Cheltenham waters —
which nearly gave me my death — I bequeath — the
empty bottles."

Sir J. Why, the ungrateful, rascally, old —

Chorus. Decency, Sir John — decency!

Sharp. [*Reading*] "Item: To Henry Graves, Esq.,
of the Albany" —   [*Chorus as before.*

Graves. Pooh, gentlemen! my usual luck: not
even a ring, I dare swear!

Sharp. [*Reading*] "The sum of £5,000, in the
three-per-cents."

Lady F. I wish you joy!

Graves. Joy — pooh! Three-per-cents! Funds
are sure to go. Had it been *land*, now — though
only an acre! Just like my luck.

Sharp. [*Reading*] "Item: To my niece, Georgina
Vesey" —   [*Chorus as before.*

Sir J. Ah, now it comes!

Sharp. [*Reading*] "The sum of £10,000, India
stock; being, with her father's reputed savings, as
much as a single woman ought to possess."

Sir J. And what the devil, then, does the old fool
do with all his money?

Chorus. Really, Sir John, this is too revolting! —
Decency! Hush!

Sharp. [*Reading*] "And, with the aforesaid lega-
cies and exceptions, I do will and bequeath the whole
of my fortune — in India stock, bonds, exchequer
bills, three-per-cents, consols, and in the bank of Calcutta, (constituting him, hereby, sole residuary leg-
atee, and joint executor with the aforesaid Henry
Graves, Esq.,) — to Alfred Evelyn, now or formerly
of Trinity College, Cambridge. [*Universal excitement*]
Being, I am told, an oddity, like myself; the only

one of my relations who never fawned on me; and who, having known privation, may the better employ wealth." [*All rise*] And now, sir, I have only to wish you joy, and give you this letter from the deceased: I believe it is important.   [*Gives letter to* EVELYN.

Eve. [*Crossing over to* CLARA] Ah, Clara, if you had but loved me!

Clara. [*Turning away*] And his wealth, even more than poverty, separates us forever!

.   [*All surround* EVELYN *with congratulations.*

Sir J. [*To* GEORGINA] Go, child; put a good face on it: he's an immense match!—My dear fellow, I wish you joy! You are a great man now—a very great man!

Eve. [*Aside*] And *her* voice alone is silent!

Gloss. If I can be of any use to you—

Stout. Or I, sir—

Blount. Or I.—Shall I put you up at the clubs?

Sharp. You will want a man of business. I transacted all Mr. Mordaunt's affairs.

Sir J. Tush, tush! Mr. Evelyn is at home *here.* Always looked on him as a son. Nothing in the world we would not do for him—nothing!

Eve. Lend me £10 for my old nurse!

[*Chorus put their hands into their pockets.*

Curtain.

COSTUMES.

Alfred Evelyn. — Black frock coat and vest; Oxford gray trowsers; cloth-top shoes; black neckerchief.

Stout. — Green, cut-off coat, with broad tails; striped vest; white cravat with large tie; nankeen trowsers, without straps; cloth-top shoes; large, red pocket-handkerchief; white hat, with black crape round it.

Sir John Vesey. — Black dress-coat and trowsers; white vest and cravat; white hair; double eye-glasses, hanging by chain round neck.

Glossmore. — Black frock-coat and trowsers; polished leather boots; black vest; white cravat; light kid gloves.

Graves. — Body-coat, and full black suit; black gloves.

Blount. — Fashionable black suit.

Sharp. — Plain, tight-fitting, black suit; old beaver hat.

Clara Douglas. — Black barege walking-dress, high neck and long sleeves, slightly trimmed with black lace; hair plain; black shoes and stockings; black satin apron.

Lady Franklin. — A gay-colored silk dress.

Georgina. — White muslin, cut high, and long sleeves, trimmed with black ribbons and jet ornaments.

THE DEATH OF CATO.

From Addison's Cato.

DRAMATIS PERSONÆ.

CATO, *A Roman Senator.*
PORCIUS, *son of Cato.*
MARCIA, *daughter of Cato.*
LUCIA, *friend of Marcia.*
LUCIUS, *old friend of Cato.*
JUBA, *a Numidian Prince, suitor to Marcia.*
FOUR FREEDMEN.

SCENE: — *A Chamber in* CATO'S *Palace.* CATO *discovered, sitting in deep meditation, holding in his hand* PLATO'S *book on the Immortality of the Soul; a drawn sword lying by him on a table.*

Cato. It must be so: Plato, thou reasonest well;
Else whence this pleasing hope, this fond desire,
This longing after immortality?
Or whence this secret dread and inward horror
Of falling into naught? Why shrinks the soul
Back on herself, and startles at destruction?
'T is the Divinity that stirs within us;

'T is Heaven itself that points out an hereafter,
And intimates eternity to man.
Eternity! [*Rising and coming forward*] That pleas-
  ing, dreadful thought!—
Through what variety of untried being—
Through what new scenes and changes must we pass!
The wide, the unbounded prospect lies before me;
But shadows, clouds, and darkness rest upon it.
Here will I hold: If there's a power above us,
(And that there is, all nature cries aloud
Through all her works,) he must delight in virtue;
And that which he delights in, must be happy.
But when? or where?—This world was made for
  Cæsar.—
I 'm weary of conjectures: this must end 'em.
 [*Goes back to the table, laying his hand on his sword.*
Thus am I doubly armed: my death and life,
My bane and antidote, are both before me:
This in a moment brings me to an end;
But this informs me I shall never die.
 [*Comes forward with a roll of paper and a sword.*
The soul, secured in her existence, smiles
At the drawn dagger, and defies its point.—
The stars shall fade away; the sun himself
Grow dim with age, and nature sink in years;
But thou shalt flourish in immortal youth;
Unhurt amidst the war of elements,
The wreck of matter, and the crush of worlds.
What means this heaviness that hangs upon me?
Nature oppressed, and harassed out with care,
Sinks down to rest. This once I 'll favor her,

That my awakened soul may take her flight,
Renewed in all her strength, and fresh with life —
An offering fit for heaven.   Let guilt or fear
Disturb man's rest: Cato knows neither of 'em:
Indifferent in his choice to sleep or die.

[*Returns and sits.*

Enter PORCIUS, R.

But, hah! how's this? My son! Why this intrusion?
Were not my orders that I would be private?
Why am I disobeyed?
    Por.   Alas, my father!
What means this sword, this instrument of death?
Let me convey it hence.   [*Takes it up.*
    Cato.   Rash youth, forbear!
    Por.   Oh, let the prayers, the entreaties of your
      friends,
Their tears, their common danger, wrest it from you.
    Cato.   Wouldst thou betray me? wouldst thou give
      me up,
A slave, a captive, into Cæsar's hands?   [*Rises.*
Retire, and learn obedience to a father!
Or know, young man —
    Por.   Look not thus sternly on me:
You know I'd rather die than disobey you.

[*Lays down the sword.*
    Cato.   'T is well: again I'm master of myself.

[*Takes up the sword.*
Now, Cæsar, let thy troops beset our gates,
And bar each avenue; thy gathering fleets

O'erspread the sea, and stop up every port:
Cato shall open to himself a passage,
And mock thy hopes.   [*Comes forward*, R.

Por. [*Kneels*, R. C.] Oh, sir, forgive your son,
Whose grief hangs heavy on him! Oh, my father —
How am I sure it is not the last time
I e'er shall call you so? — be not displeased,
Oh, be not angry with me, whilst I weep,
And, in the anguish of my heart, beseech you
To quit the dreadful purpose of your soul.

Cato. Thou hast been ever good and dutiful.
                         [*Lays his hand on his head.*
Weep not, my son; all will be well again:
The righteous gods, whom I have sought to please,
Will succor Cato and protect his children.

Por. Your words give comfort to my drooping
      heart.   [*Rises.*

Cato. Porcius, thou may'st rely upon my conduct:
Cato will never act what misbecomes him.
But go, my son: take care that naught be wanting
Among thy father's friends. See them embarked;
And tell me if the winds and seas befriend 'em. —
My soul is quite weighed down with care, and asks
The soft refreshment of a moment's sleep.

      [CATO *goes up.* PORCIUS *follows him and kneels
      at his feet;* CATO *looks kindly upon him, and
      then exit,* L.

Por. My thoughts are more at ease; my heart
      revives.

Enter MARCIA, L.

Oh, Marcia! oh, my sister! still there's hope:
Our father will not cast away a life
So needful to us all, and to his country.
He is retired to rest, and seems to cherish
Thoughts full of peace. He has dispatched me hence,
With orders that bespeak a mind composed,
And studious for the safety of his friends.
Marcia, take care that none disturb his slumbers.

[*Exit*, R. E.

Mar. (c.) Oh, ye immortal powers that guard the
    just,
Watch round his couch, and soften his repose!
Banish his sorrows, and becalm his soul
With easy dreams! Remember all his virtues,
And show mankind that goodness is your care!

Enter LUCIA, L.

Luc. (L.) Where is your father, Marcia? where is
    Cato?
Mar. Lucia, speak low: he is retired to rest.
My friend, I feel a gentle, dawning hope
Rise in my soul: we may be happy still.
Luc. (L. C.) Alas, I tremble when I think on Cato!
In every view, in every thought, I tremble.
Cato is stern, and awful as a god:
He knows not how to wink at human frailty,
Or pardon weakness that he never felt.
Mar. Though stern and awful to the foes of Rome,
He is all goodness, Lucia, always mild,

Compassionate, and gentle to his friends:
Filled with domestic tenderness; the best,
The kindest father.   I have ever found him
Easy and good, and bounteous to my wishes.

    Luc.   'T is his consent alone can make us happy:
But who knows Cato's thoughts?
Who knows how yet he may dispose of Porcius?
Or how he has determined of thyself?

    Mar.   Let him but live: commit the rest to heaven.

Enter LUCIUS, L.

    Lucius. (C.) Sweet are the slumbers of the virtuous
       man! —
Oh, Marcia, I have seen thy godlike father!
Some power invisible supports his soul,
And bears it up in all its wonted grec:
A kind, refreshing sleep has fallen:
I saw him stretched at ease, his fancy lost
In pleasing dreams: as I drew near his couch,
He smiled, and cried, "Cæsar, thou canst not hurt
    me!"

    Mar. (R. C.) His mind still labors with some dread-
ful thought.

Enter JUBA, R.

    Juba. (R.) Lucius, the horsemen are returned from
       viewing
The number, strength, and posture of our foes,
Who now encamp within a short hour's march.
On the high point of yon bright western tower

We ken them from afar: the setting sun
Plays on their shining arms and burnished helmets,
And covers all the field with gleams of fire.
 Lucius. Marcia, 't is time we should awake thy
  father.
Cæsar is still disposed to give us terms,
And waits at distance till he hears from Cato.

Enter PORCIUS, R.

Porcius, thy looks speak somewhat of importance:
What tidings dost thou bring? Methinks I see
Unusual gladness sparkling in thine eyes.
 Por. As I was hastening to the port — where now
My father's friends, impatient for a passage,
Accuse the lingering winds — a sail arrived
From Pompey's son, who, through the realms of Spain,
Calls out for vengeance on his father's death,
And rouses the whole nation up to arms.
Were Cato at their head, once more might Rome
Assert her rights and claim her liberty. —
    [*Groans are heard within.*
But, hark! what means that groan? — Oh, give me
  way,
And let me fly into my father's presence! [*Exit,* L.
 Lucius. Cato, amidst his slumbers, thinks on Rome;
And, in the wild disorder of his soul,
Mourns o'er his country. [*Groans are heard again.*
Ha! a second groan! Heaven guard us all!
 Mar. Alas! 't is not the voice
Of one who sleeps: 't is agonizing pain:
'T is death is in that sound!

Enter Porcius, l.; *advances between* Marcia *and* Juba.

Por. (l.) Oh, sight of woe!
Oh, Marcia, what we feared is come to pass!—
Cato has fallen upon his sword

Lucius. (l. c.) Oh, Porcius,
Hide all the horrors of thy mournful tale,
And let us guess the rest!

Por. I've raised him up,
And placed him in his chair, where, pale and faint,
He gasps for breath; and, as his life flows from him,
Demands to see his friends. His servants, weeping,
Obsequious to his orders, bear him hither.

Mar. O Heaven, assist me in this dreadful hour,
To pay the last sad tribute to my father!

Enter Cato, l., *preceded by two* Freedmen, *and sup-
ported by two others. The two first* Freedmen
remove the table, r., *and remain by it.* Marcia
runs to assist Cato ; *takes his right arm, and helps
to bring him to a chair,* c.

Juba. (r. c.) These are thy triumphs, thy exploits,
   O Cæsar!

Lucius. (l. c.) Now is Rome fallen, indeed!

Cato. (c.) Here set me down.
Porcius, come near me :— are my friends embarked?
Can any thing be thought of for their service?
Whilst yet I live, let me not live in vain.—
Oh, Lucius, art thou here?—Thou art too good!—
Let this our friendship live between our children ;

Make Porcius happy in thy daughter Lucia. —
Alas, poor man, he weeps! Marcia, my daughter —
Oh, bend me forward! — Juba loves thee, Marcia.
A senator of Rome, while Rome survived,
Would not have matched his daughter with a king;
But Cæsar's arms have thrown down all distinction:
Whoe'er is brave and virtuous is a Roman.
I 'm sick to death! — Oh, when shall I get loose
From this vain world, the abode of guilt and sorrow!
And yet, methinks, a beam of light breaks in
On my departing soul. — Alas! I fear
I 've been too hasty. — Oh, ye powers that search
The heart of man, and weigh his inmost thoughts,
If I have done amiss, impute it not! —
The best may err — but you are good, and — oh!
       [*Dies. Curtain descends to solemn music.*

COSTUMES.

CATO. — Flesh-colored dress; black Roman sandals; white Roman tunic; white kerseymere toga, edged with scarlet.

PORCIUS. — Roman breastplate and lambrekins; scarlet mantle; flesh-colored legs; black sandals; helmet.

LUCIUS. — Blue Roman toga and tunic; breastplate; flesh-colored legs; black sandals.

JUBA. — Scarlet satin jacket; tiger-skin mantle; rich bracelets and coronet; flesh-colored legs; red sandals.

MARCIA. — White muslin dress; drapery; black bracelets.

LUCIA. — White muslin dress, with white Roman drapery; tiara of pearls; black bracelets.

THE FORLORN HOPE OF MONA.

From Mason's Caractacus.

DRAMATIS PERSONÆ.

CARACTACUS, *General and King of the Britons.*
ARVIRAGUS, *son of Caractacus.*
ELIDURUS, *a brave British youth.*
CADWALL, *high-priest of the Druids.*
MADOR, *a venerable bard.*
EVELINA, *daughter of Caractacus.*
DRUIDS *and* BARDS — *ten or more.*

Prologue.

Mason's *Caractacus*, though a dramatic poem of so great merit, that Sir Walter Scott described it as inimitable, has probably not been represented on the stage for almost a hundred years. We have selected from this artistic work several connected scenes, to the performance of which we solicit attention. The place of action is supposed to be near the sacred altars of the Druids, overshadowed by gloomy oaks, in the center of the isle of Mona. The first events shown are the accusation, trial, and release of Elidurus, a brave British prince, suspected of treachery; and the return of Arviragus, son of Caractacus, from long absence. But the main part of the drama is concerned in setting forth the stern and solemn preparations of Caractacus and others, about to engage in a last desperate conflict with the Roman enemy, hovering near the sacred grove. In language of stately magnificence, the arch-priest of the Druids offers adjurations, and then delivers into the hand of the king the magic "sword of old Belinus," which had slept for ages within the hollow trunk of an old oak. Evelina, the king's daughter, utters a prayer for her father, her brother, and her lover, as the three stand ready to go forth to conquer or perish. The scene closes with a fierce ode of war, sung by a master bard; at the end of which a Druid blows the sacred trumpet, and Caractacus pronounces a few determined words, as a signal for advancing against the hated foe.

SCENE:—*The Island of Mona, or Anglesea; a forest
of gnarled oaks; rocky altars of the Druids.
Enter* ELIDURUS, L., *followed by* EVELINA.

Eli. (c.) Cease, royal maid! permit me to depart.
Eve. (L. c.) Yet hear me, stranger! Truth and
    secrecy,
Though friends, are seldom necessary friends —
    Eli. I go to try my truth —
    Eve. Oh! 'go not hence
In wrath; think not that I suspect thy virtue:
Yet ignorance may oft make virtue slide.
And if —
    Eli. In pity, spare me!
    Eve. If thy brother —
Nay, start not; do not turn thine eyes from mine.
Speak, I conjure thee! is his purpose honest?
I know the guilty price that barbarous Rome
Sets on my father's head; and gold, vile gold,
Has now a charm for Britons. Bribed by this,
Should he betray him? — Yes. I see thou shudder'st
At the dire thought; yet not as if 't were strange,
But as our fears were mutual. Ah! young stranger,
That open face scarce needs a tongue to utter
What works within. Come, then, ingenuous prince,
And instant make discovery to the Druid,
While yet 't is not too late.
    Eli. Ah! what discover?
Say, whom must I betray?
    Eve. Thy brother.
    Eli. Ha!

Eve. Who is no brother, if his guilty soul
Teems with such perfidy. Oh, all ye stars!
Can he be brother to a youth like thee,
Who would betray an old and honored king —
That king his countryman, and one whose prowess
Once guarded Britain 'gainst th' assailing world?
Can he be brother to a youth like thee,
Who from a young, defenseless, innocent maid,
Would take that king. her father? make her suffer
All that an orphan suffers — more, perchance:
The ruffian foe! — Oh, tears, ye choke my utterance!
Can he be brother to a youth like thee,
Who would defile his soul by such black deeds?
It can not be — and yet thou still art silent.
Turn, youth, and see me weep. [*She kneels*] Ah, see
  me kneel!
I am of royal blood — not wont to kneel;
Yet will I kneel to thee. — Oh, save my father!
Save a distressful maiden from the force
Of barbarous men! Be thou a brother to me;
For mine, alas! — Ha! [*Sees* ARVIRAGUS *entering,* R.
  Arv. Evelina, rise!
Know, maid, I ne'er will tamely see thee kneel
Even at the foot of Cæsar.   [*Lifts her up.*
  Eve. 'T is himself;
And he will prove my father's fears were false —
False as his son is brave. Thou best of brothers,
Come to my arms! Where hast thou been, thou
  wanderer?
How wert thou saved? Indeed, Arviragus,
I ne'er shed such tears since thou wert lost;

For these are tears of rapture.

Arv. Evelina,
Fain would I greet thee as a brother ought:
But wherefore didst thou kneel?

Eve. Oh, ask not now!

Arv. By heaven, I must! and he must answer me,
Whoe'er he be! What art thou, sullen stranger?

Eli. A Briton.

Arv. Brief and bold.

Eve. Ah, spare the taunt!
He merits not thy wrath. Behold the Druids:
Lo, they advance. With holy reverence, first,
Thou must address their sanctity.

Arv. I will:
But see, proud boy, thou dost not quit the grove,
Till time allows us parley.

Eli. Prince, I mean not.   [*He goes up.*

Enter CADWALL *and other* DRUIDS, L.

Arv. (R.) Sages, and sons of heaven! illustrious
        Druids!
Abruptly I approach your sacred presence
Yet such dire tidings —

Cad. (C.) On thy peril, peace!
Thou stand'st accused, and by a father's voice,
Of crimes abhorred — of cowardice and flight;
And therefore may'st not in these sacred groves
Utter polluted accents. Quickly say
Wherefore thou fled'st: for, that base fact uncleared,
We hold no further converse.

Arv. O ye gods! Am I the son of your Caractacus?
And could I fly?

Cad. Waste not or time or words;
And tell us why thou fled'st.

Arv. I fled not, Druid:
By the great gods, I fled not! save to stop
Our dastard troops, that basely turned their backs.
I stopped, I rallied them; when, lo! a shaft
Of random cast did level me with earth;
Where, pale and senseless as the slain around me,
I lay till midnight: then, as from long trance
Awoke, I crawled upon my feeble limbs
To a lone cottage, where a pitying hind
Lodged me and nourished me. My strength repaired,
It boots not that I tell what humble arts,
Compelled, I used to screen me from the foe:
How now a peasant, from a beggarly scrip
I sold cheap food to slaves, that named the price,
Nor after gave it; now a minstrel poor,
With ill-tuned harp, and uncouth descant shrill,
I plied a thriftless trade; and by such shifts
Did win obscurity to shroud my name.
At length, to other conquests in the north
Ostorius led his legions. Safer now,
Yet not secure, I to some valiant chiefs
Whom war had spared, discovered what I was;
And with them planned how surest we might draw
Our scattered forces to some rocky fastness
In rough Cærnarvon; then to breathe in freedom,
If not with brave incursion to oppress
The thinly-stationed foe. And soon our art

So well availed, that now at Snowdon's foot
Full twenty troops of hardy veterans wait
To call my sire their leader.

    Cad. Valiant youth —

    Eve. (R. C.) He is — I said he was a valiant youth;
Nor has he shamed his race.

    Cad. We do believe
Thy modest tale : and may the righteous gods
Thus ever shed upon thy noble breast
Discretion's cooling dew. When nurtured so,
Then, only then, doth valor bloom mature.

    Arv. Yet vain is valor, howsoe'er it bloom.
Druid, the gods frown on us. All my hopes
Are blasted; I shall ne'er rejoice my friends,
Ne'er bless them with my father. Holy men,
I have a tale to tell will shake your souls :
Your Mona is invaded; Rome approaches —
Even to these groves approaches!

    Druids. Horror! horror!

    Arv. Late as I landed on yon highest beach,
Where, nodding from the rocks, the poplars fling
Their scattered arms, and dash them in the wave,
There were their vessels moored, as if they sought
Concealment in the shade : and as I passed
Up yon thick-planted ridge, I spied their helms,
'Mid brakes and boughs, trenched in the heath below,
Where like a nest of night-worms did they glitter,
Sprinkling the plain with brightness. On I sped
With silent step; yet oft did pass so near,
'T was next to prodigy I 'scaped unseen.

    Cad. Their number, prince?

Arv. Few, if mine hasty eye
Did find and count them.

Cad. Oh, brethren, brethren!
Treason and sacrilege, worse foes than Rome,
Have led Rome hither. Instant seize that wretch,
And bring him to our presence!

> [*Two of the* DRUIDS *approach* ELIDURUS, *but he
> waves them off and advances toward* CADWALL.

Say, thou false one,
What doom befits the slave who sells his country?

Eli. (L. C.) Death! — sudden death!

Cad. No; lingering, piecemeal death:
And to such death thy brother and thyself
We now devote. Villain, thy deeds are known:
'T is known ye led the impious Romans hither,
To slaughter us e'en on our holy altars.

Eli. That on my soul doth lie some secret grief,
These looks perforce will tell. It is not fear;
Druids, it is not fear that shakes me thus:
The great gods know it is not. Ye can never;
For what though wisdom lifts ye next those gods,
Ye can not, like to them, unlock men's breasts,
And read their inmost thoughts. Ah, that ye could!

Arv. What hast thou done?

Eli. What, prince, I will not tell.

Cad. Wretch, there are means —

Eli. I know — and terrible means;
And 't is both fit that you should try those means
And I endure them: yet I think my patience
Will, for some space, baffle your torturing fury.

Cad. Be that best known when our inflicted goads

Harrow thy flesh.

    Arv. Stranger, ere this is tried,
Confess the whole of thy black perfidy;
So black, that when I look upon thy youth,
Read thy mild eye, and mark thy modest brow,
I think, indeed, thou durst not.

    Eli. Such a crime,
Indeed, I durst not; and would rather be
The very wretch thou seest. I'll speak no more.

    Cad. Brethren, 'tis so; the virgin's thoughts were
      just:
This youth has been deceived.

    Eli. Yes, one word more:
You say the Romans have invaded Mona:
Give me a sword and twenty honest Britons,
And I will quell those Romans. Vain demand!
Alas! you can not: ye are men of peace:
Religion's self forbids. Lead, then, to torture.

    Arv. (R.) Now, on my soul, this youth doth move
      me much.

    Cad. (c.) Think not religion and our holy office
Doth teach us tamely, like the bleating lamb,
To crouch before oppression, and with neck
Outstretched, await the stroke. Mistaken boy!
Did not strict justice claim thee for her victim,
We might full safely send thee to these Romans,
Inviting their hot charge. Know, when I blow
That sacred trumpet, bound with sable fillets
To yonder branching oak, the awful sound
Calls forth a thousand Britons, trained alike
In holy and in martial exercise;

Not by such mode and rule as Romans use,
But of that fierce, portentous, horrible sort
As shall appall even Romans.
    Eli. Gracious gods!
Then there are hopes, indeed. Oh, call them instant!
This prince will lead them on: I'll follow him,
Though in my chains, and some way dash them round
To harm the haughty foe.
    Arv. A thousand Britons!
And armed! Oh, instant blow the sacred trump,
And let me head them! Yet, methinks, this youth—
    Cad. I know what thou wouldst say—might join
        thee, prince.
True, were he free from crime, or had confessed.
    Eli. (L.) Confessed! Ah, think not I will e'er—
    Arv. (R.) Reflect:
Either thyself or brother must have wronged us:
Then why conceal—
    Eli. Hast thou a brother?—No!
Else hadst thou spared the word: and yet a sister
Lovely as thine might more than teach thee, prince,
What 'tis to have a brother. Hear me, Druids.
Though I would prize an hour of freedom now
Before an age of any after date;
Though I would seize it as the gift of heaven,
And use it as heaven's gift, yet do not think
I so will purchase it. Give it me freely,
I yet will spurn the boon and hug my chains,
Till you do swear by your own hoary heads
My brother shall be safe.
    Cad. Excellent youth!

Thy words do speak thy soul, and such a soul
As wakes our wonder.   Thou art free; thy brother
Shall be thine honor's pledge: so will we use him
As thou art false or true.

 Eli.   I ask no other.

 Arv. [*Crosses to* ELIDURUS] Thus, then, my fellow-
  soldier, to thy clasp
I give the hand of friendship.   Noble youth,
We'll speed or die together!   [*They clasp hands.*

 Cad.   Hear us, prince:
Mona permits not that he fights her battles
Till duly purified: for though his soul
Took up unwillingly this deed of baseness,
Yet is lustration meet.   Learn that in vice
There is a noisome rankness, unperceived
By gross corporeal sense, which so offends
Heaven's pure divinities, as us the stench
Of vapor wafted from sulphureous pool,
Of poisonous weed obscene.   Hence doth the man
Who e'en converses with a villain, need
As much purgation as the pallid wretch
'Scaped from the walls where frowning pestilence
Spreads wide her livid banners.   For this cause,
Ye priests, conduct the youth to yonder grove,
And do the needful rites.   Meanwhile, ourself
Will lead thee, prince, unto thy father's presence. —
But, hold! the king comes forth

   [*Exeunt* PRIESTS *with* ELIDURUS, R.   *Enter*
    CARACTACUS, L.

 Car.   My son! my son!   [*They embrace.*
What joy, what transport doth thine aged sire

Feel in these filial foldings! Speak not, boy,
Nor interrupt that heart-felt ecstasy
Should strike us mute. I know what thou wouldst
    say;
Yet, prithee, peace: thy sister's voice hath cleared
    thee:
And could excuse find words at this blest moment,
Trust me, I'd give it vent. But 't is enough;
Thy father welcomes thee to him and honor —
Honor, that now with rapturous certainty
Calls thee his own true offspring. Dost thou weep?
Ah, if thy tears swell not from joy's free spring,
I beg thee, spare them. I have done thee wrong;
Can make thee no atonement — none, alas!
Thy father scarce can bless thee as he ought;
Unblest himself, beset with foes around,
Bereft of queen, of kingdom, and of soldiers,
He can but give thee portion of his dangers,
Perchance and of his chains. Yet droop not, boy;
Virtue is still thine own.

    Arv. It is, my father,
Pure as from thine illustrious fount it came:
And that unsullied, let the world oppress us;
Let fraud and falsehood rivet chains upon us,
Still shall our souls be free. Yet hope is ours,
As well as virtue.

    Car. Spoken like a Briton!
True, hope is ours; and therefore let's prepare;
The moments now are precious. Tell us, Druid,
Is it not meet we see the bands drawn out,
And mark their due array?

Cad.   Monarch, even now
They skirt the grove.

   Car.   Then let us to their front —

   Cad.   But is the traitor youth in safety lodged?

   Car.   Druid, he fled —

   Cad.   Oh, fatal flight to Mona!

   Car.   But what of that?   Arviragus is here —
My son is here: let, then, the traitor go.
By this he has joined the Romans.   Let him join
    them!
A single arm, and that a villain's arm,
Can lend but little aid to any powers
Opposed to truth and virtue.   Come, my son,
Let's to the troops, and marshal them with speed.
That done, we from these venerable men
Will claim their ready blessing.   Then to battle:
And the swift sun, even at his purple dawn,
Shall spy us crowned with conquest or with death!
         [*Exeunt* CARACTACUS *and* ARVIRAGUS, L.

   Cad.   What may his flight portend?   Say, Evelina,
How came this youth to 'scape?

   Eve.   And that to tell
Will fix much blame on my impatient folly:
For, ere your hallowed lips had given permission,
I flew with eager haste to bear my father
News of his son's return.   Inflamed with that,
Think how a sister's zealous breast must glow!
Your looks give mild assent.   I glowed, indeed,
With the dear tale, and sped me, in his ear,
To pour the precious tidings.   But my tongue
Scarce named Arviragus, ere the false stranger,

(As I bethink me since,) with stealthy pace,
Fled to the cavern's mouth.
    Cad. The king pursued?
    Eve. Alas! he marked him not; for 'twas the
        moment
When he had all to ask and all to fear,
Touching my brother's valor. Hitherto
His safety only, which but little moved him,
Had reached his ears; but when my tongue unfolded
The story of his bravery and his peril,
Oh, how the tears coursed plenteous down his cheeks!
How did he lift unto the heavens his hands
In speechless transport! Yet he soon bethought him
Of Rome's invasion, and with fiery glance
Surveyed the cavern round; then snatched his spear,
And menaced to pursue the flying traitor:
But I with prayers (oh, pardon, if they erred!)
Withheld his steps; for to the left the youth
Had winged his way, where the thick underwood
Afforded sure retreat. Besides, if found,
Was age a match for youth?
    Cad. Maiden, enough:
Better, perchance, for us, if he was captive:
But in the justice of their cause, and heaven.
Do Mona's sons confide.

      Enter BARD *and* ELIDURUS, R.

    Bard. Druid, the rites
Are finished; all save that which crowns the rest,
And which pertains to thy blest hand alone:

For that he kneels before thee.   [ELIDURUS *kneels*
 Cad. Take him hence;   *to* CADWALL.
We may not trust him forth to fight our cause.
 Eli. Now, by Andraste's throne — [*Rising.*
 Cad. Nay, swear not, youth;
The tie is broke that held thy fealty:
Thy brother's fled.
 Eli. Fled!
 Cad. To the Romans fled.
Yes, thou hast cause to tremble.
 Eli. Ah, Vellinus!
Does thus our love, does thus our friendship end!
Was I thy brother, youth, and hast thou left me!
Yes; and how left me? — cruel, as thou art,
The victim of thy crimes!
 Cad. True; thou must die.
 Eli. I pray ye, then, on your best mercy, fathers,
It may be speedy.   I would fain be dead,
If this be life.   Yet I must doubt even that;
For falsehood of this strange, stupendous sort
Sets firm-eyed reason on a gaze, mistrusting
That what she sees in palpable, plain form —
The stars in yon blue arch, these woods, these cav-
  erns —
Are all mere tricks of cozenage; nothing real:
The vision of a vision.   If he's fled,
I ought to hate this brother.
 Cad. Yet thou dost not.
 Eli. But when astonishment will give me leave,
Perchance I shall. — And yet he is my brother;
And he was virtuous once.   Yes, ye vile Romans!

Yes, I must die before my thirsty sword
Drinks one rich drop of vengeance. Yet, ye robbers,
Yet will I curse you with my dying lips!
'T was you that stole away my brother's virtue.

 Cad. Now, then, prepare to die.

 Eli. I am prepared.

Yet, since I can not now (what most I wished),
By manly prowess guard this lovely maid,
Permit that on your holiest earth I kneel,
And pour one fervent prayer for her protection.
Allow me this; for though you think me false,
The gods will hear me.

 Eve. I can hold no longer!
O Druid, Druid, at thy feet I fall!
Yes, I must plead (away with virgin blushes!) —
For such a youth must plead. I 'll die to save him!
Oh, take my life, and let him fight for Mona!

 Cad. Virgin, arise: his virtue hath redeemed him;
And he shall fight for thee and for his country.
Youth, thank us with thy deeds. The time is short;
And now with reverence take our high lustration.
Thrice do we sprinkle thee with daybreak dew,
Shook from the May-thorn blossom; twice and thrice
Touch we thy forehead with our holy wand.
Now thou art fully purged: now rise restored
To virtue and to us. Hence, then, my son;
Hie thee to yonder altar, where our bards
Shall arm thee duly, both with helm and sword,
For warlike enterprise. [*Exit* ELIDURUS, L. *Enter*
       CARACTACUS *and* ARVIRAGUS, R.

 Car. 'T is true, my son :

Bold are their bearings; and I fear me not
But they have hearts will not belie their looks.
I like them well: yet would to righteous heaven
Those valiant veterans that on Snowdon guard
Their scanty pittance of bleak liberty,
Were here to join them. We would teach these wolves,
Though we permit their rage to prowl our coasts,
That vengeance waits them ere they rob our altars.
Hail, Druid, hail! We find these valiant guards
Accoutered so as well bespeaks the wisdom
That framed their phalanx. We but wait thy bless-
    ing
To lead them 'gainst the foe.
   Cad. Caractacus,
Behold this sword, the sword of old Belinus;
Stained with the blood of giants; and its name
Trifingus. Many an age its charméd blade
Has slept within yon consecrated trunk.
Lo, I unsheath it, king! I wave it o'er thee:
Mark what portentous streams of scarlet light
Flow from the brandished falchion. On thy knee
Receive the sacred pledge;—and mark our words:
By the bright circle of the golden sun,
By the brief courses of the errant moon,
By the dread potency of every star
That studs the mystic zodiac's burning girth—
By each and all of these supernal signs,
We do adjure thee, with this trusty blade,
To guard yon central oak, whose holiest stem
Involves the spirit of high Taranis.
This be thy charge; to which in aid we join

Ourselves and our sage brethren.   With our vassals,
Thy son and the Brigantian prince shall make
Incursion on the foe.

   Car.   In this and all
Be our observance meet.   Yet surely, Druid,
The fresh and active vigor of these youths
Might better suit with this important charge.
Not that my heart shrinks at the glorious task,
But will with ready zeal pour forth its blood
Upon the sacred roots my firmest courage
Might fail to save: yet, fathers, I am old;
And if I fell the foremost in the onset,
Should leave a son behind might still defend you.

   Cad.   The sacred adjuration we have uttered
May never be recalled.

   Car.   Then be it so.
But do not think I counsel this through fear.
Old as I am, I trust with half our powers
I could drive back these Romans to their ships:
Dastards, that come, as doth the cowering fowler,
To tangle me with snares, and take me tamely.
Slaves, they shall find that ere they gain their prey,
They have to hunt it boldly with barbéd spears,
And meet such conflict as the chafed boar
Gives to his stout assailants.   O ye gods!
That I might instant face them!

   Cad.   Be thy son's
The onset.

   Arv.   From his soul that son doth thank ye,
Blessing the wisdom that preserves his father
Thus to the last.   Oh, if the favoring gods

Direct this arm, if their high will permit,
I pour a prosperous vengeance on the foe!
I ask for life no longer than to crown
The valiant task. Steel, then, ye powers of heaven,
Steel my firm soul with your own fortitude,
Free from alloy of passion. Give me courage
That knows not rage; revenge that knows not malice:
Let me not thirst for carnage, but for conquest;
And conquest gained, sleep vengeance in my breast,
Ere in its sheath my sword.

    Car. Oh, hear his father!
If ever rashness spurred me on, great gods,
To acts of danger, thirsting for renown;
If ere my eager soul pursued its course
Beyond just reason's limit, visit not
My faults on him. I am the thing you made me —
Vindictive, bold, precipitate, and fierce:
But as you gave to him a milder mind,
Oh, bless him, bless him with a milder fate!

    Eve. Nor yet unheard let Evelina pour
Her prayers and tears. Oh, hear a hapless maid,
That even through half the years her life has num-
      bered,
Even nine long years, has dragged a trembling being,
Beset with pains and perils. Give her peace;
And to endear it more, be that blest peace
Won by her brother's sword. Oh, bless his arm,
And bless his valiant followers, one and all!

    Eli. [*Entering armed*] Hear, heaven! and let this
      pure and virgin prayer
Plead even for Elidurus, whose sad soul

Can not look up to your immortal thrones,
And urge his own request: else would he ask
That all the dangers of the approaching fight
Might fall on him alone; that every spear
The Romans wield might at his breast be aimed,
Each arrow darted on his rattling helm;
That so the brother of this beauteous maid,
Returning safe with victory and peace,
Might bear them to her bosom.

    Cad. Now rise all;
And heaven, that knows what most ye ought to ask,
Grant all ye ought to have! Behold, the stars
Are faded: universal darkness reigns.
Now is the dreadful hour; now will our torches
Glare with more livid horror; now our shrieks
And clanking arms will more appall the foe.
But heed, ye bards, that for the sign of onset
Ye sound the ancientest of all your rhymes;
Whose birth tradition notes not, nor who framed
Its lofty strains. The force of that high air
Did Julius feel, when, fired by it, our fathers
First drove him recreant to his ships: and ill
Had fared his second landing, but that fate
Silenced the master bard who led the song.
Now forth, brave pair! Go, with our blessing go!
Mute be the march as ye ascend the hill;
Then, when ye hear the sound of our shrill trumpet,
Fall on the foe.

    Car. Now glory be thy guide!
Pride of my soul, go forth and conquer!

    Eve. Brother,

Yet one embrace! Oh, thou much-honored stranger,
I charge thee fight by my dear brother's side,
And shield him from the foe: for he is brave,
And will, with bold and well-directed arm,
Return thy succor.

    Cad. Now, ye priests, with speed
Strew on the altar's height your sacred leaves,
And light the morning flame. But why is this?
Why doth our brother Mador snatch his harp
From yonder bough? why this way bend his step?

    Car. He is entranced. The fillet bursts that bound
His liberal locks; his snowy vestments fall
In ampler folds; and all his floating form
Doth seem to glisten with divinity.

        Enter MADOR *with a harp.*

Yet is he speechless. Say, thou chief of bards,
What is there in this airy vacancy
That thou, with fiery and irregular glance,
Should scan thus wildly? Wherefore heaves thy
    breast?
Why starts —

    Mador. Hark! Heard ye not yon footstep dread,
That shook the earth with thundering tread?
'T is Death! — In haste
The warrior passed:
High towered his helmed head.

    I marked his helm; I marked his shield;
I spied the sparkling of his spear;
    I saw his giant arm the falchion wield;

Wide waved the bickering blade, and fired the angry
    air.
"On me," he cried, "my Britons, wait;
To lead you to the field of fate
I come.   Yon car
That cleaves the air
Descends to throne my state:
   I mount your champion and your god.
My proud steeds neigh beneath the thong:
   Hark to my wheels of brass that rattle loud!
Hark to my clarion shrill that brays the woods among!
    [*Here one of the Druids blows the sacred trumpet.*
On, my Britons!   Battle slain,
   Rapture gilds your parting hour:
I, that all despotic reign,
   Claim but then a moment's power."
Swift the soul of British flame
Animates some kindred frame;
   Swiftly to life and light triumphant flies,
   Exults again in martial ecstasies;
   Again for freedom fights, again for freedom dies!
Car. It does, it does!   Unconquered, undismayed,
The British soul revives!   Champion, lead on!
I follow: give me way.   Some blessed shaft
Will rid me of this clog of cumbrous age,
And I again shall, in some happier mold,
Rise to redeem my country.
    [*The sacred trumpet is again sounded; the* DRUIDS
    kindle a strong flame on the altar; the three SOL-
    DIERS *unsheath their swords, and the whole com-*
    pany form a tableau, upon which the curtain falls.

COSTUMES.

CARACTACUS. — Close trowsers of red cloth; plaid tunic; short cloak of blue or black; sandals; necklace of silver chains, hanging low on the breast; round shield about two feet in diameter, with a hollow boss in the center, and ornamented with concentric circles of brazen knobs, like brass nail-heads; heavy spear and sword; the hair long, and falling over the back and shoulders. The general appearance of the dress is like that of a Highland chief, but more rude.

ARVIRAGUS. — Brown, close trowsers; tunic of bear's skin; flesh arms; dark hair; very long and heavy mustaches, but no beard on the chin; bronze bracelets, sword, spear, shield.

ELIDURUS. — Flesh-colored arms and legs; blue tunic; red and blue short cloak; long curling hair; gold bracelets. His armor is like that of Arviragus.

CADWALL. — A long white dress reaching to the feet, confined about the waist by a girdle with a golden buckle; over this, an ample robe of white, worn like a shawl or cloak, but not fastened in front; necklace of gold; long gray beard; wreath of oak leaves, surmounted by a tiara of gold. (See frontispiece to *Palgrave's History of the Anglo-Saxons*.)

MADOR. — White flowing robes; white beard. His harp must be gilded, so as to glisten in the light.

THE OTHER Druids and bards may wear robes of white, blue, or green. They all have long beards. One Druid may carry a golden crescent; another may hold a bough of mistletoe. The bards are distinguished by their shining harps.

EVELINA. — Tunic of several colors, in rich folds; and over this a robe fastened with a dark brooch; a necklace composed of many rings of gold; long light hair, descending loosely over the shoulders; a head-band of jet.